# DR. ORPHEUS

*See, wild as the winds o'er the desert he flies;*
*Hark! Haemus resounds with the Bacchanals' cries.*
*Ah, see, he dies!*
—Alexander Pope
"Ode for St. Cecilia's Day"

# DR. ORPHEUS

*a downtime myth by* IAN WALLACE

New York  G. P. PUTNAM'S SONS

*B + T*

Copyright © 1968 by Ian Wallace

Library of Congress Catalog
Card Number: 68-25464

PRINTED IN THE UNITED STATES OF AMERICA

To JAKE, to GOSSEYN,
and to THE CATEGORICAL and TERRITORIAL IMPERATIVES

*(Jake, ole buddy, it could be worse—*
*no matter what Brett may say.)*

# PROLOGUE

"Pythagoras," muttered the very old man, "is a fink."

He had his skinny wide-sleeved arms stretched out on the table ahead of him; he had been considering the subtle contours of the swollen veins on the backs of his arthritic hands. Old age, he was reflecting, facilitates the study of anatomy; and for one who was heir to Milesian science, this was a value of old age. But the thought of neighbor-city Miletus had stirred a thought of its intellectual enemy Crotona across the water; hence the not very freely translated epithet about Pythagoras of Crotona.

"Dagnab!" the old man complained. "Here's this young Orpheus, a demigod, a musical genius, dead for a thousand years so he can't defend himself. So what does this goddamned cynical Pythagoras do? He *rapes* him!" ("Cynical" is an anachronistic translation.)

The old man began to potter about the business of pouring himself a clay cup of weak wine. The "is" and the "does" were stretching the present a little: he had been a young man a generation earlier when Pythagoras had been in his prime. Age reillumines old enmities.

Orpheus the demigod! Orpheus who had made with his lyre music so sweet that it had charmed wild beasts and had magicked the great ship *Argo* so that she had leaped off the beach into the surf, carrying Jason and Hercules and Theseus and a crew of heroes out upon the Golden Fleece piracy into the Black Sea. Orpheus, who—having lost to Gray Death his young bride Eurydice—had gone down to Hades in search of her, charming the nine-headed watchdog Cerberus with his music, courageously crossing the River Styx, charming even the Lord of Hades into giving up Eurydice.

And how had Orpheus tragically lost his Eurydice? Why, in a perfectly human mistake, in an honest young man's mistake: as he and his following bride had been on the verge of bursting through Earth's crust up into the outer world, Orpheus had been unable to wait any longer: he had *looked back* at his bride—thereby breaking the spell: he had desolately watched her snatched back into the underworld forever.

Small wonder that thereafter his music had gone so wild as to madden the Bacchante women until ultimately they tore him into small pieces. . . .*Ohé! Here* was a hero, for an aging philosopher who found substance in fire!

But now this dadburned Pythagoras: makes a demigod of himself, claims he has visited Hades himself and has returned with a golden thigh; says he's a reincarnation of everybody that Zeus ever got on a nymph, but especially a reincarnation of Orpheus. . . .

The plaguing thing was that this Pythagoras was a real intellectual! Had some spanking good theories about numbers. Even had some theories about the planets; but he invented a planet that he called Counter-Earth which was located behind some invisible Central Fire so that nobody could ever see Counter-Earth from Earth. That was a little like the notion of ghosts which exist but which you can't see because when you look at them they become invisible; but to a man who found substance in fire, the Central Fire idea was intriguing. Let's give Pythagoras that much: an intellectual he *was*, with something real to contribute. If only he were here in Ephesus, maybe we could. . . .

You see, now? That's the thing! He's a fink! He could have been an honest intellectual, but he wasn't satisfied with that—he needed the vulgar crowd, he had to be adored! So he claims to be a reincarnation of Orpheus—with a golden leg, yet; and he turns his numbers into a mystery religion, so they can't ever change, so the theory can't ever be improved, so it's fixed and eternal, so it's *unnatural*. . . .

*Sure* they listen to him! *He* will live *forever!* All that he preaches will stay unchanged—and therefore increasingly unnatural. And as for us poor duffers who honestly seek *truth*. . . .

Aa!

He'll be reincarnated, too.

Someday. Maybe a thousand years from now, or two thousand, or three, or four. . . .

Bet he calls himself Orpheus! What do you bet?

Aa! Nobody to bet with!

Maybe after all I ought to take my knife and bury it where somebody will someday dig it up. *That* would cause a stink, now—wouldn't it? *That* would throw some new Pythagoras into a tizzy. . . .

A shadow fell across his table. Slowly, painfully, he twisted his head up to look.

The stranger was tall and fairly young, though his deep blue eyes had a queerly mature seeming about them. His clothes were odd.

## PROGRAM NOTES

*Dr. Orpheus* is the second of the Croyd myths. These two adventure-myths resemble each other only in these three ways: both are adventures of the same epoch-hero in a fanciful era far in our future; in both, mind is the adventurer among brains, bodies, space, time, and stars; and neither is entirely free from scientific and philosophical hypothesis-tossing. They should be approached, however, as sheer adventures, independent of each other and different in mood and construction from each other: it is totally unnecessary to have read *Croyd* (which is a swift mind-fugue) in order to enjoy *Dr. Orpheus* (which is a leisurely space-time weaving).

Any fancied personal, political, medical, or nominal resemblance between this fictional future and the real twentieth-century world exists only in the mind of him who may seem to see it, and was not intended by the author. Anagonon is an invented name (from obvious Greek roots) for an invented drug of the far future, having invented properties; and I am sure that its blandishments could not seduce many doctors of our time.

The metagalactic "surface tension" and the peculiar behavior of light thereunder are hypothetical inferences from certain Relativistic concepts which may be merely epistemic. The convolutions of the metagalactic surface, and the presentative attitude of Sol Galaxy thereto, are invented but perhaps not impossible. The structure of Sol Galaxy (better known to us as the Milky Way Galaxy, which is silly because all galaxies must have milky ways) is hard definite invention from excessively vague data. I think that all other inventions in this fiction are obviously such and require no comment here.

I am grateful to Little, Brown & Company for permission to use a quote from Edith Hamilton's *Mythology*.

IAN WALLACE

*Nonspace, 1968*

**Thoth Actuality D-Day minus 3**

Part One

THE LOTOS-EATER

A land where all things always seem'd the same!
And round about the keel with faces pale,
Dark faces pale against that rosy flame,
The mild-eyed melancholy Lotos-eaters came.

— Alfred, Lord Tennyson (1833, 1842)

*Human* (def.)—Having sufficient neural complexity to use symbolic language in order to sublimate survival and reproductive interests in more complex levels of aesthetic development, individual or social (but without necessarily denying the more fundamental levels of living).

*Minimum Human Value System*—No human shall, by force or by guile, be deprived of his ability to resist volitionally the will of another creature—except under due process of law, and even then, not by guile.

—CODE OF THE INTERPLANETARY UNION

# 1

**Eurydice, New Year's Day 4-5 EA:**

Thoth had never realized his utter personal emptiness until he learned that Dr. Orpheus had knifed his girl.

In a way, it was the use of a *knife* by Dr. Orpheus that was most significant. Even before Anagonon, knives had been only for knaves; and now there were no knaves, because everybody in the entire world was Anagononic. The newskenner had projected this deed as an archaic-bizarre extravagance, adding hastily, of course, that no extravagance was too good for Dr. Orpheus; and having briefly discharged this news obligation, the kenner had moved to far more electrifying news: the continuing ominous presence of the ships from Earth.

Thoth tried to remember what had led up to the act; but his memory for particulars always grew foggy and died when the particulars were many hours old. Orpheus had become quite naturally inflamed for Greta and last night had asked Thoth for a pro tem yielding. Who could say no to Orpheus? Who would *want* to refuse him anything?

The extravagance of Orpheus with the archaic knife troubled Thoth only vaguely, and only because it meant he would no longer see Greta. Certainly Orpheus could not have done it out of pique at Thoth: in the first place, since blessed Anagonon, nobody was ever piqued at anybody; in the second place, Orpheus particularly liked Thoth. It was merely that Orpheus had knifed Greta for some reason

1

that Dr. Orpheus did not have to make explicit to Thoth or to anyone.

When he learned that Orpheus had kidney-knifed his girl, Thoth stoically faced the problem of adjusting his own life to the situation. A major component of that situation was this emptiness which he now felt. Thoth concluded that self-liquidation—or, in the old wording, suicide—was appropriate. For one who recognized his own emptiness and saw no chance to fill that emptiness, the planet Monon had no place.

It was logical, he knew, that his inwards should rebel against his own decision; but logic has its levels. It was the inferior logic of the premental organism that was producing his inward rebellion; and this level of logic, while not the lowest, was not the highest and should not be ultimately self-determinative. He wrote off this rebellion of his autonomics. It had the same value level as sexual desire. His decision for suicide was irrevocable and must be acted upon.

What seemed logical was three activities: (1) to go to the Morgue and contemplate Greta's body; (2) to go to the Museum of Ancient Man and contemplate the raw conditions of humanity in the old days when the knife that had slain Greta had been new and useful; (3) thereafter to proceed to the Terminal Institute and be terminated—an operation which, in these days of Anagononic immortality, was accomplished by means of electronic heart-stoppage.

And now it was noon. Thoth pushbuttoned an austere lunch, ate it meditatively, stepped into the dresser, pushbuttoned his best high-striped cap-and-bell ensemble, inspected it after it was put on him (since logic told him that machines dealing with humans were no more perfect than the humans they dealt with), and stepped into the force-field shaft to go to the Morgue and contemplate the body of his girl.

Something deep unsteadied him, telling him that he had more pressing demands, less selfish urgencies. He dismissed the feeling as free-floating anxiety. Nevertheless it continued, but dimly.

(In 2502 AD, the number of Anagononics rose to ninety million. In 2503, the invading ships from Mandomen Galaxy came nearer.)

# 2

Hovering momentarily motionless in the shaft, Thoth mentally fingered his mood spectrum in order to find the
transport level that suited the mood of his final day. He concluded
that he wanted to move leisurely at an altitude of about a thousand
feet, choosing his altitude because it was about half as high as the
next tallest buildings in the planetary capital city called Eurydice:
this level would suit his melancholy felling of semidetachment by
lofting him along below some building tops and above others, half in
and half out of the city, half in and half out of humanity.

Having selected the altitude, he simply dropped until his mood
stopped him there (it was a brainwave device) and then willed to
move horizontally, and did so. He could move either in a straight line
through intervening buildings among guest-loving people, or around
them, at his will: he chose the latter, wishing to stay external.
Watching him, one would say that he was floating through the air at
a speed around thirty miles an hour; in fact, he was moving along a
kind of invisible aerial highway, an established route, with others
ahead of him and behind him but none too close.

In a good-bye mood, he contemplated the splendid and various
neo-Gothic architectural beauties of Eurydice. No building was other
than a force-field complex, of course; but each force field had its
own frequency mélange which every spectator could visualize in his
own way according to his fancy; so that to Thoth, the buildings were
only semi-transparent in a blending of pale blues and radiant gold,
with the people who moved within them or floated around them
ranging from gentle pink to strong maroon.

Pausing in midair, he turned to contemplate his home, the aristocratic high-rise hotel that he had just departed. Some other buildings intervened; but he cleared them from his mood and saw his own directly. It was a mile distant, and therefore miniature although it towered a quarter-mile high: he could have enlarged his vision of it, but that would have been alien to his mood: to this home he had already said a final good-bye, as he had done to life, and he preferred that it be a dollhouse on his horizon.

What should he be remembering about his home as poignantly he surveyed it for the last time?

Ridiculously his memories had all begun the night before. There had been nothing earlier. They had started with the growing sound of a droning litany, and moved into the conferring upon him of a special-friend bracelet by Dr. Orpheus, and hovered over the ten-day claim of Greta by Dr. Orpheus, and meandered through a conversation with Dr. Orpheus. . . .Then Orpheus had left the room, and Greta had reappeared, ready to leave.

She came quickly over and sat by Thoth, gripping his hands. Peering into his eyes, she demanded: "Don't you know what is happening?"

"How do you mean? What."

"I just got it figured out, sort of. This is five years *later!* You've been in stasis for five years! He just brought you back—but you're still under some kind of narcosis—"

He patted her shoulder tolerantly. "Now, Greta, I don't remember anything like that—"

"Of *course* you don't! You don't remember *anything* before you woke up just now—do you?"

He blinked. "Well—I'm pretty drowsy—"

"Of *course* you're drowsy! Of *course* you don't remember! He drugged you so you *wouldn't* remember!"

"What do *you* remember?" he demanded.

Greta frowned and stood up, and stamped a foot, and hurried from the room. . . .

Hovering, foggily remembering, Thoth shook his head. Greta had been making some kind of a false problem. *He* knew who he was: he was a philosopher and the special friend of Dr. Orpheus.

Nevertheless, deep in his mind's underground, there was a confused sense which clarity might have resolved into the following components: (1) that he was more than this Thoth-in-cap-and-bells; (2) that he had more than ordinary human powers; (3) that *something* was threatening his world from within; (4) that—very vague—something related to the threat from within was threatening his world from without—and it *wasn't* the ships from Earth. . . .

Shrugging, Thoth turned in midair and moved on toward the Morgue. Again he noticed unaccountable anxiety; again he quelled it.

Now a minor traffic slowdown began to develop for necessarily his own highway was converging with others as he approached the center of the city and began to move downward. Although each traveler moved at his own speed, some at high velocity, there was no danger of collision, since a property of these force-field arteries and capillaries was to keep their occupants separate: those moving rapidly were automatically routed around those moving slowly until convergence made traffic too clotted for this.

Nearing the center of the web, human bodies were bunched at minimal five-foot intervals, and speed slowed to ten miles an hour; but there were no absolute stoppages, and the prevailing mood of Eurydice infused patience into every traveler. The buildings were low now—none rising higher than five hundred feet, since the city was zoned so as to scale the altitudes upward as one moved outward in any direction from center. Some of these buildings were very old, constructed of solid materials like glass instead of force fields. (One did not have the option of moving through a solid!)

There was one exception to the low zoning of the central town. Rising out of an exquisitely tailored park a mile in diameter, the Pythagorean Palace, whose base was a kind of translucent ziggurat a quarter-mile square, ascended in a series of leisurely noble setbacks until it culminated in a slender tower whose gracefully multipointed crest speared clouds three thousand feet high. Indeed, the relative altitude of the Pythagorean Palace—the governmental center of the planet Monon, the official seat of Dr. Orpheus and his TAC Board—was written in the zoning: it must be always a full 50 percent higher than the next-highest building in Eurydice; and whenever a new, loftier high-rise appeared on the city's periphery, up went the Pythagorean Palace accordingly. Even though much of the tower consequently stayed empty for a while after each rise, it did not matter, really—there was no particular problem, other than a problem of expending boundless energy, about using and subdividing or ignoring a volume of a force field.

Thoth was bound for the Pythagorean Palace. All that he now wanted was there. The Morgue occupied a number of subterranean levels, as did the Museum of Ancient Man. The Soul Hospital occupied a number of stories at the three-hundred-foot level, where a deep setback provided a broad outdoor terrace for patients: later, Thoth would pause there, just to make sure he was wholly ready for death. And nearly at the crest of the tower, three thousand feet up, floated (and wove gently in high wind) the Terminal Institute.

*At* the crest was the shrine—or, as one might say in a secular mood, the governmental office and residential apartment—of beloved Dr. Orpheus, Planetary Chairman of Monon.

(In 2502, the number of Anagononics rose another two million. In 2503, the ships from Mandomen were entering the metagalaxy.)

# 3

Although jester-privileged Thoth might have entered the Pythagorean Palace at any level directly, his mood led him to touch down before the main entrance: here on the broad plaza he contemplated the numerous lofty doorways: the tallest and central doorway arched fifty feet above the plaza, and the four on each side ranged symmetrically down to ten feet. Above each doorway was blazoned a gigantic Pythagorean Number done in the imperishable silver gleaming suprametal called Anagonium which had been synthe-sized (or, some said, mystically *rediscovered*) by Dr. Orpheus, and which compelled the love of every beholder by reason of the Ana-gonon with which it was impregnated.

In the ancient Pythagorean tradition, these numbers were Greek letters: Romans or Arabics would have been anachronistically and architecturally crude. One small impure concession had been made to grandeur: instead of being small Greek letters after the ancient number practice, they were capitals. Above the lofty central doorway rose a commanding B; flanking it were Γ and Δ; next at left and right came E and Z; and as the doorways lowered, H, Θ, I, and K were their designations. As for A — the all-in-all *One* that was exclusively the meaning of Dr. Orpheus—it *constituted* the high-flying central tower in the sky, no matter how high the building might rise, no matter how frequent its metamorphoses.

High-ranking Jester Thoth—noble by friendly caprice of Dr. Or-pheus—could enter by the proud central B door, in common only with the ten members of the highest priesthood called the TAC Board. (He didn't remember having seen any of them lately—but then, what *did* he remember prior to last night?) For just a few moments he paused, contemplative, in the foyer, enjoying its spacious magnificence: the vulgarity of the murals did not trouble him, since they were entirely within the logic of the culture.

He then went to the elevators (which were force-field shafts precisely like the one in his apartment hotel), palmed a button (which merely opened a door onto an empty shaft), entered, and thought *Morgue*.

Instantly he dropped several hundred feet, and when his thought brought him to a stop, doors opened and he debouched into the Morgue's reception foyer.

Of course there was a receptionist — blond, of course. She sat public-relations serene at her opaque force-field desk. "Good to see you, sir. What can I do?"

Thoth named the girl—Miss Greta Groen.

One blond eyebrow twitched, but there was no other sign of special interest. "Take the door to your left," she directed, "and keep going down the corridor to the next desk." She must have pressed a button, for the double doors in the portal to his left vanished.

He strode through. The corridor was narrow and doorless, but the murals in this corridor were vital and disturbing.

It was a young brunet man at this desk—a thin-moustached dandy who said obsequiously: "You want to see Greta Groen."

"Right."

"As a cadaver? Or in her vitality?"

The latter possibility was one that Thoth had not considered; it bore no relation to his mood. "Her cadaver," he said flatly.

Rising, the man said: "Follow me." Apparently he was just a demonstrator, no more. Down a branch-off corridor (equally vital) he led Thoth for several rods, until finally this corridor opened into a vast vault whose walls were lined with drawer doors. The demonstrator paused at one tier: the fourth door from the bottom was labeled in shining Anagonium: *GRETA GROEN*.

The demonstrator paused, one hand reaching high to rest on the bronze handle (if it was bronze). He said, eyeing Thoth: "You are sure you want to see her? She has been identified, you know—there is no doubt."

Thoth bit: "Nevertheless, please show her to me."

The demonstrator restrained a smile. "Sentiment, eh?" He touched a button and stepped aside while the drawer moved out.

There lay Greta—sleeping, one would say, beneath a silken coverlet, and her lips smiling in sleep.

The demonstrator said considerately: "This drawer is rather high— the top is above my head; the body is at eye level even for you. I could get a ladder."

"Do so."

The man brought the kind of ladder that you open and mount to find yourself, at its summit, scarcely three feet up. It was enough. Thoth mounted, steadying himself by holding the side of the drawer. By some bureaucratic oversight, the architects had omitted local force-field elevators.

Now he was looking down on his ash-blond Greta.

She was precisely as Thoth had known her. Would her eyes open? They would be forest green. . . .

But what of the knifed kidney? The drawer was wide enough so that he could turn her over, if he chose. He chose against it. He knew that the wound would not be visible on this replica.

Greta, in fact, was gone—soul *and* body. They had sliced her into fine slices during the autopsy, after thorough internal and external icrophotography. Then, as usual, they had reproduced her. Here was her reproduction—her *duplicate* done in a protein synthetic which had been named *Serenitite* by a board of funeral directors. No human, by sight or touch, by day or by X ray, could distinguish this body from Greta alive but in suspended animation. Her face was vitally peaceful, her body (nude beneath the shoulder-high coverlet) peacefully vital.

Ironical that precisely the relative immortality conferred by Anagonon had operated to make a kidney-stabbing instantly and irrevocably fatal. The kidney, enlarged and hyperactive to absorb toxins from every other kind of ailment including fatigue and age, had instantly discharged its stored poison into her blood and felled her like cobra venom. So rare were accidental deaths on the planet Monon that five years of fatal accidents in all Eurydice had filled scarcely 10 percent of the drawers in this vault. (But intentional deaths—Terminations—had filled another 5 percent during the past year.)

"Well," thought Thoth, "so I have contemplated her." He sighed, shrugged, and descended the ladderlet. "Close the drawer," he said; "I have seen what I wished to see."

Considerately the demonstrator stroked his young little moustache. He said presently: "It is no business of mine to ask why you wanted to see her. But perhaps you would wish a live assignation?"

That perplexed Thoth. "What do you mean?"

Up went the slender black brows. "You do not know about our vitalizations?"

"Perhaps I have forgotten. I forget easily."

The man permitted himself a slight smile. "Well, it *is* a new thing. We can vitalize the lady temporarily for you. This includes an activated brain. You could pass a few hours with her in"—he consulted a small desk chart—"Room -493. We could send up a tray of drinks and snacks—"

Thoth considered this: the meaning was perfectly clear, and no new development within reason surprised him anymore. Perhaps he needed to know about *this* development, before he presented himself to the Terminal Institute. "What is necessary?" he inquired.

The man glanced at Thoth's bracelet. "In your case, sir, the command is enough—or any command. Besides, she has the option of throwing you out. Well, -493 is two floors up—although still four floors down, if you follow me. Take the small elevator there—"

Abruptly reconsidering, Thoth shook his head slowly. "Perhaps," he murmured, "it was a bad idea." And he turned and went away—profoundly disturbed now, trying to shake off the persistent feeling that there was something more vital to be done.

(In 2502, the number of Anagononics rose another two and a half million. In 2503, the invaders from Mandomen were changing course and beginning to run along the plane of the galaxy toward Earth.)

# 4

Thoth rigorously thrust himself into a higher level of logic while he rose higher in the elevator shaft. He emerged in the vast foyer of the Museum of Ancient Man. "Ancient" here included the time range from the fine-flake flint techniques up to and including the postmedieval nuclear reactors.

He had come to examine a murder knife, but momentarily he was diverted by the TV newskenner screen. "THEY *are getting closer!*" it snarled. He had to force himself into a lower level of logic to appreciate this news. When he had reached this level (somewhere in his parietal area, with ancillary frontal contributions), he sank into a supporter-ray seat and allowed his consciousness to swing out into the vastness of three-dimensional space with the time dimension supplied by the continuity of action.

*They* were, of course, the weird irrational crowd from—well, from "Earth," which was the oddly earthy name that *they* used for their little planet on the far side of the Central Fire. (Here on Monon, "earth" just meant topsoil.) Somehow, apparently, *they* had arrived at breaking through the surface tension of the gravitic curvature of their own galactic system—and they must have required some years of supralight velocities to snarl hitherward like a pestilence of locusts.

Their ships were visible now on the screen. They had been hovering for days in the same location relative to the Monon surface. Only by means of the search rays of Planetary News, operating at a horrible distance, could these ships be made pseudovisible—and then only sometimes, not always. It was impossible to count the ships, since after the leader mass the following ships became practically indistinguishable from fifth-magnitude stars.

Planetary's announcer was explaining in a softly soothing voice that was quite at pleasant odds with the attention-getting growl which had started the newsken. Thoth, however, did not listen closely, being entirely enthralled by the beauty of the three-dimensional space screen, his thoughts wandering into contemplation of the colossal magnitudes and of the mental genius involved in bringing so mighty a thing so cheaply to the eyes of the populace. Besides, the announcer's voice was making him drowsy. Anyhow, it could not matter to him whether they would ever land or not: he would be dead tomorrow. . . .

Someone asked him: "How do we know they're from Earth?"

Thoth replied: "Dr. Orpheus says so."

"Oh," said the stranger. It was authority enough. Abandoned, Thoth returned to his brood.

It would be ironical, wouldn't it, if the invading Earthmen were to duplicate *him* and send his duplicate for a live assignation with the duplicate of Greta. Activated, would they have conscious minds—or only computer brains? And to an alien watcher from Earth, would it make a difference?

People were beginning to leave: deep space palls. Seeming to sense this, Planetary News brought its flash cut-in to a swift close and moved to more mundane concerns. There was at the moment a prime primitivistic sports event—tree diving! It brought Thoth to sharp attention, out of his semidrowse. He intently watched these heroic young men who, simulating tropical blacks of an ancient era, were diving headlong from the tops of trees, the winner being the one who could come closest to the ground before a spring cord jerked him back. If you came any closer, you lost another way.

It reminded Thoth of the primitive death-knife. . . .

He tore himself away from this spectacle, so much closer to human living than the faraway Earth monsters were. He arose and penetrated the Museum of Ancient Man.

(In 2502, the number of Anagononics rose another three million.)

Thoth stood now before the knife. Presented to the museum that morning by Dr. Orpheus, with a benign suggestion that it might be worth showing immediately, this knife occupied a midfloor case all its own, with guide-rope aisles approaching it to control the morbid crowds. Thoth had reached the museum at an off-time: spectators were ranged around the case, but there was no lineup, and he was able to reach the exhibit easily without pulling jester rank.

The word "case" was as misleading as "guide rope." Nobody used material anymore if he could possibly use a force field, especially in view of the subtle techniques for coloring these fields. The "guide rope" was in fact a field twisted and corded to simulate a heavy ornate theater-aisle-type rope (rather, mused Thoth, as primitives had designed their first automobiles to simulate carriages and their first pottery to simulate baskets).

The knife case was an octagonal plane ten feet in diameter, parallel with the floor, floating at waist level, unsupported, its color a luminous velvety black startlingly marbled with a ruby veining that shifted restlessly.

In the center lay the knife.

Contemplating the very ancient artifact, Thoth caught himself looking for stainings of Greta-blood; and he glanced about him, wondering if perhaps his openmouthed neighbors might not be looking for the same. Then he returned to the knife. It floated there seemingly naked and just reachable if you leaned far across; but of course one could never touch it by reason of the invisible hemisphere that protected it.

There were, however, things one might do to bring the knife closer. By pressing a button, one materialized a three-dimensional phantom duplicate of the knife, just at normal focal distance from one's eyes; a miniature joy stick close to this button slowly rotated the knife in two planes as one might choose to control it; a second button dismissed the phantom. Several spectators were playing with these realistic phenomena; but others, like Thoth, merely stared at the actual reality in the center of the plane. The phantoms did provide better and perfectly accurate viewing, private and at close range—yet somehow they were not the real thing. Thoth chuckled, remembering that people were still patronizing the legitimate theater.

Now, yielding to curiosity, he pressed the button. The phantom floated before him. Twenty-nine centimeters in overall length, the weapon was essentially a fifteen-centimeter blade of burnished bronze, thick at the haft but tapering concavely to a wicked point, and fluted on both sides; it possessed no handguard; its tang was broad and flat, knurled around the edges of ivory half handles crudely inscribed with ancient art. There was no blood: it had been cleaned.

A wispy contralto narration whispered privately in the auditory centers of his cerebrum: "Before you is the knife that Dr. Orpheus used to blessedly terminate Greta Groen in the larger interests of Monon. The knife is a primitive. In its own warlike epoch, it could only have been used for termination by stealth or for infighting: it is obviously not fitted for skinning animals. It is difficult to contemplate this weapon without shuddering as one recalls the barbarity of those times: no death without pain, and in this instance no death without a cold, slow sense of foreign matter invading the vitals. Orpheus chose to confer upon Greta this slow, cold sense—without the pain, of course, because of holy Anagonon.

"As you rotate this weapon, you will be impressed, I think, by the primitive grace of its craftsmanship, its authentic artistry in a time when the most delicate works of Man were incredibly crude by our standards. If you wish to study the three-dimensional microphotographs of this blade, they are available in the Microhall for this antique epoch; but be warned that these microphotographs are not for persons having queasy stomachs, because of the psychic trauma entailed in looking at a blade edge as jagged as a leptotherm and imagining these jags entering one's own guts. Nothing causes pain anymore, of course—but *this* blade would *really* tickle. End of lecture."

Thoth shuddered, feeling it in his guts. In her kidney. Slow, cold sensation of invasion. Jagged. . . .

(Now there were a hundred million Anagononics in 2502.)

"Quite a thing, isn't it?" murmured a thrillingly melodious male voice at his right.

"Quite," agreed Thoth, not looking around, *feeling* the psychic power that could only be his master. Orpheus never failed to charm him, and he found the fact queerly disturbing. "How did it feel going in?"

"To me, or to her?"

"To you, Dr. Orpheus. To her, I can imagine."

"I'm no sadist. Masochistic, if anything. So my interest in the knife is elsewhere. I want to know where it came from—or *when* it came from."

Puzzled, Thoth gazed up at the hypnotic eyes of Dr. Orpheus—who was taller than Thoth (whereas most men were shorter than Thoth). "You *don't know* where it came from—or when?"

"Frankly, no," Orpheus confessed. (Modestly he disregarded the admiring gazes that people were sending his way: the beloved world dictator loved to walk unannounced and unguarded among the people wearing a simple Grecian tunic, he could never be in danger.) "Look, Thoth, I won't bother to tell you *why* I used it on Greta—there were sufficient reasons. But I'll tell you something different. You aren't going to believe this—but when the reasons did become sufficient, I just *found it in my hand.* It just *came into my hand—* from *nowhere.*"

Staring at the knife, Thoth had to believe it. Orpheus was the sole owner *and the meaning* of the unique Alpha: it was unthinkable that he was not saying truth.

"Study it," Orpheus insisted. "What era did it come from?"

Thoth knew a little archaeology, he didn't know from where. "It is bronze," he observed, "and it is fitted with two half handles of incised ivory, riveted on. And the blade is crudely fluted. And the tang is knurled around the half handles. The knurling and fluting and riveting make it later than the tenth century BC, don't they?"

"BC?"

"Before Christ."

"Oh. Eh. Well—well, su-perb, Thoth, despite your Counter-Monon BC dating. Only, there are problems. In the era you mention, they had iron already, so why bronze?"

"Why not? A technology doesn't change overnight."

"Yes, but there's more. Look at the pictures on the ivory handle. That's an Egyptian river galley with sixteen oars, and earlier than the beginnings of the crescent hull. So now we aren't talking about tenth century BC—we're talking about *fourth millennium* BC!"

Thoth was feeling again the sense that something fundamental in his life was out of joint. "So what? So a first-millennium artisan imitates fourth-millennium art. Don't *we* simulate antiques?"

"When we do this, do we use contemporaneous tools?"

"Eh?"

"Look at the fine cutting marks in the ivory incision. Here, use the magnification. See? It was done with a crude microflint burin. Your first-millennium artisan used a fourth-millennium tool!"

Thoth felt weak. "Even that might have been done, but I'll grant that the evidence for your point is piling up. Only, what *is* your point, Doctor? Because, look: in the fourth millennium, Egyptians had only flint and obsidian and soft copper; they had no bronze—and yet that's a good hard bronze dagger, concave-tapered like a third-millennium Minoan weapon."

"You've just added weight to my argument that this knife is an anachronistic problem. It does not correspond to any single archaeological era on Monon; it is a composite of eras. On the other hand, Thoth, on *some other* planet, all these diverse technologies *might* have come together in a single era. *Now* do you follow me?"

Thoth blinked: he had to entertain all possibilities that had not been excluded. (Something in him was damning this cold intellectual discussion over the weapon that had slain his Greta.) "You are seriously suggesting that this knife is a plant from another planet. But *what* planet?"

Orpheus pointed to the smaller TV screen that hung here in the Hall of Ancient Man. Again the Earthships hovered.

*"Earth?"* Thoth whispered.

"Conceivably." Orpheus meant *probably*.

Thoth fought for clarity. "You are suggesting that in some way the Earth invaders planted this dagger in your hand by remote control just at the instant when you thought you had good reason to terminate Greta. For working purposes, let us assume that this far-fetched hypothesis is valid. There remain two issues. First, *why* did they do it? Second, *how* did they do it?"

"As to the *how*," Orpheus commented darkly, "Croyd may be on one of those Earthships."

"Croyd?"

Pause. "Then you don't remember him?"

"Memory is not my strong point."

"I know. Never mind. Well, I can imagine at least two reasons *why*. First, Earthfolk regard arbitrary termination of a human life as a felony no matter who does the deed; by making me a felon, they hoped to put the leader of this planet in jeopardy—not understanding that this couldn't happen here. Second, they thought the active presence of this ambiguous dagger might introduce into this planet an element of confusion that could pyramid into risk. Imagine, Thoth— on *this* planet, on our Monon, in our Eurydice—*confusion!*"

The paradoxical notion set them both chuckling. Thoth recovered first. He countered: "But if you don't know *how* they did it, the very difficulty of the method throws the entire hypothesis into a dubious light. After all, it *still* could *possibly* be a witty antiquity created by a first-millennium artist mingling third-and fourth-millennium themes and techniques with a fourth-millennium burin."

"But still, Thoth—even so, *how did it get into my hand?*"

Someone blurted: IT'S GONE!"

Thoth and Orpheus whirled to look. The dagger was no longer in the impenetrable exhibit case.

People crowded around. There was babble.

Just to Thoth's right, a male voice asserted softly: *"Uh."*

After a moment the sound penetrated, and Thoth looked.

Dr. Orpheus was wavering down: Blood was bubbling from a slash in his tunic just above the right kidney.

That was when Thoth discovered that his own hand was gripping the ivory handle of the ambiguous dagger whose bronze beak now dripped with blood that had once belonged to Dr. Orpheus.

Croyd Actuality D-Day minus 4
Krell  Actuality D-Day minus 7

Part Two

THE ANAGONON CIRCLE

**Did you realize, Doctor. . .**

. . .that the computerized therapeutics which today we consider so ultramodern actually stem from primitively computerized diagnostic aids devised in postmedieval times, and only binary in their base until four centuries ago?

. . .that a mere two centuries ago, personalized diagnosis and therapy were still as frequent as computerized diagnosis and therapy, despite the incredible waste of doctor minutes in a teeming, pain-screaming Earthworld?

. . .that the first fully computerized hospital did not appear until 2320, was all in one geographic location, and occupied the full time of a directing doctor?

. . .that only a century ago there were still several million doctors in Earthworld, and that a single doctor could control a maximum of five computer-decentralized hospitals?

. . .that by contrast, in our signal year 2500, Earthworld health is vigorously sustained by fewer than a hundred thousand doctors (assisted, of course, by millions of trained aides, program checkers, computer attendants, etc.). . .that there are doctors who control as many as a hundred computer-decentralized hospital nets each, using only half time for completely adequate direction. . .that visionaries in biotherapeutics consider this condition primitive and foresee thousand-hospital doctors within the lifetimes of some of us?

–BIOTHERAPEUTIC REVIEW **(May 2500)**

# 5

**Tannenport Space Station, 2502 AD:**

At first naked-eye sighting far above sky, the deep-space frigate, coming in tail-on, braking from high-G approach, was only a blue match-flame of incandescent repulsor gas. Aboard the satellite space station, only the appropriate docking crew bothered to watch. The flame enlarged, then seemed to remain the same size for about a minute, then went out. As soon as the crew's eyes accommodated, which was immediately, they could see the dark shadowed disc which was the foreshortened tail-end view of the frigate as it coasted in, with small intermittent jets of blue gas all around the disc edge signaling operation of the feather brakes. As she came around, the sun caught her great flank in a flash of blinding silver (but the glare hitting the crew's sunglasses automatically raised the opacity index of the lenses). Presently, massive-gentle, the two-thousand-foot frigate softed to relative rest beside the station, totally shadowing the crew, clearing their sunglasses.

The frigate had made it from Alpha Centauri in just under two days, threatening the record run by the fastest flagship of the galactic fleet.

*"Ceres,"* muttered a new man, reading the nameplate on her dust-striated hull. "Who's the commander?" He had touched a button activating a long, spidery covered bridge that telescoped outward a hundred feet until it accurately fitted its muzzle around the ship's crew hatch.

"Groen," said a veteran, tongue-touching his grinning lips, "and that's a commander to see. Watch!"

They stood at attention at the hither end of the companionway.

Echoing eerily through the thin, metal tunnel-bridge *peeped* the bosun's pipe.

At the far end of the brilliantly illuminated tunnel appeared the blue-uniformed, gold braided, blue-and-white-capped figure of Commander Groen. It was carrying white gloves. It wore a skirt.

The new crewman had his lips fixed to echo the bosun's pipe. The veteran frowned. The youngster stopped sound.

A similarly uniformed ensign—but with pants—awaited her just outside the tunnel mouth. She emerged and paused; behind her, a yeoman carried her overnight bag. The ensign saluted; she returned it. He said: "Ensign Anderson, ma'am. Welcome aboard."

She said: "Commander Groen"—she pronounced it mostly like Green but something like Grinn. "Thank you, Mr. Anderson. Will you take me to my taxi?"

Composing his reply, Anderson appreciated her. She was older than he, but she seemed too young to be a commander. Standing easily at attention, hands crossed in front of her holding the gloves, she was tall and slender, her face long and high-cheekboned and fair, her ash-blond hair falling straight below her cap to cheekbone level, her brows (darker than her hair) level above forest-green eyes; he suspected that her generous mouth, which was composed, was capable of wide smiling. It was going to be hard to reply. He said crisply: "Ma'am, I regret to report that the taxi we were holding has been preempted by an admiral."

Her mouth tightened a little. "My priority was too urgent for preempt by just an admiral."

He reddened. "I have been instructed by my captain to confess that we bungled. We had another stowed away that we were going to hold for you—but after yours was gone, the stowage turned out to need critical service. It will be ready in about an hour."

Her brows were gathering. "Instruct your captain that he must give me *his* vehicle immediately."

"Ma'am—that stowage *is* his vehicle." He coughed and added: "If you wish, I can take you to the captain."

Unexpectedly her mouth corners twitched. "I think he would not welcome me, and he seems to be impotent anyway." The smile suspicion vanished; she frowned; she gazed downward, thinking. She slapped a hand once with her gloves. Absently tucking the gloves under an arm, she drew a book of matches, lit one, held it at eye level, gazed into the flame. Anderson was fascinated. When it had burned down to finger danger, she coolly, slowly, blew it out. A crewman stepped forward and took it from her.

She said: "Ensign, take me to a private room where there is a tight-beam visiradio with thalamic ID equipment. And ring me there ten minutes before my vehicle is ready."

Told to wait outside, the yeoman left her bag on a bench and departed, closing the door. Commander Groen locked it, opened her bag, produced an electronic bugcheck, and checked the room systematically for spy gimmicks. Satisfied, she replaced the bugcheck, closed the bag, took off her cap, dropped it on the bench, fluffed up her hair with both hands, sat on another bench before the visiradio, activated it, selected a little-used frequency, and dispatched a signal.

Presently the visiscreen registered the correct answering code.

She responded with a third.

It responded with the correct fourth.

Producing her thalamic-pattern ID card, she dropped it into the slot. The screen responded with the expected answering pattern.

She placed her forehead between electrodes, held it there for a moment, then withdrew and studied the screen. Immediately it said: PATTERN CORRESPONDENCE CORRECT. The words vanished and were succeeded by: PATTERN CORRESPONDENCE OF YOUR CONTACT ALSO CORRECT.

At that, she snapped on the scanner that would transmit her image to her distant contact. Immediately the solid-projection screen lit up with *his* brilliantly lighted image, his wonderfully familiar image—*his* long, lean sun-browned face, his big hard-humorous mouth, his Mediterranean-blue eyes, his short auburn hair. . . .

"Hi, Croyd," she said eagerly, her mouth fulfilling the smile promise.

"Hi, Greta," he answered warmly, grinning big.

"Seems like a lot of niff-naw with the ID routine, when we know each other as well as we do."

"Both of us know that bodies can be stolen. Both of us could be aliens."

"You wouldn't fool me long."

"Nor you."

There was a silent while of appreciation, necessarily brief. When, sobering, they began to talk intently about the inward and outward threats to Earth and the galaxy that had led him to call her to Earth, this did not mean that mutual appreciation had faded—only that it had turned itself outward to operate harmoniously upon a stupendously dangerous objective. Face to face, they were shoulder to shoulder.

They were a free-ranging pair, parsecs apart more often than together—but a pair they were, and *quite* a pair. They had it! And as far as she was concerned, nobody was going to fracture it—least of all herself!

It would be kind of nice, though, if—just privately, and not for permanent holing-in but just for occasional delicious-familiar recourse—this roving pair could have a secret territory of their own, a bit more intimate than the whole galaxy: a housing home, like a brained body, for themselves to inhabit together sometimes. . . .

Croyd broke the brood. "How come you're calling me, kid? I was about to leave for our RP in Boston."

"Snag here. Can't get a vehicle for an hour."

His face went wholly hard. "That's too long."

"I know it's too long, but I don't know why. You were going to brief me at RP."

"To save time, I'll brief you now—though an hour is still too long. We'll have to think of something."

"Brief me now, then we'll think. Just incidentally—what is the Galactic Chairman doing on Earth?"

Both of them knew that this beam had to be theirs exclusively; both of them had adequate disturbance-detectors.

"*Temporary* Chairman," he countered, "and don't you forget it."

"Five years you've been temporary. What's permanent?"

"Which question do you want answered?"

"Why on Earth?"

"Why on Earth what?"

"I thought you said time was short."

"Sorry. Well, I'm investigating a drug for the Medicine Board."

"For *this* kind of duty you call me all the way in from Alpha Centauri?"

"It's quite a drug."

"Time is short, you said."

He demanded: "Tell me what you know about a certain Dr. Fellanel and a drug called Anagonon."

"Never heard of either."

"*Ne*ver *heard* of. . .*where* have you *been*, Greta?"

"Alpha Centauri for six months, and before that you know where for two weeks, and before that the Lyra sector—quit sparring, Croyd."

"All *right*. Dr. Fellanel heads an organization known as TAC or The Anagonon Circle. For six years they've been pushing a drug called Anagonon: one shot, and you've had it for life. Right now we estimate that more than a hundred doctors, controlling maybe a thousand computerized hospital nets, and a good many million lay men and women are Anagononic members of TAC—"

"Good God, Croyd! That society is as large as some nations! How come?"

"Dr. Fellanel gives it only to selected doctors. His doctors give it to other doctors. They give it to their computers, and *they* give it to lay people. We haven't quite figured out the system."

Personally Greta was enthralled; professionally she was aroused, alert—this was big stuff on the very face of it, without considering that Croyd wouldn't be in it if it weren't the very biggest. "What's this Anagonon got," she demanded, "to pull all these groovies?"

"Greta, you should take it. You would never again feel pain, your energy would be permanently boundless, and—listen—you'd never die—almost!"

Silence on the tight beam.

Greta said quietly: "What's the catch, Croyd?"

"The catch is that we are beginning to think there may be side effects."

"Like?"

"Digest this, Greta. You take Anagonon. It makes you painless, fatigueless, and deathless—for life. But: from that moment on, *you are unable to refuse any command issued by another person who has received Anagonon and whom you recognize as having higher authority.*"

Silence. Then:

Greta: "*Any* command?"

Croyd: "*Any* command."

Greta, low: "How fast is the membership of TAC multiplying?"

Croyd, low: "Geometrically."

Greta, presently: "We aren't fooling, are we, Croyd?"

"We aren't fooling."

"This Fellanel could end up bossing the galaxy."

"Right. And there's another thing—"

"Go on."

"I have a feeling that Dr. Fellanel isn't smart enough to have cooked this up himself."

"There's a hidden organization?"

"Maybe extragalactic."

"Extra. . . .How?"

"Remember the incident of the Large Magellanic Cloud?"

"I sure do. We met over that."

"All right. My thought is that a crowd from that galaxy or another has planted Anagonon with Dr. Fellanel in order to weaken us for invasion."

After a moment Commander Groen said tightly: "We have now used ten minutes."

"We would have used it anyhow, at the RP. Now listen, Greta. Tomorrow afternoon Fellanel and his ruling hierarchy, which is called the TAC Board, appear for review before the Earthworld Bureau of the Galactic Medicine Board. If Anagonon is approved again, the lid is off. If the Board of Review again finds the drug harmless—if only the benign effects of analgesia, energy, and relative immortality can be shown—Fellanel wins the day, and I don't see anything in God's world that can keep him from selling the drug to everybody in the galaxy. This is the *dream* drug— isn't it?"

Greta mutely nodded.

"Tonight is it," Croyd told her. "I am going in to challenge. I need you with me as a witness—not just *any* witness, Greta: *you*. My appointment with Dr. Fellanel is in half an hour—and for certain reasons, it has to be *right then*. When is your vehicle?"

"Forty-five minutes at the earliest. Where is Fellanel?"

"Boston."

"That means at least an hour before I arrive—even if this damned

Navy comes through. Croyd—*what?*"

Pause.

Croyd said: "You'll have to jump."

Greta went cold. She couldn't jump by pullman: the maximum safe pullman range was five thousand miles because of the inverse-square problem. He had to mean a PK jump!

She said, small: "You've barely taught me the rudiments. The most I've done is a hundred miles intime and ten minutes uptime or downtime."

Croyd went gentle; his face was concerned. "I know it's a risk. I also know that fear won't stop you. Make your cold judgment, Commander. Can you do it?"

She forced herself to think clearly, unemotionally. She took precious seconds to think through the consequences of failure, the probabilities of success, the operational difference between the hundred miles that she *had* experienced and the twenty-five thousand miles that she *hadn't*. . . .

She said simply: "If I'm not there in thirty minutes, it didn't work; go on in without me and worry later. Coordinates?"

He gave her the Boston address. Then he added simply: "I want for you to make it."

She nodded with a strained smile. She said: "Kisses, Croyd."

"Kisses, Greta."

"I won't be the first you've lost."

"No. But I don't want to lose you."

"Out, Croyd."

"Out, Greta."

Presumably his visiradio snapped off at the same instant as hers.

She took no time to breathe heavily: the decision had been made. Opening her traveling case, she got out of uniform, changed into a suit of civilian clothes, packed the uniform, shut the case. Then she opened the door and called in the yeoman.

"Ma'am?"

"Strange things are about to happen, yeoman. I am about to disappear, traveling case and all. Ask no questions—chalk it up to weird experiences in space. Stay on duty outside the door. When someone calls to inquire, tell 'em I've returned to the ship and will be in touch. Then go back to the ship yourself. Got it?"

"Yes, ma'am."

"I bless you for being laconic. Yeoman—"

'Ma'am?"

"You do a good job."

"That sounds ominous, ma'am."

"Watch it! Back outside the door, my friend."

"Ma'am—"

"Yeoman?"

"Whatever it is—good luck."

"Thank you. Out."

He saluted, a bit more prolongedly than necessary, and disappeared.

Grasping her traveling case, Greta went to a porthole and looked out and down. Earth was twenty-five thousand miles below. She thought she could distinguish North America. Wherever Boston might be—ten or fifty miles one way or another on the diagonal made little difference: she didn't have to be able to see it or visually gauge it—the trick was for her midbrain to handle the coordinates.

Closing her eyes, she willed it as one might will to jump a long distance.

Her guts twitched. . . .

**Metaspace, in time slippage**:

"Now hear this!" chirred the voice in the intership squawkbox. "We are approaching the metagalactic barrier. We are approaching the metagalactic barrier. Sol Galaxy sector. Sol Galaxy sector. Batten down for turbulence, expected duration three lantini. Out."

The dark-brown eyes of Maelbrug dwelt upon the light-brown eyes of Krell. Maelbrug's eyes were confident, yet not wholly devoid of fear. She queried: "Will it be bad, Krell?"

"About the same as going out," 'e told her. "This time we are going back in."

Three of her eyes closed, and she shuddered. "Going out was pretty bad," she confessed.

Gently Krell patted her right secondary shoulder with 'is left tertiary claw. "Take it easy, princess," 'e told her. "When you've had one turbulence, you've had them all."

Now she gazed at 'im with all her eyes, drawing courage from 'is calm experience. "I know," she told 'im shyly, "it isn't really bad, it's only a shaking up, the ship can stand this. It's only that I—"

Krell contemplated her with shepherding love. "If you hadn't been brave," 'e told her, "you wouldn't have come. I know that. Lie down, now: I'll buckle you in."

Decisively she negated, shaking her head. "*You* won't be buckled in. Why should *I* be buckled in?"

"Because," 'e reminded her patiently, "you aren't a ship's officer. Because you and your sisters are supremely valuable to all of us. Because you personally are supremely valuable to *me!*" With four of 'is podia 'e was gently forcing her down into the hammock. "Be a good girl, now. Don't try to be masculate, Maelbrug. Be my girl, now—won't you?"

She submitted, lying passively—and watching Krell with adoration—as 'e went through the long, repetitious buckling procedure.

Presently it was all done, and 'e stood back and surveyed her.

She said quietly: "I am at your mercy, Krell. I trust you. I love you. I wish you could enjoy me. It is ridiculous that those who have enjoyed me are otherwise worthless, while you who have worth cannot enjoy me. Krell—isn't there *some* way for you to enjoy me?"

'E told her calmly: "I love you. Consequently I would not be able to enjoy you."

"You could enjoy me if you did not love me?"

"Yes, but only with cruelty. But with you I cannot be cruel."

"You really do love me, don't you—"

*"Now hear this! All commanding officers report immediately to flag bridge."*

All Maelbrug's eyes were wide. "Krell! Isn't that something unusual?"

Krell multiply shrugged. "Rest easy, Maelbrug—it won't be bad alone. We have an exceptionally intelligent ship."

"If it won't be bad—why all commanding officers to the flag bridge immediately?"

Making 'imself relax, Krell drawled: "Beers all around, probably. 'Bye, princess." 'E bent tenderly over her, brushing her mouth parts with 'is.

Then 'e hurried to the flttr. Evidently—out here beyond the rind of the metagalaxy—there was some kind of crisis.

It must not prevent their invasion of Earth—not even delay it. Not merely their species life, but *Maelbrug's* life depended on a prompt arrival.

# 6

**Tannenport Space Station, 2502 AD; then Boston, 2495-6 AD; then Eurydice, New Year's Eve, 4-5 EA:**

What we do indirectly with our bodies we do directly with our brains, and what we feel indirectly in our bodies we feel directly in our brains. Hence it was body action that Greta willed when she jumped from the Tannenport Space Station twenty-five thousand miles above Earth, and a bodily gut-twitch constituted her guiding feedback, although the work was being initiated in her forebrain and being done by her midbrain which also was coordinating the feedback. The difference from simple walking was, from a control viewpoint, merely brain topological.

The trouble was that Commander Greta Groen lacked expertise. She was *going* to get it—since Croyd was her teacher—but she didn't have it yet. For instance, the quality of the teleportation twitch was in her discernment only partially distinguished from the uptime-downtime twitch qualities. That she could learn these at all seemed miraculous—and yet it supported Croyd's contention that superhuman it was not.

Her practically instantaneous jump from the space station to Earth felt like a single fast whirl on her toes. . . .

She materialized in a clinic, happy to have materialized at all.

Then, collecting thought in a split second, she knew that she had made some kind of mistake. RP with Croyd was to be *out*doors. To add to the trouble, a man wearing a white jacket, his back to her, bent over a desk at the far end of the fairly large room: if he should turn around. . . .Desperately she tried to recall a special technique that Croyd had told her about but hadn't yet taught her: strobo-temping, an uptime-downtime feathering procedure that permitted one to see without being seen.

But she caught sight of a wall calendar: the year was 2495. *Seven years in the past!*Perversely relieved, she forgot about strobotemping: this was uptime past, when events were unchangeable—so her presence here wouldn't be noticed even if the man should turn around and look straight at her.

All this thinking had required something under ten seconds.

Greta noticed now a rather pretentious brass nameplate on the man's desk: *DR. FELLANEL.* Well; and wasn't he their quarry? On a good guess, she judged that she had made a small mistake in space and a big mistake in time: fifty or a hundred feet off in space had landed her in the doctor's office instead of outside his house—but seven years too early was something else!

That was when she went *cold.* She *could* have materialized *in the wall.*

Dr. Fellanel worked on. Apart from being seven years early, Greta was a quarter-hour early anyhow: she could afford to look him over a little. . . .

Fellanel flung aside his work and spasmodically stood facing her, tearing off his white jacket. Greta gasped. He was staring at her, desperately pulling off his clothing: clawing at his necktie, ripping his shirt zipper, viciously attacking his shoes and flinging them into corners, kicking off his trousers. Clad now only in a slender golden *pénistache,* Fellanel jerked open a desk drawer, produced a laurel wreath, adjusted it on his head, and stood erect, gazing at Greta, his great chest arched and spasmodically heaving, his belly taut, his physique impressive. He was an athlete fresh from the games, ready to claim his prize.

Here in uptime, necessarily the man was mindless, and Greta was viewing him as no more than a full-color tri-D cinematic projection; yet the force of the mind that *had* possessed this body in its 2495 germinality, and *would now* be animating this body in its 2502 germinality, flooded the face with inspiration and ecstasy, power and anguish. This spiritual force centered on the eyes, large and exoph-thalmic and wide apart: the irises were pallid blue, almost faded blue, and yet these vital eyes conveyed a sense of seeing both inward through tortured murk into ineffable beauty and outward through events into eternity. Above those weirdly radiant eyes towered a broad, high forehead creased by fine lines of introspection, crowned by sparse, disorderly blond hair and now by the laurel wreath; around and below the eyes, a long, hard face with a long, bony, flare-nared nose and wide cheekbones emphasized his intensity; the strong chin was haloed by a sparse, disorderly blond beard; the extraordinarily wide mouth was parted now in something between a cry-readiness and a fey smile, revealing excellent teeth with a little gap between the upper incisors. This head dominated a long, rangy, athletic body, at least as powerful as Croyd's body and perhaps even a bit taller. It was a personality that could not be satisfied by anything drably real, that would labor obsessively and compulsively to realize a fantastic dream, that would greet with dismay the new drab reality of the dream and cast it aside to pursue some new fantasy.

She comprehended with a troubled frown that this Dr. Fellanel *had to be loved,* and was *not* loved, and would kill in order to be loved. . . .

Fellanel advanced upon her.

Commander Greta, erect and stone cold, held steady, reminding herself that this was uptime.

Fey-eyed Fellanel walked past her.

Commander Greta turned.

Fellanel opened a door that revealed darkness beyond, and he disappeared downward into it.

Greta followed.

She found herself descending a rotten wooden spiral staircase down into darkness.

The darkness ahead dissolved in flooding green pallor, revealing the silhouette of Fellanel. He had reached the bottom of the stair; he was stepping off into green dimness. Greta hurried, following close, knowing she could not be sensed.

The limitless grotto was filled with the crashing music of a harp— or a lyre.

Fellanel stood at the edge of misty water. A vast seeming, like a multiheaded dog with serpent tails, fawned before him. A gray boat with a gray boatman undulated in fog. Fellanel stepped gracefully aboard, giving something to the boatman, who bit it and nodded. Greta leaped abroad too; the boat did not feel her weight.

The transit of the water, which Greta never saw for mist, took perhaps a minute. They grounded gently. Fellanel disembarked and moved resolutely forward. Greta trailed, her nerves tortured by supernal music. Knowing the techniques of her time, Greta grasped that all this was an incredible expansion of effects producible on any theater stage; but the realization did not mitigate her wonder that Fellanel or any man should expend what was necessary for so much and then allow himself to become so rapt within its fantasy. (She also noticed that five minutes of her lead time were gone.)

They moved forward now through a foggy Carlsbad grotto.

They paused before a vaguely curtained atrium. How far had they trod? A hundred feet? A hundred miles?

Fellanel fell to his knees before the atrium, presenting to Greta his hard slim buttocks and back. The hollow-echoing lyre diminuendoed but stayed low-barbaric.

The voice of Fellanel shocked the grotto: it was an indescribably resonant tenor: he was muscular-tense, his taut arms half raised before the shrine, as he chanted high a broken chant in a mellid tongue that Greta did not know. Two words she recognized over and over, mingled with all the other words, because they were myth names that she knew:

*"Orpheus!"*

*"Eurydice!"*

The chant cut itself off with shocking sharpness.

Tense Fellanel loosened, knelt limp, stared at the curtains.

Somnolently the curtains parted.

Behind them a grave and possibly beautiful nymph was seated foggily on some kind of throne.

Fellanel called, hollow: *"Eurydice!"*

Slowly Eurydice arose

and fell apart.

Instant of Fellanel-silence, with Greta equally paralyzed.

A yell tore from his throat: *"AHHHhhh*hhhh−"

He collapsed, forehead on the oozy clay.

What stood there, instead of his Eurydice, was a. . .green-armored multijointed. . .*thing*.

It was more than man-size. It had too many eyes and limbs: all were in motion.

Greta comprehended that this thing was not part of the customary mystery play.

Fellanel's head came up. Absurdly he quavered: "What have you done with Eurydice?"

In this Hell cavern he was evidently willing to believe that the creature was a devil. So almost was Greta.

The thing replied in a high-pitched English that seemed to emanate from somewhere near 'is middle; 'is mouth parts were moving, but only in a compulsively rhythmic way that did not correlate with the words; the voice was toneless, echoing dead in Hades, but the antennae moved expressively:

"Both of us know that she was only a flexible robot-effigy of Eurydice. I have destroyed her because I am about to give you something ineffably more precious, and you must put her out of your mind and offer this new love object your full heart."

By now Dr. Fellanel knelt high and courageous, though he trembled. "I am not insane," he declared defensively—his voice was Irish-melodious. "I know that this Hades is my own creation. If I am now hallucinating a demon, then I am in the grip of a transient hysteria and therefore in no mental condition to be making pacts with a devil." Greta felt that this logic sideslipped somewhere, but she couldn't quite finger the slip.

"I am no devil. I am Sira Ssen." The name was chirr and a hiss. " And it is no pact that I offer you, but a gift. Consider this gift, Dr. Fellanel: consider it carefully. It is freedom from pain. It is enhancement of energy. It is freedom from most kinds of death, including the death of old age. And it is total dictatorial power over all Earth and your entire galaxy."

When the creature said "your entire galaxy," a convulsive swing of the right antenna emphasized *your* in a way that interested Greta.

Fellanel stared.

Fellanel got to his feet.

Fellanel whispered: "Your name is—Sira Ssen?"

"The substance of my gift," Ssen droned, "is a hormone that is genetic in my species. We have isolated and analyzed this hormone; its elements are plentiful and easily obtainable here on Earth. You can synthesize small quantities of it at small expense; and as its use expands your power, you will easily obtain funds to synthesize larger quantities. It is yours. Do you want it?"

The Fellanel shoulders went back and his straggle-bearded chin tilted up. "Why me?"

"I have studied you and many others. You are one of twenty-nine thousand four hundred eighty-three men on Earth who believe that they are reincarnations of your prehistoric demigod Orpheus. Among these, you are one of three who understand the relationships between Orpheus and ancient Greek Pythagoras. I have backtracked time from each of you three—and I know that *only you ARE* the reincarnated Orpheus!"

The effect of this assertion on naked Dr. Fellanel was galvanic.

A full minute late he partially recovered, and his voice broke as he demanded: "What interest might *you* have in Orpheus?"

"I am a reincarnation of Eurydice. He loved me." Was there a slyness in the position of 'is mouth parts?

Fellanel stiffened. "I trust you do not imagine—"

Ssen stiffened—losing 'is sly, Greta felt. "I said it was a *gift*. And this is the devil of a place for technical talk. May we ascent to your clinic—"

Greta's instincts demanded that she stay with this colloquy; but her spacetime RP with Croyd was *right now*—and her downtiming could not safely take off from this catacomb!

Turning, she fled to the edge of the water. No Charon! She waded into the mist-invisible water—but there wasn't any: a buoyancy field had supported the ferry. Hurrying then, Greta found her way back to the spiral stair, precariously mounted it, reentered Dr. Fellanel's office, and reclaimed her travel bag. This was uptime: it would stay eternally the same, she could return later and review it like an old film. But her rendezvous with Croyd would be *action now,* and it could not wait, because what they would be doing would immutably change the future!

Having triple-checked her coordinates, Greta downtimed.

* * *

Locally she had done all right: it was the same Fellanel office. Assuming that she had now reached her rendezvous time point with Croyd, she had only to find her way outside without being noticed. With the aid of a little strobotemping, she could open the door and walk out invisible. Only. . . .

A wall calendar said 2496. She had moved only a year toward actuality—she was still six years into uptime. "Groen, Groen," she moaned, "*why* didn't you pay better attention in Map Reading?"

That was when she heard voices in the next room. One was female, the other was Fellanel. Passing through the door, she found herself in a medical clinic room. Fellanel—rawbone-tall, wearing a long smock, carrying in his right hand a small injection gun, exuding chthonic charm—confronted a portly middle-aged brunet woman clad in a hospital gown.

Greta listened. The conversation was perhaps longer than it needed to be; from it she gathered that the woman was also a doctor, a gynecologist, and that she was going to be the first doctor (after Fellanel) ever to receive the bug-drug—which already had been named Anagonon.

"Just climb on the table, Doctor," said the sonorous Fellanel tenor "and assume the fetal position. You will have to raise your gown high enough to expose the sacral vertebrae."

She replied crisply: "That is silly, Doctor. You are old enough to know that I have breasts." Shedding her hospital gown, she mounted the table and assumed the position.

Having polished her sacrum with alcohol, Fellanel turned to a side table and gave the injection gun (already well baked in a radiosterile cabinet) a final minim-spray of Antiseptane. He now approached his patient, saying with jocularity: "I am about to inject. Personal service, Doctor: no computer injection for *you—*"

"Just a moment, Doctor." Her voice was peremptory, strained.

Fellanel paused. "Yes, Doctor?"

"Before you inject, there are two or three questions that I need answers to."

He said a little pettishly: "While you are asking the questions, the sterile area above your sacrum will become septic again."

She said dryly: "Give me credit for knowing this, Doctor. Will it kill you to sterilize me again?"

"Of course not," he said—yielding necessarily, since she had straightened out, turned over, and was facing him, breasts and all. "Ask your questions, and I do hope I have answers."

"I have read all your literature on Anagonon, and it satisfactorily confirms what you have told me; and I have even used your samples on some laboratory animals and again confirmed. Nevertheless, at this last moment, I have certain doubts, and I must be reassured."

"Well, Doctor?" Fellanel was defensively aggressive about it.

"Tell me again, Doctor, while I watch your eyes. Is it *absolutely* true that Anagonon will confer upon me total freedom from pain, permanently enhanced energy, and conditional immortality?"

His pale blue eyes were totally convincing. "It is *absolutely* true— no qualifications, except those implied in the conditionality of the immortality."

"One more question, then, while I watch your eyes. I have heard rumors of certain side effects. What comment do you have, Doctor?"

His eyes stayed on hers, but they became shifty: it is a rare villain whose eyes can be steady. "These rumors are theoretical. I have already quashed them."

"But do you *now* deny it, Doctor? You are a doctor talking to a doctor. Do you *now deny* it?" She had swung her legs over the edge and sat tense, gripping the table with both hands.

He drew himself to full height, elevating his aureoled chin. "At this late hour, Doctor, if you do not trust me, perhaps Anagonon is not for you."

With alacrity and weight she hit the floor. "I agree, Doctor. Anagonon is not for me." Naked, wobbling, she stormed out.

As she passed through the door, she fell like a stone.

Fellanel sauntered toward her, unzipping his jacket. Greta caught her breath: *Was* he going to. . . .Was *this* sort of frustration the reason for. . . .

But time was gone; she was already one minute late for RP with Croyd.

Icily checking midbrain coordinates, again she jumped.

Same clinic. Empty.
Automatically she glanced at the calendar.

The year made no sense. It said 5.

Baffled, she walked quickly to the desk, studied the calendar closely. The year said 5 EA. The month and day said January 1. The window said it was night.

Another mistake—but the calendar did not tell her *what sort.*

She backed away. Then her eyes fell on the desk nameplate. It did not say DR. FELLANEL. It said DR. ORPHEUS.

As she looked closely, the letters seemed to blur a little—but not much, only the way things do to close vision after long hours of study under conditions of slight eyestrain.

Greta pondered, feeling cold, but also quite unemotional, totally frontal. She had made still another mistake. This was the worst one because it had no date-meaning.

She heard low voices. They came, not from the waiting room quarter, but through a door in another wall.

She opened the door—very cautiously, because she could not be sure that this was uptime.

She saw—*herself.*

Herself and Fellanel.

In a violent, compromising situation. They were both in night-clothes. He was behind her, clasping her waist; she was protesting; he was gesturing wildly

and a knife fell into his hand, and he drove it into her back.

Greta wailed: "CROYD!"

From somewhen, his mind reached out for her. . . .

# 7

**Boston, 2502 AD:**

> He was holding her tightly, tall above her, calming her
> shuddering.

It was night.

In moments she was in shape to help him, to calm her own
shuddering. Pushing gently against his chest, she stepped back and
looked up into his face.

Croyd, all right. Even apart from the hair and the eyes and the
hard unforgettable face—Croyd, for sure.

He was gripping her shoulders. She gripped his upper arms.

She looked around. It was not deep night; it was rather early;
there was a young moon. They seemed to be standing on the walled
grounds of a towering large old brownstone house.

"This RP?" she inquired.

He nodded.

She looked at him steadily. "I goofed it up. How did I get here?"

'I felt you yell. I pulled you in. What happened?"

"How late am I?"

"Almost a quarter-hour. Not bad, really."

"Then how late did I make *us?*"

"I left us some margin. We have a few minutes. What happened?"

She told him, telepathically.

The third incident wasn't easy to tell. But she told it.

Silence.

She said hard: "You are talking to Commander Groen. This 5 EA
was downtime, wasn't it?"

"Looks that way," he brooded.

"Then my future is to be seduced and stabbed by this character?"

*"Doesn't* it look that way!"

"Stabbing, maybe; seduction, no. I'm no prude, my friend, that you know—but I have a man now, and I won't play games."

"That's how I want it. If it changes, don't apologize; I love you, I'll absorb it, I'll call it combat reciprocity—but that's how I want it. Anyhow, if you know about this probability, you are armed against it. The future is always uncertain."

"But you said that downtime is always blurred. But it *wasn't* blurred."

"Not blurred at all?"

She thought hard, remembering the nameplate. "Maybe a little, on fine stuff. Not much. Maybe not at all, I can't be sure."

They were eye to eye. He told her: "All I can say is, now you have a firsthand idea how big this Fellanel affair is. For some reason that I haven't figured, it may be dangerously lousing up the future. I'm glad you goofed it, Greta—I'm gladder that you ended up *here now;* I was afraid you might *not,* but I'm glad you goofed it because you learned some things. That alien demon in Hades, for instance: evidently Anagonon *did* come from somewhere else, though I don't know where—another galaxy, maybe; and that has to mean some kind of invasion threat. And the chubby-hard gynecologist—her I'll watch for. I don't know what the downtime stabbing meant, but we'll keep it in mind." He glanced at his fingernail cutichron: "We're on the minute, Commander. Are you in shape?"

"Do I look in shape?"

"This is a hell of a time to ask me a question like that. Yes. Let's move in."

The salon was all space: vast, baroque, high-curving into infinity. Had Fellanel been haunting the ceiling, the two people seated side by side on the little rococo settee centered on square miles of richly rugged parquet flooring would have seemed infinitesimal, dwarfishly foreshortened, lonely. But Fellanel wasn't at the ceiling: he had passed through a side curtain, promising to return in a moment.

They were served drinks by a topless female; a topless male stood facing them at Greta's side of Fellanel's empty chair which also faced them; both servants wore oriental sashes, pantaloons, and curl-toed slippers. The visitors selected drinks, and the female stepped back to

Fellanel's chair, standing on the other flank. Both male and female were physically even more powerful than Fellanel.

Croyd contentedly inspected the pendulous toplessness of the female. He thought quietly at Greta: *If I seduce her, will you seduce him?"* Croyd's big, lean youngish body and his lean, hard face and his big strong-sensitive hands were totally composed; only a certain stiffness at the roots of his hair and a certain gleam in his eyes revealed his readiness for the action that would come.

Greta's eyes were somewhat dilated. The neat knees of her long legs were tight together, and her long slender hands were too still; her torso was taut-erect; her semi-long neck, not taut, was flexibly alert, her face was composed but at attention; her eyes were scouting the range. Greta drew out a book of matches, struck a match, gazed steadfastly at the eye-level flame, and thought back: *I do not like thee, Dr. Fellanel. Two reasons why I sure can tellanel: he has the wrong sort of interest in my legs, and this is the room where he is going to stab me in a kidney. Your briefing didn't include why I'm here.*

*Are you armed?*

*Natch.*

*Good. Don't use it.*

*All right. What do I do?*

*You watch, and listen, and tomorrow you testify. You're the only person I know who has both good sense and an audiophotographic memory. Also, if you have to, you know how to jump.*

*Again—for* this *you brought me from Alpha Centauri?* Greta demanded.

*Also I may be spending my last hours in this life. I want you here. Kisses. Only, since I'm here, they may be my last hours.*

*So you have me here,* Croyd reminded her coolly.

*Why maybe your last hours?*

*If my plan works, Fellanel will give me a lethal dose.*

*How's that again?*

*And if those side effects are there, the life I will lead won't be the life I led.*

The spent match had long since gone into an ashtray. Greta mind-murmured: *I know better than to try changing your intentions. But I thought you said the bad side effects were permanent.*

*Listen, Greta. My mental defenses are adequate. I have trained for this. I can resist changes in my brain cells even while they are occurring in other parts of my body. My attitude will come through. I'll stay my own man. The galaxy will rise or fall on what you and I do here—*

Far to their right, Dr. Fellanel reentered. He paused, posing in his entry, then walked jauntily to his chair and sat facing them, selecting a drink from the topless female's tray. But within him there was no cheer: his computer had told him that Thoth was Croyd. And although Croyd was not quite the highest man in the galaxy—the highest being the elected President of the Interplanetary Union— Croyd nevertheless headed Galactic, Incorporated, the professional corporation hired to govern the galaxy, situated on Nereid, the little satellite of Neptune. Croyd was therefore more threatening than the President would have been.

"I am for the good life," murmured Dr. Fellanel, the back of a finger toying with his light-blond aureole beard. "I am pleased that both of you agree. Won't you talk, now? Ask me anything."

Croyd said: "What we have heard is that you are somehow using Anagonon to develop a fascist organization."

Fellanel's drinking glass shattered on the floor. "Do you know what you say," he demanded angrily, "when you say *fascist* to me?"

Croyd nodded: "I do." Greta sipped quietly. (Both of them had taste-tested the drinks and found them innocent.)

Fellanel's hands grasped the brocaded arms of his chair; the huge hands worked convulsively at the chair arms, fraying the fringes. "Let me tell you," he said low and tense, "what *fascist* means to me. It means Hitler—have you heard of that postmedieval terrorist? Not his contemporary, Mussolini—he was an actor, a cheapskate comedian— but *Hitler*. And do you know what *Hitler* means? Paranoid egomania. Pseudo-Wagnerian heroics. Strength through the Joy of the Marquis de Sade—or don't you know medieval history? Self-interest. Demasculinized brutality. Millions upon millions of slaughtered people: Jews by mass murder, all nations by blitzkrieg. The Reign of Law exterminated in favor of a reiteration of Rule by Caprice of the Overlord. Tragedy so vast as to be unspeakable; unspeakable horror so chthonic as to transcend the cheap label of tragedy. Self-deception. *Self-decep-*

*tion,* HUMAN SELF-DECEPTION—"

He had half risen, quivering in a semicatatonic pose.

Croyd and Greta sipped quietly.

Fellanel slipped back into his chair. He meditated. He said then: "No, my friends, I bring the opposite. *I* bring *life.* Do you *know* what my Anagonon does? There are three basic sources of human misery—and Anagonon counteracts every one. *Anagonon permanently eliminates pain:* once having taken the drug, an injured or sick person experiences only local vibrations that signal trouble but are not subjectively painful. *Anagonon enhances and perpetuates energy:* once having taken the drug, a person is able to do as much as he wants to do, and wants to do as much as he is able to do: he never wearies: he can sleep at will, but sleep is now a luxury rather than a necessity. Finally, *Anagonon annihilates mortality:* once having taken the drug, a person will never die unless disease or violence kills him by a direct and massive attack on heart or brain; and senescence is permanently out of the picture. Does *that* sound like *fascism?* No, I am bringing a new world, Paradise—"

The fascinated visitors had set down their drinks: Fellanel sat erect, eyes blazing, gripping his great knees. "This world is musty; its antiquity smells, it is painful and indolent and mortal! Consider our very dating system: what do we call our year, my friends? it is 2502 *AD,* a barbarous *AD* date. *Anno Domini!* And what does *that* mean? A dating from the reputed birth of one among many saviors—and four years wrong, at that, even if you grant that this savior ever existed.

*"My* world of the future will be *differently* dated! It will take origin from some critical turning point in the career of my Humanistic Converter—ANAGONON. Perhaps that turning point will come tomorrow; for then I hope and intend that your Medicine Board will agree and decree finally and forever that Anagonon is *Good* Medicine. In so doing, your Board will be remaking Earth and all the galaxy *for man!* Not AD—but *EA,* the years will be after that: *Eniautos Anagonou—Year of Anagonon!* They will be years of *order!* Pythagorean years, they will be! My chthonic name Fellanel will be forgotten: in the EA years I will be *Dr. Orpheus*—my real private identity!

"It is no longer a dream! *It is within my grasp—"*

He seemed to be reaching for more words. He paused. Then he

seemed to be coming into some self-realization. He quieted. He slumped a little. His hands spread, went back to his knees; he smiled a little in his touseled beard.

At the identification of **EA**, Croyd had felt Greta's mind tense, although her body remained composed. He caught her thought: *It was an EA year when he stabbed me!*

When Croyd's voice came, it continued hard. "I don't suppose your secret identity as Orpheus was revealed to you by supernal sources?"

Fellanel met his eyes. "Among cultured people, that was a manner of speaking. I shall legalize the name Orpheus because I like it and because it means life. That is all I meant."

"Also you kept speaking of this world of the future as though it would belong to you. *My* world, you said; *my* Anagonon—"

"Mother love. No more than that. Possessiveness about my dream."

"Nevertheless, again I put it to you that you are a fascist."

Fellanel tensed. "If you think that—how did you have the nerve to enter my sanctuary?"

"Miss Groen and I are experienced investigators. We felt it best to come to you openly and challenge you frankly. We know the dangers—your clinic is guarded, even your two athletes here could probably kill us by karate or some such thing: it is all part of the fascist pattern. Nevertheless we have come with a specific purpose, and it is one that can clear you tomorrow if you are clear."

The doctor leaned forward. "Clear me? Why do I need clearing?"

"If your claims are true—and *if these claims alone* are true—then your discovery of Anagonon is a very important contribution to human progress. But: in enumerating its benefits as painlessness, energy, and relative immortality—*have you exhausted the proper account of its effects?*"

There was a pause. Then Fellanel made a signal that was subtly unlike prior signals. Again the servants brought drinks (which were refused); but then, instead of retiring, the man positioned himself behind Croyd and the woman behind Greta. The guests did not miss the quietly threatening maneuver.

Croyd nevertheless pressed: "The word we are getting is that Anagonon has certain permanent side effects. These effects come to this: *A person who has been changed by Anagonon is thereafter unable to refuse any command issued by another person who has received Anagonon and whom he recognizes as having higher authority*. Tell me about these alleged side effects: are they real, or are they slander?"

Fellanel was on his feet, pacing, hands in pants pockets. "They are slander! Slander! Slander!" He turned to face Croyd: "What do you want me to do to prove that they are slander?"

Croyd said blandly: "You could inject me with Anagonon."

Greta slowly turned to eye him.

After staring at Croyd, Fellanel seated himself and leaned forward. "I do not know, sir, whether your courage or your duplicity is more to be admired. On the one hand, apparently suspecting side effects, you dare offer yourself as a guinea pig. On the other hand, being self-interested, you use the pretext to get Anagonon."

"That, Doctor, raises a point that will be at issue in tomorrow's hearing. You *restrict* the use of Anagonon. *Why?*"

"Two reasons," shot back Fellanel, prepared for that one. "First, it is still in short supply. Second, it is a doctor's duty to determine who should properly use a medicine."

"That statement is too broad. A doctor determines *what sort* of medical case should use a given medicine, and any patient who fits the psychophysical specifications may receive it. But your procedure with Anagonon during six years has been quite different. You have established a society known as The Anagonon Circle, or TAC, organized in a hierarchy, with a hundred or more doctors as a sort of multiranked priesthood, and with a lay membership running into many millions. All are Anagononic. This is hardly a short supply of Anagonon—but it *is* selective use."

"I will testify about these matters at the hearing. I thought your question was about suppositious side effects."

"If the alleged side effects exist, Dr. Fellanel, then this is a world-menacing fascist organization, and you are its absolute dictator because of Anagonon. So if you want to disprove this allegation—why don't you give me Anagonon?"

Fellanel pondered. Then he queried: "If I did, what would be gained for purposes of this hearing? There is hardly time to decide whether you will or will not experience side effects.'

"Yes, there is—just. We have Anagonon thoroughly theorized; and this theory, with a detailed proof procedure, has been filed in a sealed envelope with the Medicine Board. The evidential symptoms will show themselves, if at all, within fifteen hours or less, and they will appear in an icroscopic examination of leucocytes. Just before coming here, I submitted a sample of my normal blood as a control. So there is time to find out."

Fellanel signed for a drink. His guests negated. Leaning back and sipping, Fellanel told his drink: "This agent who calls himself Thoth turns out after all to be heroic, not self-interested. But he is also a fool. For if I were to give him Anagonon, and if his hypothesis were correct, then he would necessarily be loyal to me, and I could order him to testify in my favor at the hearing."

"Not quite," put in Greta. "His blood examination would testify against you."

"Correction," murmured Fellanel. "If he is a fool, it is not for the reason I said." He set down his drink and pondered further. Then he looked straight at his guests. "Are you a philosopher, Mr. Thoth?"

"I am not unphilosophical. Why?"

"Your theory is ingenious: I neither affirm it nor deny it now. But if this theory were right—would not these side effects be humanly good? Even Christ-like?"

"Whether they would be judged humanly good," asserted Croyd, "would depend on one's value system. Mine is the Minimal Human Value System that constitutes the Preamble to the Code of the Galactic Union, adopted by democratic-representative procedures. The third of these Minimal Values is described as follows: 'No human shall, by force or by guile, be deprived of his ability to resist volitionally the will of another creature—except under due process of law, and even then, not by guile.' The side effects I mentioned would be interpreted by any court as a violation of this value."

"Why?" demanded Fellanel, excited now, on his feet in a slight crouch over his guests. "We do not give Anagonon by force—we give it by consent! If there were any known side effects, then such side effects would be explained in full to the candidate, and on this basis his consent would be obtained before administering Anagonon. So the charge of guile would hardly fit."

Greta suggested obliquely: "What would the signed consent forms prove? They wouldn't say what *hadn't* been explained. Besides, Ana-gonon being what it is, you could give it by force first, and then order the recipient to sign a prior consent form."

"Oh, no," said Fellanel earnestly, troubled; and again, "Oh, no." He sat working on a fist with a hand. Then he looked up candidly at his guests. "Really, you know, you have me in an unfair box. Look, Mr. Thoth, how can I give you Anagonon now, even for the test? In order to give it to you, I must first have you sign the form on which all the conditions are stated. But if I show you the form, you will know what if any side effects are stated thereon. But I've said that I will not testify as to side effects until the hearing. So you've tied my hands, have you not? No, I cannot give you the drug."

"If you do not give me the drug tonight," countered Croyd, "there will not be time for the fifteen-hour maturation before the hearing. In this case, the hearing will be postponed. Do you want that?"

"Postponement is impossible," said Fellanel, shaking his head vig-orously. "I know my rights under the Earthworld Code of Jurispru-dence. A postponement now would require my consent, and I will not give it."

Croyd and Greta looked at each other and shrugged; then both of them arose. "Well," sighed Croyd, "It is too bad; for if Anagonon is as great a thing as you say it is, the world ought to have it. Don't say we didn't try to help you. Good night, Doctor." They started for the door.

Desperate, Fellanel could not avoid the cliché: *"Wait!* What do you mean?"

They turned to face him. "At the hearing," Croyd explained, "the sealed envelope that I have filed will be opened and its contents offered in evidence, and I shall have to state that you refused to test Anagonon by giving it to me. Since you will not consent to post-ponement, the Board will have to reach a decision on this basis. You know what it will decide: it will deny further use of the drug and order all stores confiscated."

Fellanel was rigid.

Then he clapped his hands three times sharply.

Behind and above him, near the far wall and the ceiling, a larger-than-life image materialized in midair: a portly, stern middle-aged woman seated in a chair. This woman spoke in a resonant bass: "Mr. Thoth—Miss Groen—*sit down.*"

And as startled Croyd and Greta stared up at her, behind *them* appeared, larger than life, the high-hung figure of a dignified, gray-bearded, bespectacled man who said in a quiet baritone: "Yes, friends—do be seated." And as they whirled to inspect *him*, there successively appeared in various aerial loci about them a handsome, gray-haired man in his middle sixties, a thin young dark German, a strong-looking Negro of indeterminate age, a wispy Oriental, and four other men—one wearing a white medical jacket.

Clearing his throat, Croyd remarked: "I assume that these are the members of the TAC Board. If you don't mind, Doctors, we will stand—it's easier to twist our necks."

Greta said in his mind: *The woman is the doctor I told you about—the first one he ever stuck. With Anagonon, I think, is what I mean.*

Fellanel told his guests: "You recognize this convocation method as a rather advanced form of tri-D projection. Mr. Thoth, will you summarize your proposal and your threats?"

Croyd did, laconically.

"Well, Doctors?" Fellanel inquired. "What do you think?"

They all looked at each other and their lips moved rapidly but no sound came. "It's a thing we do at Board meetings," Fellanel told Croyd and Greta affably. "They can hear each other, but I can't hear them. It helps them arrive at independent judgments."

Greta suggested: "Does that mean that in the hearing of their Anagonon boss they could not think independently?"

"It does not!" said Fellanel curtly.

The bass voice of the female gynecologist cut in. "Doctor, we have arrived at a recommendation. We think that you should give Mr. Thoth Anagonon tonight, with two provisos. The first is that he sign a waiver of his right to first read the conditions in order to leave you free to introduce pertinent evidence and testimony at the hearing."

"Good," said Fellanel. "Will you do this, Mr. Thoth?"

"Of course," Croyd agreed. "And the second proviso?"

"Merely," said the woman, "that Miss Groen is also to be given Anagonon."

Greta's lips paled.

The doctors flickered out.

Croyd went grim. "Good night, Dr. Fellanel." Rising, he took Greta's arm and they started for the door.

It was locked.

Croyd turned. "I think you should open the door. We want to leave, you know."

Fellanel said mildly: "You may have misunderstood. My Board and I have agreed that I *should* give you Anagonon: not that I may, but that I *should*. So I shall simply *have* to give both of you Anagonon tonight."

Croyd said hard: "When you open this door, *as you will,* I will take Miss Groen to the Medicine Board offices and place her under heavy guard; and I will then return to receive Anagonon."

Fellanel said, hard: "You should not have brought her in the first place; but since you did, she also will receive Anagonon."

Croyd challenged: "Have you heard of a man named Croyd? Do you know his personal powers?"

Fellanel asserted: "I know your powers, Mr. Croyd."

Impassive, Croyd responded: "I suspected that you'd recognized me. Pray do not force me to use my powers."

Fellanel said: "Try."

"I will," said Croyd, "in a small way." From the back of his head he threw a telekinetic blast. The door flew open behind him, and he turned to lead Greta out.

As they passed through the doorway, they fell like stones.

For precisely one minute, Fellanel and his male and female servants remained in their frozen positions. Then Fellanel relaxed, smiled gently, and started languidly toward the bodies. He bent over Croyd and Greta. He was a little surprised that they had succumbed, having anticipated that Croyd might have defenses against such attack; evidently, though, the sophisticated Mr. Croyd *(Thoth!)* had been armed only against field forces, not expecting anything so crude as body-penetrating gas. Once in a while, in the past, a recruited doctor had refused Anagonon and had walked out; but even in the very first instance, Fellanel had been ready.

The gas, of course, had been saturated with Anagonon—which was quite plentiful after all.

So now Fellanel had absolutely nothing to fear from either Mr. Croyd or Miss Groen at the Medicine Board hearing tomorrow. This Croyd was a challenging fellow, all right: Fellanel was forming a plan to keep Croyd at his personal elbow—as a privileged jester, for instance. Call him Thoth, eh? That name would be the *ultimate* irony.

As for this delicious Miss Groen. . . .

# 8

**Entering the Metagalactic Barrier, Date Under Inquiry:**

The six guest officers on the admiral's bridge wore six colors of armor—Krell's was radiant gold—but otherwise, except for conservative rank insignia on their forehead plates, all were slenderly identical. No, wait: if one scrutinized the brown fibers that. extruded from interstices in their armor, one noticed that the fibers on one or two were gray.

All were silent, waiting. All stood: they did not plan to sit.

Ahead of the officers, the almost totally transparent nose of the flagship (faintly tinted to minimize personnel accidents) revealed outside—nothing. No stars. Not quite blackness: it was gray, a little, like more than an hour before dawn; nevertheless in the glassine they could see their own reflections rather clearly.

The silver-armored flag captain entered, followed by the black-armored admiral. There were no beers.

Scarcely raising 'is voice, the flag captain chirred: "Are you listening, gentletens?"

Silently they nodded.

"The admiral has a word to say, gentletens." The flag captain stepped back.

Forward stepped the admiral: white-fibered, gleam-eyed, coal-black. "Gentletens, I apologize for taking you away from your responsibilities, but it does appear that a bit of a crisis may be brewing."

Krell, most junior among these officers and experiencing 'is first metaspace command, tensed a little—but not much, because prior cruises in and beyond 'is home Andromeda Galaxy had presented 'im with 'is fair share of crises. ("Andromeda," or Messier 31, to *us*; to *them* it was Mandomen Galaxy, and they called their home planet Flr.)

The admiral proceeded in good order. "I hate to bore you with old stuff; nevertheless let me swiftly review our mission. We *have* to take territorial possession of another galaxy that presents a suitable environment. We have selected Sol Galaxy because it is by far the largest among three galaxies that are closest to us by the metaspace charting, although others are closer via roads within the metagalaxy. We seven ships have therefore embarked from Mandomen, burst through the metagalactic barrier, crossed the intergalactic fissure, and are now reentering the metagalactic barrier near the locus of Sol Galaxy. The fact that we have not yet completed our penetration of the metagalactic surface tension is evident: see, gentletens—no stars!" Dramatically 'e flourished a claw in the direction of the forward transparency.

They all nodded, impatient for 'im to come to the point.

But 'e was in no hurry. "Our prime target within Sol Galaxy is the planet Earth—that is to say, Sol III—immediately because our hyper-telemetry tells us that Earth is rich in *you know what*, and more generally because Earth dominates that galaxy." (Some of them shifted a bit at 'is coarse and scarcely veiled you-know-what reference.) "So when we have Earth, we have the galaxy. Until now, I assume that I have been merely reviewing material that we all understand. Right?"

"RIGHT!" they chorused.

"Now, gentletens—of all the commodities that a new planet and a whole new galaxy can offer us, what would you say is the most precious?"

Now *all* of them were reduced to embarassment: frozen still, glancing surreptitiously at each other with side eyes.

The admiral cleared 'is voice discs. "Captains, I know you know; but we have to face this openly at all times, whatever inhibitions our lifelong taboo training may have imposed upon us. In these matters the young think and speak more freely—so permit me to call on the youngest among us. Sira Krell?"

Doubly embarrassed by the delicate topic and by 'is juniority, young Krell began: "Well, sira, in the first instance, a suitable environment—"

But a dirty-minded chuckle rippled across the bridge; and behind Krell a red-armored commander sniggered: " 'S matter, chum—didn't they tell you the facts of life?"

The admiral was not amused. 'E waited, watching Krell.

"Sira," said Krell, "I am of course aware that there is an ultimate need which is most precious; but without the suitable environment, that value would be no value."

"Very good. Is anything else besides a suitable environment necessary to make that value a value?"

"I believe that 'suitable environment' covers all the contributory values. In a way, it covers even that one prime value."

"Which is?"

"Suitable mammals."

Several officers cleared their throats. They knew, they knew, it was all but instinctive for them to know; and just for that reason, the topic of mammals was taboo among civilized representatives of Flr. Officers and other masculates told mammalian jokes, naturally; but in a sober gathering like this. . . .

The admiral snapped: "Sira Krell, just because of your youth and your small command, your words are authoritative: what you know, all of us must know—and frankly and outspokenly recognize. You are the sole crew of your little ship *Champu*, the smallest in the fleet; and you carry only one female. The rest of us have more crew and more females; this flagship carries a crew of thirty-nine and is transporting seventy-one females. We will not go into the question why you and your female are here at all—"

The red one behind Krell said: "Haw!"—but very softly. Krell silently marked 'im out for destruction—but much later. Krell and 'is princess were here because 'is "princess" was the lowest-ranked of those in the expedition, and there had been no room for her, and she had begged, and so Krell's little two-place ship had been brought into it. This made his Maelbrug the last nubile female in Mandomen.

"Your words," the admiral was continuing, "are therefore authoritative. This is a technical session, a clinical session: spare us the embarrassed hesitation; let us be perfectly explicit about this prime value. Go on, Sira Krell."

Steeling 'is resolution, Krell spoke calmly. "Sira and gentletens, it comes down to this. Our race must have mammals to survive. There was a time when our females—well, *laid their eggs"*—it evoked voice disc clearing—"in other arthropods. It was an instinct laid upon us before there were any mammals. But after mammals arose on our home planet Flr, and when we were driven by their challenge to become intelligent instead of mechanical, we learned that mammals were more succulent hosts. By shifting to mammals, we proliferated so rapidly that we soon gained command of our galaxy. But in the process, we so evolved that our eggs now *require* mammals—they will not proliferate in arthropods."

"Which mammals best?" the admiral persisted.

"Sira, in the highest primates."

"And why is this fact taking us to Sol Galaxy and particularly to Earth?"

"Sira, five generations ago our own Mandomen Galaxy ran out of primates—excepting, of course, the high primates who took force-field refuge in the Glistr Star-Cluster. So we were reduced to other mammals, and we are down now to the miserable unguiculates, and our birth rate is fatally low; and we are backed up to our original planet Flr, for the high primates have recaptured our other planets and are poised to destroy us finally. But if now this thin fleet can take command of Sol Galaxy with its teeming trillions of primates—"

"They call the highest ones *humans,* Lieutenant."

"Exactly, sira!" No longer embarrassed, Krell was a flaming young zealot. "And on the day when my Maelbrug first overwhelms a human and begins to thrust her ovipositor into him again and again and again—"

"Krell! That will be enough!"

"Sorry, sira, I did not mean to be indecent."

"Very good, Lieutenant; you exceeded yourself at the last, but your lecture was basically correct. Now, unhappily, I have one of my own to give. Are you listening, gentletens?"

They nodded. Krell stepped back.

"We must stay for a moment, gentletens, on the delicate topic. All of you realize that time is of the essence on this excursion. Are you all aware that there are three reasons for this?"

A gray-armored captain spoke. "I am aware of two reasons, and I will speak of one. Because of our high speed and great distance, we must aim, not at where Earth *is*, but at where Earth *will be*. Unfortunately this lead time is qualified by a large uncertainty factor, owing both to distance and to the limitations of extrametagalactic hypertelemetry. In this sense, time is a major factor. As to the second sense in which time is a major factor, I yield to our courageous young lieutenant."

It drew chuckles from four officers. The admiral demanded: "Well, Krell?"

Krell said, very low: "Our males are too frail to make the trip. The eggs of our females, once fertilized, have a preposit gestation period of nineteen Flr-days. We calculated that we could make the voyage in thirteen days, plus or minus two. We therefore chanced impregnating our females on the day of embarkation. That is the second reason why time is a major factor."

"And the third reason, Sira Krell?"

'Is voice was almost inaudible. *"All* our surviving nubile females are with us on this voyage. It is our species—win or lose."

Mercilessly the admiral pressed: "And if our females do not find mammals in nineteen days from embarkation?"

Thinking concernedly of Maelbrug, Krell responded: "Pain. Insanity. Death." Then 'e added:: *"Species* death."

The admiral allowed silence to dwell upon them.

The admiral then asserted: "As you know, we are now reentering the the metagalactic barrier. Have you noticed anything missing?"

The universal silence grew turgid: each of them had been hoping that 'e alone was missing something, but now the admiral had made it objective.

The gray-armored captain finally responded: "Sira, yes. There is no turbulence. Do you have a theory, sira?"

Krell was recalling ironically how carefully 'e had buckled down 'is Maelbrug against this missing turbulence that was always, in theory and in fact, a vicious feature of transit through the metagalactic skin.

The admiral slowly shook 'is head. "I don't have a theory—not yet—except that I know of no way to consider this lack of turbulence good. In the back of my mind I have a very small and disturbing intuition, with no intellectual support as yet: namely, that this lack of turbulence is somehow related to *time.*"

They stiffened. *Time* was their mortal adversary.

"I called you together," 'e told them, "primarily to draw your attention to this oddity with its obscure possible hazard—and to do one other thing which Sira Krell has now made clear.

"Theoretically, a military masculate's acceptance of 'is mission on command is sufficient. In practice, all of us know that 'e must inwardly *comprehend the meaning* of 'is mission in terms of its thrusting cause and its intended consequences—that it must be 'is mission personally. Now in the possible emergency created by this lack of turbulence where there should be turbulence, I call upon each of you to hold high in 'is hearts these meanings that Lieutenant Krell has so well reviewed for us. We are daring space and time and chance, not for conquest alone, but for home and hearth and the survival of our race. We shall win—or we shall die; and in the case of our females, their deaths will be horrible. Are there any questions, gentle-tens?"

Just to Krell's left, a blue claw hesitantly started up, wavered, and went down again.

The black admiral nodded to the silver flag captain, who rasped: "Formation—dismissed." 'E followed the admiral out.

As officers headed for the flttr, Krell tapped one of the top shoulders of the blue-armored commander who had raised 'is claw and then had bugged out. "What was your question?" Krell demanded.

The commander shrugged other shoulders. "I was going to be clever and ask 'im how a person can notice *no turbulence.* But 'e wouldn't have understood."

"I don't, for sure," Krell snapped. "Glad you backed out, Fstr."

"It's an epistemological question—" began Fstr; but then Commander Fstr shrugged still farther down and muttered: "Let's get the hell into that flttr."

**Greta Actuality D minus 3 and 2**
**Krell Actuality D minus 6 and 4**

Part Three

FLIGHT OF MIND

Love, as I think, is an instant's fusing of shadow and substance. . . .

—James Branch Cabell, FIGURES OF EARTH (1921)

Every end (said old John Dewey), once attained, becomes a means to ends beyond. (Allowing, one may add, an interval for exploratory appreciation and comprehension of the end attained before moving on.) So it is with love at its best. Until the fulfillment of love is attained, it is a goal; but once the love is attained and absorbed in full knowledge and faith, it becomes a *climate* for conjoint pursuit of goals beyond. . . .

—Nike Pan, PLATO AND THE STARS (2318)

# 9

**Within the Metagalactic Barrier:**

They were a resplendent pair, Maelbrug and Krell—close together in flashing panoply on the compact bridge of their little ship: 'e pressed gently erect against the pilot pole, held lightly to it by the quarter-G artificial gravity that exuded from the pole; she gracefully semicoiled on the navigator's couch whose gravity was quarter-G. Dutifully Maelbrug read and reported the instrumentation, not understanding any of it. Beyond the transparent forward curvature of the bridge, still there was only dark opacity rendered more solid by the artificial illumination of the bridge, which created odd reflections in the concavity of the shell: Maelbrug and Krell saw themselves, not in the shell of the mirror, but nestled small in its hollow.

"Tri-D azimuth 250-220, origin Skirl, whatever that is," reported Maelbrug, "holding steady. Exterior light rising slowly, 7 csl in the past 91 clicks, but still up only to 29 csl—"

"That's as it should be, Maelbrug. Go on."

"Exterior hull curvatures: forward normal, aft normal, forward/port normal, forward/starboard normal, port/forward—well, to shorten it, all readings normal except port/aft/aft/semidown. Interior hull readings—"

"What's with port/aft/aft/semidown?" demanded Krell sharply.

"Nothing much, I'd say: some teentsy-weentsy meteor—"

"Out here we don't have meteors! What does the instrument *say?*"

"There's just a little pink dot."

"Pink, eh? How big?"

"Maybe about like a baby's spiracle."

"Oh. All right, then. You should say: magnitude 5."

"How can I tell?"

"In the training. . . .Never mind. Baby's spiracle, I get it."

"Why doesn't the stupid instrument just flash on a 5?"

"You may have a thing, there. Go on."

"Velocity relative to Mandomen center, $4.582397 \times 10^6$ C, but slowing. Is that pretty fast?"

Hesitation; then a surprisingly curt reply: "It's fast. Go on."

Fixing 'im with an eye, she bent the others on her task. "Date: H-hour plus 12 days 27 hours 43 clicks. Temporal kymography fluc-fluctuating minimally around zero line for entire back two-day range. . . .Krell—"

"Maelbrug?"

"Are we—on schedule?"

"Why do you ask?"

"What a silly question, you sound almost male! But you're putting me off; *you* don't ask silly questions. Then we *are* behind schedule, aren't we. How much?"

Krell understood her concern, feeling it 'imself. "Not much. How are you feeling?"

"I'm beginning to feel a little full. Not seriously, though. How *could* we fall behind schedule?"

"It seems to have been the lack of turbulence. We were counting on the standard turbulence to give us tail thrust."

"How would *that* work?"

"Like water pulsating through a hose."

"How does *that* work?"

"Well, it does. But don't worry, we aren't *that* far—"

"I thought you figured thirteen days for the whole trip. "

"That's right—but we're almost there. We've already covered four fifths of the distance."

"That means we'll be there in—what? Three or four days?"

"Well—five days, maybe."

"I do know my arithmetic, Krell. That doesn't work out right."

"Well, you see, this is going to be the slowest part of the trip. We can't travel as fast inside the metagalaxy because of space curvature and dustclouds. But I can guarantee five days."

Silence. Then: "That's tight, my friend."

Softly: "Not too tight, Maelbrug. We'll touch down on Earth a day before you are ready to extroject. The microspectrographs show that Earth is teeming with mammals."

"But the spectrographs are nearly two million years old!"

"Yes, but our hypertelemetry is practically instantaneous; and crude as it is, the inferences are unmistakable that a complex humanoid political structure has evolved with its center at Earth. And this was confirmed by the recent death communiqué from our heroic pioneer, Sira Ssen. So you'll be wealthy with hosts almost immediately."

"Krell—"

"Mm?"

"In Mandomen, the humanoids have made us all but extinct. *Totally* extinct there, now."

"In Sol Galaxy, we plan to return the compliment by domesticating the humanoids."

"Unless they kill us first."

"They won't—because what our martyred pioneer Sira Ssen left with them has presumably made them powerless to resist us."

"But what if that didn't work?"

"They still can't kill us. In this one little ship I have power to destroy a planet, modulable to power precise enough for killing one small mammal. Only, we don't want to destroy them—for you know what reason."

"So why didn't we use this power in Mandomen, and take our galaxy back from the humanoids?"

"They neutralize it."

"Oh."

Silence.

"Cute little face," said Krell softly, turning 'is main eyes upon the purple iridescence of her countenance.

"Pardon?"

"I said, cute little face. Yours, I mean."

"Krell! Are you *sure* you aren't male—just a little bit?"

'E told her quietly: "Not the slightest little bit. But I know a pretty face when I see one."

"Do males have pretty faces for you?"

"Some do, but weak. But yours is a strong pretty face. And yet cute."

"Why cute, Krell?"

"Perhaps now you'd better check the external light gauge again."

Shrugging six, she looked at the gauge and tensed. "This is interesting. It has gone up to 93 csl. Isn't that nearly—"

'E left the control pole to join her on the navigator's couch, peering at the gauge. 'E nodded. Reaching up the pole, 'e touched a button that extinguished the bridge illumination except for the black light that made the instrument dials luminescent. Outside the shell, all was pale pearl gray.

Krell got on the communicator. Giving 'is ship's name, 'e said: "*Champu* to flagship. Over."

"Flagship here."

"I read 93 csl. What do you read?"

"Confirm 93 csl." In a prolonged exchange, the two craft confirmed mutually that they were running close together on parallel courses, and the flagship informed the *Champu* that the entire formation was holding constant.

Flagship then said: "Anticipate immediate breakthrough into metagalaxy. Hold your present course for two hours; then we will veer port downside and run along the galaxy toward Sol. Repeat."

Krell repeated.

"Very good. After changing and setting course, come to flagship for an Admiral's Conference. Not an emergency, however."

"Understood."

"Out." Click.

Krell turned to Maelbrug.

Maelbrug was staring at the forward shell.

Abruptly they were blinded by three light images: port, starboard, forward.

Krell touched another switch that reduced the transparency and the glare.

'E and Maelbrug were now able to resolve the lights into three gigantic star images at right, at left, and forward.

"Why three?" she whispered.

For Krell the experience was new, but 'e had done 'is homework. "As this clears," 'e said, "You are probably seeing, as I am, that these are three great lights set in a totally black hemisphere of space. Keep your main eyes on the center light, let your side eyes take care of the other two. Now, what are you seeing?"

"The light to my right is the greatest of the three. The light to my left is next. The one in front is faintest."

"The one in front is Sol Galaxy."

"Oh." Disappointment. "I thought it would be bigger."

"Actually it is almost as big as our Mandomen. But you are seeing it edge-on, and a great thickness of dustclouds in its central flat disc is obscuring much of its light for us. Can you begin to see the shape now?"

Awe: "It is very beautiful. It is like a straight vertical shaft of darkness, darker than night, with rich white lightfire glowing on both sides in the middle of the shaft."

"When we turn and fly across it, you will see that Sol Galaxy is a great spiral disc of white fire like our own Mandomen."

"Where is our Mandomen? Can we see it?"

"The mass of white light that you see to the right is more than half of all the galaxies in the metagalaxy, and the fainter mass of light to the left is the remaining minority. Our Mandomen is part of the light to the right. We are still so close to the inner surface of the metagalaxy that all the light from all those galaxies is confused together as a single great light. But as we move farther in, the galaxies to left and right will begin to distinguish themselves from each other, and you will be able to find Mandomen."

"Will it be big?"

"It will look only like a fairly large star."

"How can it be so far away?"

"By crossing the extrametagalactic fissure, we came here in only thirteen days. Had we stayed inside the metagalaxy, the trip would have taken nearly a year."

"Why, Krell?"

"The surface of the metagalaxy is convoluted. Each galaxy, thrusting outward, makes a lobe; between galaxies there are fissures. Within the metagalaxy, light hugs the inner surface, traveling far inward and then again far outward to go from one galaxy to the next. But we took the shortcut across."

"Krell—"

"Maelbrug?"

"I want to stay here with you."

"How?"

"Here in space with you. Alone in this beauty with you."

"So do I with you. But—"

"I know. We can't. Even if we wanted to be defiant, we couldn't—because I have hundreds of little time bombs inside me, and besides, our air and food and water would give out. But I want to. Can we leave it like this?"

"So do I want to."

"Let's be quiet for a while."

# 10

**Boston, 2502 AD:**

Exactly fifteen hours after Greta and Croyd had been felled in the doorway, Dr. Fellanel-Orpheus entered the bedroom where he had caused her to be carried. She was asleep, but not deeply so.

Pulling up a chair beside her bed, Orpheus gently shook her shoulder.

She awoke alert, ready to respond, to initiate, to know, and to go. She was radiant at the sight of divinely handsome Orpheus. Sitting up and seizing his hand with both hands, she demanded eagerly: "Tell me what happened, Doctor!"

"You and Croyd received Anagonon when you tried to leave last night. The shot was concealed in my doorway; I had it set; you triggered it by going through."

"*Clever* Dr. Orpheus!" honestly exclaimed Greta. "Where is Croyd?"

"He is all right—I'll tell you about him in a minute. It is more important for you to know that both of you are now honored members of The Anagonon Circle. I have your bracelet, my dear: hold up your left hand."

He affixed the slave bracelet with a small tool that emitted a tiny spark. She raised her hand to admire the talisman. "I have never been so proud," she told him. But then, forgetting the bracelet, she pressed: "What about Croyd?"

"I have him under sedation, because I think he may still be dangerous, Anagonon or no Anagonon."

"Very wise of you. I am sure that he would still be dangerous."

From a pocket Orpheus produced an aluminum cylinder about six inches long and two inches in diameter. "This is a thermal container," he told her, "and what it contains is a very small glass tube of whole blood. We extracted this blood specimen from Croyd seven hours ago. Let me explain. You are too smart to be fooled, Commander Groen—yes, I know who you are—and I am sure you realize that it is true about the side effects."

"Of course," she glowed. "How good of you to be honest with me!"

"The point is," Orpheus expanded, "that although it does take fifteen hours for the side effects to maturate, it takes only eight for the advertised effects of painlessness, energy, and relative immortality to operate. At the hearing this afternoon, we are therefore in position to offer this blood sample in evidence to prove that Croyd took Anagonon and did experience the main effects but did *not* experience the alleged side effects!"

Greta, ignoring the fact that she was almost nude, threw back her coverlet and swung her legs over the bed. She said, low: "It is brilliant, Doctor. I see several technical difficulties, but I am convinced that you know exactly how to overcome them."

"Every one!" he assured her. "However, it is all going to depend on your testimony—and we have to start right away. I'll coach you aboard the helijet to New York, and there will be some papers for you to sign. How fast can you be ready?"

She was on her feet. "Five minutes, I think. Will you hand me that traveling case, Doctor? It would be better for me to be in uniform—"

The Medicine Board of Final Review had five members, one of them a computer with a full vote.

Greta, trim in the uniform of a galactic naval commander, appeared as a special witness for the Investigation Section of the Medicine Board.

Under affirmation, she testified coolly that she had been detailed by Temporary Chairman Croyd to assist him in an investigation which had been requested by the Medicine Board. She stated that she had been given all details of the theory and procedure which Croyd had filed with the Board in a sealed packet.

She then stated that Croyd had appeared at Dr. Fellanel's clinic and, in her presence, had accepted Anagonon. It had been administered by Dr. Fellanel himself.

A few hours later—still in her presence—Croyd, she stated, had been summoned away on urgent galactic business of a secret nature that he could not communicate either to Greta or to the Medicine Board. This accounted for his absence from this hearing.

Before leaving, however, he had been able to remain in the clinic for the prescribed fifteen-hour maturation period. He had then submitted to a blood extraction under the supervision of Dr. Fellanel and two other TAC doctors, with Greta observing.

Commander Groen testified that she had been present at all times, along with Chairman Croyd, while the blood was quick-frozen, placed in a small thermal container, and handed to Croyd by Dr. Fellanel. Croyd had then handed this container to Greta, and she had kept it on her person continuously until now and had it on her person now. All who had been present—Fellanel, the two witnessing doctors, Croyd, and Greta—had then cosigned a document asserting that the thermal container which Croyd had handed to Greta contained the blood, untreated except for quick freezing, which Croyd had yielded fifteen hours after receiving Anagonon. Responsive to questioning, Greta now produced this document, and it was entered in evidence.

Greta then exhibited a thermal container, testifying that it was indeed the container which Croyd had handed her and which by her own eye witness did contain Croyd-blood. This container was also entered in evidence.

The hearing now adjourned to a laboratory for analysis of the leucocytes in this experimental blood sample in comparison with those in the control sample previously filled. Antigrav equipment got the computer there along with the other board members.

No matter how sophisticated scientific procedures may become, no system of abstractions ever quite convinces until there is confirming visual and tangible evidence—the more dramatic the better, as long as it is precise. Thus, after all qualitative and quantitative analyses were in and computed, the high point—climaxing two hours of studies—was visual, tangible, and sizable.

It was a pair of full-color solid projections: the double helix of the DNA chain constituting (to use crude wordage) Croyd's gene for intuitive interhuman responsiveness *before* the use of Anagonon, and the parallel double helix of the equivalent gene from one of his leucocytes *after* Anagonon. This gene had been pinpointed in the theory as the pivotal gene with respect to the alleged side effects.

The scientists slowly stalked around these projections which were larger than a man. They scrutinized them, felt their surfaces and curves and angles, thrust their arms between helices, calibrated them.

In the end, it was consensus that between the control blood sample and the experimental blood sample there was no significant difference with respect to this gene. But then, after the prescribed fifteen hours, *there had been no side effects!* (Greta knew, of course, that Fellanel had cheated—but Anagononic Greta was not the least bit interested in telling.) By contract, the genes involved in the central effects, the boasted effects—the genes associated with pain projection, energy diffusion, and mortality— all *had* changed, in ways that accorded with theory and entirely upheld the claims by Dr. Fellanel and all prior research.

Various doctors and lay members of TAC, all eminent people, then testified, corroborating Fellanel's plea that there were no side effects. Courtroom tests on these people proved dramatically that they felt no pain and that their energies were boundless; but proof of the immortality allegation, as Fellanel's attorneys with difficulty convinced the Board members, would have to rest on theory.

Dr. Fellanel was then asked why he insisted that he and TAC

maintain monopolistic control of Anagonon. His testimony was presented with expressive emotionality but nevertheless with scientific elegance, involving factors of controlled optimum production volume and utilizing also some pertinent sociological parameters. His basic plea was that there must be centralized control of the drug. Conceding that the government was theoretically competent to exercise such control, he showed not only that the medical hierarchy of TAC had experience of Anagonon which would be hard to replicate, but also that the finest minds in biotherapeutics were members of this hierarchy. He went on to cite a number of precedents in the public-utility field. He rounded it off with an impressive recitation and explication of the Hippocratic Oath. He then stood down.

The Board found 5-0 for the safety of Anagonon, 5-0 for its efficacy, and 3-2 for the exclusive competency of TAC to administer its production and use. The computer voted *for* on all three issues.

Nobody thought to suggest that somebody ought to keep tabs on vanished Temporary Chairman Croyd. A man of his stature had to come and go as he might judge best, and he could rarely talk about it.

This was the triumphant day that Fellanel—Dr. Orpheus—chose as the origin point of his Monon: for the years EA—*Eniautos Anagonou.*

## II

**Boston, 2502 AD; then Eurydice, 4-5 EA::**

Clinging to an arm of Orpheus after the hearing and the helijet ride back to Boston, Greta passed with him through the outer foyer and into the majestic baroque salon that was his residential sanctuary.

Having closed and locked the door, he helped her off with her jacket; gently he loosened and removed her necktie and then his own, and he went to the bar to make zacs. Perhaps there he touched a button: the hall was filled with the seductive music of a harp.

Presently they sat in facing chairs. He gazed at her with heightening pleasure. She gazed back at him with heightening concern, with a growing discomfort in her belly—a wrongness that her mind began to recognize as guilt about something or other.

Presently said Orpheus, leaning excitedly forward, showing his great handsome white teeth: "If you would like to make yourself more comfortable, you will find some lounging pajamas in that bedroom—"

Greta shot back: "No! Not yet!" She was beginning to know what the guilt was about.

The Orpheus eyebrows went up.

Greta stared at him, shaking her head a little, trying to clear it. Dimly she remembered an emotic shutoff procedure that Croyd had taught her, involving just a little adjustment in her own forebrain that prevented emotional arousal from coming to consciousness. Mind fumbling, she executed it—but it didn't help very much, because her forebrain was saturated with the persuasibility of Anagonon.

Orpheus was saying with a kind of nettled bewilderment: "I thought I heard you say *no* to me. Greta—you aren't a deviate?"

She shook her head and blurted, "Please wait! Just wait a minute—" What had she just been doing? Worshiping this man, all day.
Admiring him for his treacherous conquest of Croyd and herself.
Betraying Croyd with happy lies. Establishing the ultimate triumph of
this very Anagonon which was going to do to the world and the
galaxy what it was doing to Croyd and herself.

And now, dear God, she *loved* this Orpheus! Shut it out of her
consciousness with brain switches, fine; but that wasn't inhibiting the
erotic action of her midbrain and hindbrain. Worst of all, even were
she totally cold to him, Anagonon would require her to do his
bidding. But she *wasn't* cold to him: he was mighty, intense, over-
poweringly attractive; and the room and her soul were flooded with
harp music. . . .

He arose and came and stood before her. She looked up at him,
consciously loving him with that *agape* which is purely of the spirit,
totally unconscious *of* any *eros* in her mind, yet hideously conscious
*that* her below-conscious instinctuality was ready to throw her upon
him. He bent low to lay a hand on her shoulder: the shoulder moved
responsively, trembling forward. . . .

A memory intruded. Her telling Croyd: "I'm no prude, my friend,
that you know—but I have a man now, and I won't play games."
Croyd telling her: "That's how I want it. If it changes, don't apologize: I love you, I'll absorb it, I'll call it combat reciprocity—but
that's how I want it."

Seating himself beside her, towering above her, Orpheus reached
across her breasts to grasp her far shoulder.

She could not say no to him, not with Anagonon—but the Croyd-
memory countered the Anagonon just enough to let her lie. She said
as distinctly as she could: "Dr. Orpheus, I suppose that I should have
expected this, it's part of the pattern, but I confess that I didn't. I
love you, and so I have to be honest with you: sexually I am not
with it."

Incredulous, he held her shoulders a moment longer; and then his
hands fell away and he stared into her green steady eyes. His face
and his voice hardened: "You have Anagonon—and you *refuse* me?"

Her inward conflict was bitter. "I *can't* refuse you—you *know* I
can't refuse you! Anything you do is all right! But—you just have to
realize that I can't respond!" The very lie sent her metabolism

higher: now fiendishly her thalamic thrust destroyed her cerebral inhibition, and *conscious* desire combined with Anagonon to assail her defenses. . . .

The face and body of Orpheus went manic. "I get it. You want to be *ravished!* All right—occasionally even *that* is good!" And he leaped upon her.

At the instant of the lustful leap, Greta's terrified mind departed her brained body.

Suddenly Orpheus released her mindless body, and moved away, and went into thought again.

Pacing, detumescing, he told the floor: "There's something wrong with this. Just possibly I *respect* you, Commander Greta. No, you I can't ravish. Instead, I am going to give you time. All the time you need. Years, if necessary. After all, if it is a woman I want, there are all the women I need; but with you, I think what I need for sure is a total voluntary surrender—and with desire." He turned to devour her with compelling eyes: "I don't want you any other way, Greta."

She did not reply. Having rearranged herself, mindless Greta was looking straight ahead, her face quite white.

He took her hand. Leaning toward her, he said urgently: "You are *sure*, Greta?"

She replied tonelessly: "I am sure." It was an automatic brain response, a computer response.

"And yet you love me?"

Her brain made her voice say: "Of course I love you. I have Anagonon."

He stood, half smiling in a half-distraught way, half spreading his arms and hands. He murmured: "I never liked any of them until I met one like you. But she told me I was too dreamy to be a man. So later I grew this beard, but I thought then *they* ought to come to *me*. But they didn't. That was when I found out that I was really Orpheus, so it didn't matter. And then Anagonon came, and then they *all* came. But *you—*"

Turning back to her, he ordered: "Go home, Greta."

She suffered his bear embrace, and she went away—mindless in the hazards of the night streets.

* * *

In the course of her elementary uptime-downtime telekinetic training with Croyd, Greta had not progressed to the point of departing her body. But the psychic trauma of the lustful leap was acute enough to send a normally educated mind into psychotic split. In Greta's case, she was already educated up to the threshold of a special escape, and reflexively she used it.

Whither would she go, though—or, since she had temporal options, whinner? Had she been trained in this disembodied mind activity (which necessarily had to be brief, since a mind unbased on a living brain is quickly eroded and scattered into psychospace), the number of planned options open to her would have been indefinite: the whither-whinner had to be predictable by one who might know enough to predict it.

Croyd could have predicted. Her mind would have to go to a place-time where there was *another Greta-body* available to her, *and* where Croyd would be found nearby *with his mind awake.* Where-whenever these two requisite conditions might exist, that spatiotemporal locus would be a live lure for her aimlessly disembodied mind.

*Another* Greta-body? Well: the *same* Greta-body *five years later* would serve as well.

And it was precisely on New Year's Eve, 4-5 EA, in Eurydice, that Thoth was awakening after five years of stasis. . . .

Croyd lay supine on the couch; his eyelids fluttered; he seemed on the verge of awakening. Greta bent over him with concern of a vague sort, her half-conscious memories a mélange of an almost-rape by Orpheus and five subsequent years of fleet activity. She knew somehow that Croyd had been kept in stasis, that until now for some reason it hadn't troubled her, that only last night he had been felled by Anagonon.

Also bending over Croyd from the far side of the couch, Orpheus was crooning: "This planet is not Earth. This planet is Monon. Earth is an enemy planet. Earth is light-years away; it is a dark evil Counter-Monon beyond the Central Fire. This planet is Monon, Thoth, Thoth: this planet is Monon, it is *Counter*-Earth. This planet is Monon—"

Croyd opened his eyes; and as he did so, Greta remembered that she must not call him Croyd, now, for Orpheus had decreed that his name would be Thoth.

Only yesterday Orpheus, by his own private channels, had communicated with her on her frigate *Ceres* : it was one of the ships "from Earth" which were the "mysterious" and hated enemies of Monon, enemies which Orpheus was building up in the minds of his people on Monon as an obvious dictatorial device for consolidating loyalty. Commander Greta and all her crew were Anagononics, but Fleet Admiral Leclerc did not know this. On a suggestion by Orpheus, Greta had advised Admiral Leclerc that a high-placed private contact of hers wanted to work with her on a fleet intelligence mission; and the admiral had given her secret orders to report below, using the pullman. When she had arrived, Orpheus had advised her that he was going to awaken Croyd as Thoth, that she was to be Thoth's girl, that he needed Thoth for his confidant; and Orpheus had also advised Greta what request he intended to make of Thoth. It troubled Greta, but she opposed no objection: Orpheus had been patient for five years. . . .

Croyd raised a hand feebly, and the voice stopped, and Orpheus and Greta looked at each other. Croyd inquired: "How long have I been sleeping?"

"Quite a while," said Orpheus. "However, you've awakened just in time, Thoth. I came here to give you something, to show you how much I like you."

Pleasure flooded Croyd's face; but Greta was in the grip of profound disturbance, and she was struggling to understand why, as she and Orpheus helped Croyd to a sitting position. Reaching into the leather wallet that hung from the girdle of his tunic, Orpheus brought out a small amulet on a chain bracelet of gold.

Taking the amulet, Croyd scrutinized it: obviously he was not sure what it meant. (Glancing at her own left wrist, Greta saw that she wore a similar bracelet.) The amulet was an ovoid, its surface queerly metallic-iridescent like silver with translucent depth; and etched in this surface was an O.

"I had your old bracelet removed while you slept," Orpheus told him. "Never mind what it was. What counts is this new one. Shall I tell you what the O means? My own bracelet"—he displayed it— "bears an A for Alpha, and Alpha means *One:* I am the only *One* in the world. I like you, Thoth, and I want you to be high on my Monon, so that you and I can associate with each other in our special relationship. But I could not make you a Beta for *Two*, because that is reserved for the ten high members of my TAC Board; and if I were to give you any lower rank, it would be less than what I want for you. So I have created this special rank O which means nothing at all and everything at all. If the O were internally crossed, it would mean Theta or *Eight;* but without the bar inside it, the O means only one thing: *The Ambiguously Ranked Friend of Dr. Orpheus.* Are you happy with your O, Thoth?"

Gaping a little, Croyd nodded. His fatuous pleasure reminded Greta of *something*: Orpheus talking to *her* on *her* awakening five years before. . .Orpheus fitting *her* with a bracelet. . *.her* zany glee. . . .

And what had followed. . . .

Five years before?

*Just now?* No, no: five years. . . .

"You will be the only person on Monon to wear the O," Orpheus emphasized. "Here, give me your wrist." And as Croyd offered his left wrist, Orpheus linked the bracelet around it; and then with a small instrument he did something that evoked a tiny light and a little heat at the linkage.

He said: "As you well know, Thoth, every human being on my Monon wears such a bracelet with one or another rank engraved upon it. Both bracelet and amulet are made of Anagonium, which is indestructible except by a technique which only a few of us know; consequently there is no chance for anybody to steal another's bracelet or to alter his own inscription of rank. When a rank is to be changed, and that is rare, only certain designated officers are able to do it. So your rank of O is absolutely secure: for life, my friend, you are my intimate friend, my philosopher. Are you glad?"

"Of course I am glad." Thoth felt the gladness glow.

"And now," asserted Orpheus, rising, "I claim Greta from you, Thoth."

Greta was impassive.

Orpheus had spoken the stimulus phrase for a ritual that Thoth somehow knew. Not by his gift of rank had Orpheus bought Greta: on his Monon, a Transient Claim was a Transient Claim whenever it might be made by a superior or by a peer. Thoth eagerly responded with the correct ritual response: "Of course, Friend, she is yours for ten days and ten nights. Return her in good condition."

Weeks ago Orpheus had concluded to awaken Croyd as Thoth his jester; and all during these weeks, intensive hypnopaedics had done their work. The lethargic Croyd-brain became thoroughly acculturated to Monon—he knew all its ways and walks and customs as though they were his own by long practice: to the conventional Ten-Day Claim he had given the correct conventional response without even thinking twice; Greta grasped that he would not be remembering anything that had happened to him at any time in the past—but he would take this as a matter of course, not missing the memory. Suddenly Greta felt anguish. . . .

"Greta," said Orpheus, "please go get ready while I talk to Thoth."

She left the room without comment. In the bedroom that she had occupied yesterday, she began to pack. It went slowly, because without much success she was trying to think straight; but there seemed to be no hurry, for the men were talking discursively.

Had she been able to remember her own mind-jumping, this would have been a hook to help unconfuse her thinking; but the downtime jump had been reflexive in trauma, and her mind had immediately coalesced *with her mind* in this 4-5 EA body. (But how did this brain come to *have* a mind for hers to coalesce with?) The harder she concentrated, the more surely her brain forced her memories into the logical sequence that was categorically imperative: first the invasion of Dr. Fellanel's house by Croyd and herself, then the Anagonon-felling, then the inquiry, then her perverse refusal of Orpheus, then five years of fleet action as a secret fleet agent of Orpheus. . . .

Somehow, though, intuition manages to survive logic. The logic was perfect—but it did not satisfy her. She had to warn Croyd—but she didn't know what to warn him *of*.

For a girl with a superior audiophotographic memory, the confusion was unsettling.

"Greta!" called Orpheus. "Hurry up. I'll wait outside."

Greta hurried into the room, carrying her grip. Setting it down, she came quickly over and sat by Croyd, seizing his hands. Peering into his eyes, she demanded: "Don't you know what is happening?"

"How do you mean? What?"

"I just got it figured out, sort of. This is five years *later!* You've been in stasis for five years! He just brought you back—but you're still under some kind of narcosis—"

He patted her shoulder tolerantly. "Now, Greta, I don't remember anything like that—"

"Of course you don't! You don't remember *anything* before you woke up just now—do you?"

He blinked: "Well—I'm pretty drowsy—"

"Of *course* you're drowsy! Of *course* you don't remember! He drugged you so you *wouldn't* remember!" She was shaking him a little, intent on conveying to him what just for the instant she was *sure* she comprehended. . . .

He demanded: "What do *you* remember?"

She frowned. She remembered a perfect logical sequence of five years. She remembered that she was Anagononic, and *he* was Anagononic, and now he was awake, and Orpheus was God, and he and she were favorites of ultra-beloved Orpheus, and that was *that*. . . .

She stood up, and stamped a foot, and hurried from the room. Orpheus awaited her in the corridor. Floridly he courted her and escorted her to his private aircar which haughtily ignored the aerial ways, taking them directly to the Palace of Pythagoras.

Her mind was numb, her brain unresponsive. The trip she endured.

The vast ground breadth of his Palace of Pythagoras had enabled Orpheus to indulge a fantasy: within it, behind the entry foyer and attainable by two secret doors, he had enshrined intact the entire brownstone house wherein he had discovered Anagonon and formed his TAC Board and established his new life. Here also, immediately after the inquiry whose success had enshrined the day as the origin day for the years *Eniautos Anagonou,* he had first courted Greta. She was his dream Eurydice come alive again—strong, mature, insatiably desirable. It was proper for him to bring her here. . . .

It was almost a repetition of the other time. They sat opposite each other in the vast baroque salon, sipping drinks. Then he made a suggestion; and this time Greta—still mentally numb—concurred as a matter of compliant course but without enthusiasm. (The multiple sizes of female pajamas in the closet did not even amuse her.) Not long afterward, having made themselves comfortable, they faced each other.

Again the long arms and hands of Orpheus were half spread. His eyes were infinitely deep as he queried: "How do you feel *now,* Greta—after five years?"

Head down, she was frowning, feeling desperately ashamed of herself for having made him a promise that she could not keep. She said candidly: "I told you that I would not be cold—but I was wrong. I am going to be cold, Orpheus. I cannot help this."

It enraged him. Rising, he stood over her. "This time, Greta, you have no choice."

Chilled, she shrank back into her chair, again prey to lacerating inward conflict between love and revulsion. There was a price for Anagononic painlessness: psychic division *hurt.* But this time her mind held steady.

Thrusting herself out of the chair, she squirmed past him and ran a little distance away, then paused with her back to him; her mind was working very fast: it was destroying the logic of the memory chain: it was affirming with total self-conviction, "It *wasn't* five years ago—it was *just now!"*

She felt him seize her around the waist from behind; and he murmured hard: "If I had a weapon, Greta, I would kill you. But since I do not have a weapon, I *will* take you by force this time."

While he said it, out of an eye corner she caught fleeting sight of someone peering in through an open door. She recognized the someone. It was *herself*—inexpertly strobotemping. Herself lost in time, seeking Croyd, witnessing her own future stabbing. Suddenly Greta went totally stoic—but her stoicism was that of a seasoned naval officer. *This is defeat in combat,* she told herself: *be a commander—be a commander*—BE A COMMANDER. . . .

Her voice was chilly. "I will not resist, Orpheus, because I have to love you; I have no choice. But I will be cold; I have no choice. But I wish you would kill me instead."

During the long instant that followed, she looked sidelong at her*self,* filled with compelling belief in the old superstition that to meet oneself meant death.

When the knife came into her, she felt no pain—only thrill.

Where now would her mind go?
To Croyd?
*But to what body?*

# 12

**Eurydice, 5 EA; then Nontime:**

Before noon the next day, benign Dr. Orpheus himself
was dead—kidney-stabbed, apparently, by bemused Court
Jester Thoth, who mysteriously had filched a weird knife out of a
museum case for the vicious work. This knife had then disappeared,
but Thoth had not. He had now to stand trial.

The ambiguity of *L'Affaire d'Orphée* was illustrated by the unusual fact that it took nearly half a day to dispose of Thoth's
conviction and appeal. Old courtroom procedures had to be used; for
in this year 5 EA, the Anagonon regime had been dominant for five
years and had totally eliminated crime two years before. However,
some remained who knew how to do these things.

In the front row of the courtroom, the entire high TAC Board of
Dr. Orpheus looked on: the heavy-set female gynecologist, the distinguished gray-bearded psychiatrist, the sharp young German doctor,
and the rest of them. They were stony. Later, they would have the
problem of determining among them which was to succeed Dr.
Orpheus as Planetary Chairman—and each of them was beginning to
comprehend that their very benign Anagonism would make choice
impossible. . . .

They contemplated the villain Thoth. None of them was sure what
one's emotions ought to be; for Dr. Orpheus had conferred upon
Thoth a bracelet with a totally ambiguous rank designation. For this
reason, they were sorry that proceedings were slow. But because
afterward they would have to come to *decision,* they were glad that
proceedings were slow. . . .

Wisely the prosecution restricted itself to the charge of treasonous assault upon the Planetary Chairman. Had it ventured mention of murder, embarrassments might have resulted from a demand for definition of "murder."

Into the judge, who had been programmed for this charge, were fed such items of evidence as the presence of Orpheus beside Thoth just prior to the dagger's disappearance from the museum case, the almost immediate death of Orpheus by stabbing, the presence of the bloody dagger in Thoth's hand, the laboratory proofs that Orpheus had owned the blood, and the prior termination of Thoth's mistress by Orpheus—a holy deed, since it was Orpheus who had done it, but necessarily unsettling for Thoth. "Guilt" was an outmoded term: the possible verdicts were "deviate" or "nondeviate." Proof that Thoth had assaulted Orpheus constituted proof that Thoth was deviate, and vice versa.

Immediately after the verdict of *deviate* and the sentencing (which was programmed "if deviate, then atomizing" but ameliorated by the qualifier "except if extenuating circumstances, then mere narcosis," the factual extenuating circumstances being the prior termination of Thoth's mistress by Dr. Orpheus), defense requested right to appeal, the judge computed such right, all tapes were fed into the appeal judge on the other side of the courtroom and the verdict was upheld on the basis that the trial judge had been properly programmed and the outcome had been logically consequent on the data.

Thoth went to jail. He was not visited by either the prosecutor or the defense attorney, since both were plugged into courtroom outlets.

Solitary in his small cell, Thoth did not philosophize; but he did meditate rather clearly—his clarity being at once heightened and obscured by a consistent irrational conviction that he was *not really here,* coupled with compulsive recurrence of worry about something unidentified left undone.

His cell was many levels below ground in the Palace of Pythagoras—far below even the Morgue. Amusing that, having apparently killed Orpheus (although he did not remember doing so), it was he who was now buried here beneath the House of Orpheus.

He sat in an easy chair with his back to a small end wall without windows; to his left and right were unbroken side walls; before him was an unbroken front wall whose door was cunningly paneled and so invisible. There were a comfortable wall cot and a tiny dresser and a corner nuclear-disposal commode; and in the soft-plastic floor a circular crack showed where an elevator table would presently sink for a moment and then arise bearing food. He could plan on staying here several days (relieved by such audiovisuals as he might think to request, including female tri-D feelies if wanted) until he would be led forth for permanent narcosis.

This civilization was humane: the narcosis would merely reduce him to blissful idiocy: it would be a punishment only to the extent that he might brood upon it beforehand, and this he did not propose to do. Had he not anyhow planned self-termination? What, for him, was the functional difference?

Thoth was undisturbed, and it somehow disturbed him that this was so. He inquired what he should think about. He concluded explicitly (and with a neat self-restriction which further disturbed him) that he should first review the pertinent series of occurrences, and that he should then study the dagger mystery.

The series of events that had brought him here was simple, its climactic points having centered on an anachronistic knife: Orpheus, having found it mysteriously in his hand, had driven it into Greta's kidney; and somewhat later it had penetrated a kidney of Orpheus, whereafter Thoth had found it mysteriously in his own hand. These events, with the intervening events, made a temporally sequential *but not a causally sequential* series, and the discrepancy was troublesome. Just for a moment he found himself philosophizing: did this mean that Random Epiphenomenalism was the correct metaphysics? He shrugged: it meant nothing, and therefore it proved nothing.

But now he was led further back in the event series. He should perhaps consider what had occurred before Orpheus had killed Greta. Well, Orpheus had made a Transient Claim, in all proper form: even with another man, Greta and Thoth would have had to concur, since form was form; with Dr. Orpheus, his peremptory had been enough. So then Orpheus had led Greta away; and she would have returned in ten days, only. . . .

What had happened *before that?*

Well, Thoth had awakened, and. . . .

Before *that?*

Thoth wrinkled his brow. Naturally there must have been a childhood and youth and early manhood during which he had become the confidant of Dr. Orpheus; and somewhen along there, he must have met Greta. But Thoth couldn't remember. Amnesia? He shook his head: nothing so severe: he was just chronically short on particular memories. . . .

His guts griped with the total conviction that he *wasn't here.*

Brushing the weird notion aside, he calmed his guts. Let him now consider the second problem—the dagger mystery.

Well; but hadn't he *already* considered the dagger mystery? Into the hand of Orpheus from nowhere—then into the hand of Thoth from nowhere! This dagger had ways of its own!

Witchcraft? Pragmatically, anything is possible, but witchcraft is highly improbable. Thoth dismissed the light hypothesis.

Another thing now came into his memory. From the premise that the dagger was anachronistic, Orpheus had suggested that the invaders from Earth had somehow planted it to confuse Monon. On an impulse, Thoth activated the TV screen in his cell: no invading ships. Well, they came and went. Anyhow, the idea was improbable just because it was so exotic. Invaders having power to play thus with a dagger anachronism would have power to confound Monon more directly. Still. . . .

Just for an instant, Thoth played with a vague idea about time travel with respect to the dagger.

At the end of the instant he had rejected the notion. Nothing ever exists but the present: the future is only a prediction made in the present, an uncertain system of *probabilities;* the past is no better than an imperfect memory recalled in the present. It is possible to say that there is no such condition as *time.* Most assuredly, time travel is a nonsense idea.

But how did the dagger get out of the case?

Just when he was on the verge of clutching a believable hypothesis, Thoth experienced a new shock. He had exhausted *all* of his memories. *There was nothing else to remember!*

After that realization, Thoth went into a defensive stupor. During it, his table circle disappeared downward, leaving a hole in the floor, and reappeared laden with solid and liquid goodies. Two preliminary brandies revitalized him: he then ate well, savoring soup and fish and steak and potatoes and salad and wine and dessert and liqueur. (For liqueur, they had provided a rare old liquid gold called *Vieille Cure.*) Snicking a big cigar off the table just as the table went down, he lit up and relaxed in blue smog.

Somewhat later he flipped the butt into the waste receptacle and gazed through haze at the front wall.

A fantasy touched him. This cell was his territory: he should therefore mark its boundaries as a caged wolf might do. Having prepared himself, he spurted a little urine at each corner of the cell. He thought. He supplemented this marking at the centers of the right-side wall, the rear wall, and (having raised the cot) the left-side wall. Then he considered the front wall. He hesitated. He desisted, rearranging himself: something told him not to close himself in too hastily.

Leaning back in his easy chair, he scrutinized the unmarked front wall. Theoretically it remained an open possibility.

*I am not really here. . . .*

Perhaps he should say: "Open sesame." What was sesame? Some seed, maybe. Then why *"Open* sesame"? Detail: forget it. . . .

It was a force-field wall. How do you control a force field? He didn't know the technology. On the other hand, he was used to utilizing force fields by allowing them to catch his mood once he had definitely decided on a mood. Perhaps if he were to adopt an open-sesame mood and let it flow toward the wall. . . .

He found the mood: it was rather like sky beyond the city.

He said: "Open sesame."

A center of dizziness identified itself somewhere in his brain and flowed everywhere outward; he had felt the sensation somewhen before, it had something to do with *willed change,* but he remembered no index; internally blinded, he waited, and his vision cleared like a camera iris opening outward.

The front wall had dissolved. Beyond it lay a corridor moving off to the left.

Thoth considered this fragment of a corridor. Deliberately he arose and went out into it, passing through the place where the front cell wall had been. To his left the corridor extended interminably, and there seemed to be doors opening off it on both sides. To the right was a dead end.

He hit the dead end with a spurt of urine, symbolizing something. Then he went back into his cell and emptied his bladder into the commode. Turning, he three-quarters expected to see the front cell wall again; but instead, there was still the open corridor. He sighed. He went out into it.

Turning left, he ambled down this corridor.

He stopped before he came to the first door. Something insistent was telling him: This house is *yours*, Thoth!

He frowned: he couldn't remember any house that had been really his. Then his forehead smoothed: he liked the idea. Not understanding the situation, he was willing to learn.

*This is* MY *house. This* IS *my house....*

The corridor seemed narrow and low and bleak. Mentally he articulated a preference that it be more noble. The dizziness followed, but not so severe, not blinding him: again he felt that sense of will-control, almost as though with an invisible hand in his own brain he were adjusting something; again it felt oddly familiar, even friendly. And now his corridor had widened a little, and it had heightened a lot; now the floor was parquet and the walls were fine marble and the ceiling was sculptured and high above.

This is *not* a force-field house!

This is *my* house?

Turning, he hastened back to where the cell had been. The wall was blank, the cell was gone.

Putting fingers to lips, gaily he tossed a kiss at the gone cell. As he did so, abruptly he realized two things: that he did not remember a prior time when he had been gay; and that he *knew* this. And yet—since now he was gay—he *must* have been gay before, *some*time.

Wheeling, Thoth ambled back along his corridor in its open direction, until he came to the first door which opened to his right. Before looking in, he placed a little bet with himself: it ought to be a bedroom, but it would prove to be a study. Then he stood before the door, looking in. It was a spacious study: vague at first, but with details gradually clarifying themselves as (feeling very minor *control* dizziness) he *allowed* them to do so. Along the far wall were high-arched curtained windows heavily draped, and near a window was a large richwood desk with some sort of dull-metal lamp shedding yellowing light, and all along the end walls were bookshelves stuffed with entrancing volumes—probably (he reflected, and somehow *hoped*) not hypnopaedic tapes at high frequency for subliminal reading, but real old-fashioned ink-printed tomes. No doubt about it: this was *his* study—but such a study as he had never owned (had he?), the sort of study that he had always desired (but how did he know about "always" before—well, before Greta had left him last night?)—a study that seemed to fit *him*. It now crossed his mind that the windows in the far wall were the first windows he had seen since his jailing; but they were dark, they told him nothing; evidently it was cloudy absolute night outside.

He hesitated at this door, wanting to go in and claim his study and look at his books.

But he did not want to break this dream.

Yet it was totally real, not like a dream. (Dreams he remembered; he'd had one last night.) It was no good pinching himself, because of course he could feel no pain; but there was another criterion. In his dreams, he was never able to exercise any control—indeed, he rarely even thought of doing so, in a dream; and whenever he did thrust himself into attempted control of a dream, the dream invariably blurred and he awoke.

But this was *particularity* remembering—sort of! At any rate, he *seemed* to be exercising some sort of mental control—a will control, as inscrutable to him as the control whereby he moved his arms and legs, and just as effective—a control that not only dissolved force fields but seemed now to be building structures of opulent beauty and old-time material solidity.

Should he test it by entering his study?

But he feared to blast his study. . . .

But was that distant music? And were those remote voices?

Down the corridor he moved, toward the voices and the music. Perhaps he was entertaining tonight? He should be there? A door opened to his left; he glanced in: it was a sumptuous bedroom, the bed was a canopied four-poster, it was unoccupied: it was a guest room; and the doors beyond would be more guest rooms. He did not enter, he moved on: the ensuing doors were closed, but he *knew* that he could have opened them and found substance beyond.

He paused. Ahead, the corridor was endless and doorless. If this house was a proper house, it would have a grand stairway. He sensed that he was on the second story: the first story would be containing the action—but how would one get there?

Setting himself, he executed the mental gesture: no dizziness at all, this time, but a familiar *act* that required some energy but nothing more. (Still, however, he was not willing particularities: rather, he was willing that something of a general sort happen, while allowing something out of his subconscious to flow in for content.) Just ahead, to his right, a whole wall section dissolved.

Thoth hurried forward to this place. He stood now at the head of a grand stairway: broad and single here at the top, halfway down dividing into double stairs leading left and right downward to the first story. The music and voices came from below.

This *was* his house! It was his *own!*

Proud as he had never been, sole owner of a territory, Thoth moved down the stair; and at the landing he arbitrarily chose the turn to the left. He debouched onto the first floor: the carpet was rich, the hall spacious, the walls new-Gobelin tapestried. There were rooms to the left, but the voices and music came from the right. He turned right.

He paused. Was his house too limited? Was its space too restricted? This downstairs corridor debouching off the hall under the stair seemed narrow. . . .

A territory may be as large and complex as its owner is willing and able to maintain—and to create?

He willed a new room to his right. Up two broad shallow steps, the wall dissolved. There was a spacious dining room filled with round tables laden with fine service, with cabinets for crystal and china all around the walls: nobody sat there, but many could; and beyond (always some unexpected bonus!) a door opened onto a very narrow corridor extending indefinitely into dimness. . . .

This house of mine is vast and beautiful. Even better, *its potentialities for new experience are infinite!*

Bypassing this dining room for now, newly conscious of his own psychophysical strength, Thoth moved toward the music. It drew him through a doorway. He found himself on a balcony looking down upon an enormous ballroom where hundreds of beautiful people were dancing. They were not invaders; they were his guests. This ballroom was also a theater; and within its mighty golden proscenium, three-dimensional color cinema enthralled the ones who did not choose to dance. . . .

Deep within Thoth struggled the dual question: *Why and how?* But it was subordinated by the pervasive assertion: *This my house. This is created by me, an extension of me, a projection of me—but not me alone, since it could not be projected without something vital and formatively responsive to project it upon, something independent of me but responsive to me.*

Watching his guests, he felt his soul illuminated by the generosity of noble possession.

But since they did not need his presence to continue their joy, he chose not to go down to the people and the music. His eyes strayed left. If he chose, he could ascend again, not by the grand stairway, but by a private beautiful small stair that now appeared curling upward from his balcony. Since arrangements at its head appeared somewhat indefinite, he concluded that he must do some more building there, and then explore it.

What would be up there?

It would be the bedroom suite of the master—and the mistress.

*What* mistress?

Greta?

But she was dead. . . .

Her *mind*, though? Where had her *mind* gone when she died? A colossal idea was coming into Thoth: he leaned on the balcony rail with his eyes closed, thinking it over carefully to get it perfect. For some reason, out of some dim experience that his particularity memory could not identify, he knew Greta inwardly, body and brain, as though he had once dwelt in her. And also he knew that Greta's mind was strongly individuate—that somehow, somewhen, he had helped her mind, which was born of her brain, to transcend her brain and dominate her brain, becoming her quintessential *self*. Then, when the knife of Orpheus went into her back, had her mind died with her body—or had its individuate selfness somehow persisted, awaiting rescue?

His eyes opened momentarily, and he gazed at the dancing people. He knew they were phantoms, mere phenomena, projected by his mind offhand into this space as a mind projects people offhand into its dream space. However, this space seemed more malleable, more vital, more independent of itself than dream space is. Could he somehow have escaped from his prison into *nontime?* And, now he thought about it, from where in his nonexistent memory of things past had he dredged up this concept of nontime: that is to say, psychospace, the raw unrestricted omnipotential premindstuff that exists everywhere infinitely and endlessly except where it is interrupted by matter generated out of itself?

Old concepts were coming swiftly back to consciousness. Nontime was necessarily in direct contact with every time and every place. Greta's death under the Orpheus-knife was more than a day behind him, and by now her mind should be scattered into psychospace; but if it were possible for him to reach out and seize her mind at the instant of its departure from her dying body. . . .

He performed an act of will.

Somewhere in his brain, he felt her mind murmur sleepily: "Croyd?"

Odd that she would call to this stranger Croyd, that she would not call to Thoth. Odd also that he felt no jealousy. Instead, he proceeded to another concern: her mind should have a body of its own. This body should now be waiting for him up there on the balcony. But it would not be adequate for him to project for her a phantom body, like the dancers below: her mind needed a real brain with its own real memories.

With this realization came knowledge that somehow he understood a brain so thoroughly and meticulously, *from within,* that he could design one in detail. Could he, unaided by the icrographic force-field equipment in the Eurydice Morgue, *duplicate* Greta as that equipment had duplicated her?

No, it would be inadequate. He could not equip her with a sufficient set of subjective memories that were all her own. Certainly he could not give her memories that he could not remember. . . .

Eh—but that duplicated Greta-body of Serenitite that lay in the Morgue. . . .

Again he performed an act of will.

He opened his eyes and gazed up the curling stair. . . .

He found himself in an atrium isolated from the rest of his house;

He entered. All the chambers within were draped filmy everywhere. And there was a woman who looked at him with half surprise but not with complete surprise: she was tall and slender and ash blond and green-eyed and quizzical, and her own draperies were like the gauze of her chambers.

He murmured: "What's a nice duplicate like you doing in a place like this?"

She came into his arms. He put her mind into her.

Serenitite is protein, as vital as protoplasm, only all but immortal. *Good lady, thy lord hath come home.*

Quietness.

Depression.

Comprehension that something was hideously wrong. That only she could make it right.

Inexplicable intuitive knowledge *how* she could make it right. . . .

Mouth against her throat, he begged: "Let me come into your brain, Greta. Take me into your brain, you can, you have, you can. Let me share your memories, and with them return into my own brain and clear it. *Help me remember what I am, and what was, and what threatens—*"

> CROYD (no given name known) (no birthdate known).—b. Nigel III. Species *croyd Thoth;* asserts he adopted species name as legal name on learning that his species was destroyed when Nigel went into nova after Croyd escaped to Earth. (NB: Nigel nova obsvd from Earth 2321, origin date estd 2292; Croyd offers no comment on implication of personal longevity.) Known assignments, all galactic: Agent, 2475-2484; Chief Internal Intelligence, 2484-2491; Assistant Secretary Internal Conformity, 2491-2496; Temporary Chairman, 2496-? Special skills: telephysical, psychokinetic. (No further data made available.)
> —*Interplanetary Who's Who* (Ed. 2502)

# 13

Later Greta took Croyd-Thoth by an arm and led him to a door in a wall. This door she opened. They walked out on a long slender exterior promenade whose railings were golden-thin: it was an elevated breezeway bridge between halves of his house.

They paused at the center. She said: "Look around, Croyd."

He dared look.

There was nothing. No sky, no sun. No blue, no gray, no color at all. No ground beneath. Nothing at all.

Presently she remarked: "For sure you are Croyd: you did not close your eyes, you are continuing to look."

He mused. He told her: "I'd rather look at my new house. It is the house that I have always dreamed of owning. It becomes whatever I want it to be; and yet, having become what I have chosen, it is solidly that, resistant to further change until my decision about the direction and need for change is total and orderly. It is my territory. It is my extended self. I—I could make it more, if I chose." He gazed at Greta: "It seems to me that at this instant, if I were to choose, I could make it more. Could I?"

"Try."

He surveyed his house, standing here on the spidery-golden bridge between its halves. It was Norman-grand; he found no significant fault. "I have a queer feeling," he observed, "that any changes I might wish to make would have to be made from the interior of my house, and not from out here. But I am not sure that they could be made. And yet I do not understand how I built it in the first place. It doesn't fit into my physical logic."

Greta kissed him lingeringly.

When they parted, she kept her face close to his, ready to be accepted again if he chose. He grinned: "You are no cadaver—you are no cadaver!"

"What do you mean, cadaver?"

"In the Morgue, you were dead."

"I—*was?*"

"Inside and out. Or anyhow, you were only a subanimate Sereni-tite duplicate."

"What was the direct cause of my decease?"

"Orpheus stabbed you."

"I was in a morgue? Is that where I got this weird garment? It could be a winding sheet."

"It's your coffin coverlet. I brought it along. It's becoming."

"Where are we, Croyd?"

"I haven't the foggiest. *Is* that fog, out there?"

"To me it looks like nothing."

"Greta—"

"Croyd?"

"Why do you call me Croyd?"

"It's your name. Are you going foggy again?"

"Only a little. I know I'm Croyd. And yet my name is Thoth—I think."

"Thoth is only your alias. Orpheus doped you and made you forget your real name—which is Croyd."

"Last night my mind milked your brain of memories, but in my brain those memories are not yet wholly clear. May I catechize?"

"Pray do."

"Who's Croyd?"

"He bosses the galaxy. He's you."

"Some boss! Who are *you*?"

"Greta."

"That much I know. Occupation?"

"In the fleet, they call me Commander Groen. I kick a frigate."

"It rings a bell that is very loud. I've known you before."

"Quite long. Quite well."

"Where is the fleet now?"

"Croyd, it depends on when *now* is!"

The odd remark somehow made him think about the impossible concept of time travel. Then, like a two-by-four hitting the forehead of a mule, it hit him that time travel was *not* impossible—that *he personally knew this*—provided one put some qualifications on the meaning of such travel, qualifications that he seemed to have once understood. He demanded: "Give me more of that!"

She unleashed it. "It was 2502 AD, and you and I bearded Orpheus in his den, only then he was Fellanel, and somehow he got us. Then I was in my frigate off Nereid. Then he was trying to seduce me, but I got away somehow, and all of a sudden it was some damned year 5 EA, and everything was different, and I was with the fleet but Orpheus called me down, and you were dressed in these monkey clothes, and he tried to seduce me *again*, and—you're right, he *did* stab me, but again I got away somehow, and I was all in nothingness—like *that* void, out there—and then, somehow, *here!* Croyd, you are looking at one chicken commander: I'm scared to death, and I seem to be AWOL—"

Croyd gripped her shoulders: she was trembling badly. Presumably the dope of Orpheus was wearing off, because Croyd's past was opening out like a landscape in dissipating fog. However, the feature-less void beyond the rail was not.

"You know what that is?" he challenged.

"Where?"

"There." He turned her around to look beyond the rail.

"What is it?"

"Nonspace. Nontime."

"How's that again?"

"Tell you later. It's the only kind of medium that would have allowed me to psychobuild this house."

She swung back to him, eyes wide. "Croyd—you *are* back!"

He gave her a tight nod. "Not all the way, though. You say your fleet is cruising off Earth?"

"Right. Admiral Leclerc commanding."

*"When?"*

*"Now.* Well. . . .Well, when I left, the year was this goofy 5 *EA.*"

"Let's get to your fleet. I think it may be the ships from Earth."

"The ships *at* Earth?"

"The ships *from* Earth. I'm beginning to form a theory, and I have to nail it down in order to act—and, oh, Lord, how I have to ACT!"

She nodded vigorously. "This I buy. But I don't know how I got *here*—I even seem to have left my uniform behind—so how do we get *there?*"

"What were the fleet's Earth coordinates?"

"Approximately a thousand miles above Eurydice."

"Mm. Any idea what Eurydice was called in 2502?"

"Boston."

"All—*right!* Hang on, Greta—"

Closing his eyes, Croyd felt around in his midbrain for the following spacetime coordinates: Boston, 2507 AD, one thousand miles up. When he had sensed them precisely, he threw a brain switch. . . .

They stood on the bridge of Leclerc's flagship. Officers and crewmen stared. Greta glanced down at her Morgue toga, up at the admiral, down at her toga. Touching his dark thin moustache with a little finger, compact Leclerc suggested: "Mr. Croyd—Commander Groen—both of you seem out of uniform, in one manner or another."

Greta said, cool: "Admiral, *do* entertain Mr. Croyd while I change." She vanished.

Officers and crew kept staring.

Rising, Admiral Leclerc delicately proposed: "Sudden arrivals do distract our people. Shall we talk in my salon? I have some excellent Bisquit—"

# 14

So far, he reflected as he followed Admiral Leclerc, his hunches had come out right—but so far they had been simple: (1) from nonspacetime you could go to any place time, although getting back might be something else; (2) the year 5 EA, dominated by Anagonon and by Orpheus *né* Fellanel, *had* to be 2507, five years after the Medicine Board inquiry, which must have been successful for Anagonon and which Fellanel-Orpheus had therefore triumphantly made the point of origin for his new-world calendar.

What had happened to the five years, though? Even with his memory practically wide open, he couldn't remember any of it prior to the Transient Claiming of Greta by Orpheus. Had he been doped and unconscious the whole time? Impossible—by now his brain would be worthless. But wait: maybe in *stasis*. . . .

Well, back to that later. Just now the major concern, the *cosmic* concern, was the fate of Earth, and of the whole galaxy by infiltration. He'd somehow lost five years: by now, Anagonon must have enslaved all Earth and would be on its way to other planets.

Besides, Anagonon might not be the only threat. Increasingly he was haunted by the evidence that Greta had given him five years ago: evidence that the inspiration for Anagonon had been *alien*. . . .

Leclerc stated simply, over Bisquit: "I am glad you are back, Mr. Croyd. Derien has been Temporary Chairman, and he has been—well, very adequate, very adequate—"

Croyd nodded, but he wondered. Derien, who had been Undersec-retary for Internal Conformity, was an excellent high bureaucrat; but to imagine that in five years as Temporary Chairman, Derien hadn't been permanently replaced. . . .Croyd filed it as another of several inconsistencies about this entire screwy situation.

"Thus meanwhile Anagonon gathered strength," Leclerc went on, "until the Orpheus organization has taken control of Earthworld and is beginning to infiltrate other planets. Mr. Derien therefore ordered me to cruise above this Eurydice, which I had always respected as Boston, and be ready to respond to orders resulting from my reports of the developing situation."

"Mr. Derien was then on the ball."

"He got on the ball when the Interplanetary President put him there."

"You are not bitter, Leclerc?"

"I am a Gallic realist."

"How far can your orders go?"

"They can extend to destruction of Earth."

"Those are extensive orders."

"You comprehend that the signal would have to come directly from Derien himself. Or from *you,* now. It occurs to me that I should be advising Nereid of your existence."

"Not yet, Admiral. Hold it off a little."

"What is it that is on one's mind?"

"Some inconsistencies, Admiral. Little things that don't add up. I lost five years, *poof!* like that! Commander Groen, too—she doesn't remember anything in particular between 2502 AD and 5 EA: just a series of instantaneous transitions. And she was dead—stabbed—but somehow I recovered her mind."

"She was dead?"

"Stabbed with a dagger. By Dr. Orpheus—"

He pondered

Leclerc ventured: "What is it that it is?"

"That dagger keeps bugging me. I seem to have stabbed Orpheus with the same dagger."

"You stabbed Orpheus? Then perhaps our troubles are solved—"

"No dice, Admiral: the TAC Board and Anagonon will carry on. But still, that dagger bugs me."

"Because it kept being an instrument of different events?"

"Partly. But more. In the first place, it was an anachronism. But even odder: Orpheus could not explain where or how he got hold of the dagger: he claimed it just fell into his hand out of the air, so on impulse he used it. And there are some other questions—but to ask them would require background that we haven't time for."

The admiral spread his hands.

"And then," Croyd added, "there is the point that an alien, a man-sized arthropod, gave Dr. Fellanel the formula for Anagonon. Do you know of any intelligent arthropoda in *our* galaxy?"

"None. The concept seems self-contradictory."

"Extragalactic, then. And what would be this alien's purpose, unless he wanted to weaken us over a period of years for eventual invasion? And if so—"

"Something, Leclerc?"

The admiral said tightly: "I am reminded of something possibly unrelated. I keep getting extragalactic pips on idar."

Croyd grew tense. "It is possibly *not* unrelated. This same invasion may be on its way here—right now. Have you reported these pips?"

"No, sir."

"Why not?"

"They have been coming in from so many different quarters, and so often, that it is preposterous. I have finally had to tell my idar man to report them only to me directly and let me judge whether to put out alerts—otherwise the fleet would go mad and never sleep. Besides, the pips never seem to come any closer."

Croyd ruminated. He said presently: "That frequency is highly improbable, isn't it?"

"Highly."

"There is a great deal of improbability in this total situation, isn't there, Admiral?"

*"Ah, oui."*

"Commander Groen seems to be taking her time. I thought she'd whip over to her frigate by pullman, and put on her uniform, and whip right back."

"You are touching," said Leclerc, "on the most improbable aspect of this situation."

*"Alors?"*

"Commander Groen and her frigate are not operating with this fleet. She was detached yesterday for duty off Rigel."

# 15

Having begged leave of Croyd and Admiral Leclerc to return to her frigate and get into uniform, Greta went to the admiral's pullman, set its coordinates for *yesterday's* fleet position of her frigate, and stepped into the pullman to be converted into electromagnetic waves which would be regrouped with accurate precision at the other end as her brained body. Her mind, as usual, would travel with the wave pattern.

She was parsed, all right, but not regrouped. There was no pullman receiver at the location she had dialed: her frigate was far away.

The electromagnetic waves of her body—which Croyd only last night had stolen telekinetically out of the Eurydice Morgue and revitalized in his house—went skittering away into space, diffusing endlessly as the square of the distance.

# 16

**Approaching Sol Galaxy, 2503 AD:**

For the alien invading fleet from Mandomen, tonight's Commanding Officers' Call was located not on the bridge but in the salon of the flagship. It was centered on business, but in a relaxed atmosphere of talking and smoking and drinks. The luxurious quarter G of space travel was maintained, allowing the officers to recline on hard couches as though they were air cushions but nevertheless with some reassuring tactile pressure and naturalness of movement.

(This intergalactic invasion fleet bore no relationship whatsoever to the "ships from Earth.")

Executive officers also were guests tonight, which raised the complement to fourteen gentletens. (Krell had no exec—in fact, no crew at all.) In the salon, the couches were uniformly spaced and close together, an arrangement that allowed spontaneous clustering of little groups, while masculate yeotens and ordinary spacetens scurried among couches carrying drinks and smokes and snacks

All bulkheads as well as the hull were transparent. The latter allowed easy inspection of the developing Sol Galaxy panorama as, relative to the flagship, the star spiral languidly rotated like a lazy shining flapjack in midair, turning its edge away to reveal its flanks (although actually it was the flagship that was turning to run along parallel with the galactic plane). The bulkhead transparency allowed officers who might wish distraction to watch the flagship's females who had foregathered and were buzzing in the Queens Lounge. (It was possible to flip a switch and listen to their chatter, but nobody bothered.)

The masculate Myrons of Mandomen Galaxy were a breed that Mandomen mammals found peculiar, although an intelligent insect on Earth (if any had evolved) would merely have found them normal in a different way. Myrons, who were not insects but decapods, had by birth three sexes: male, female, and masculate. The females were the brooders, the mystique centers of clans, the rulers: queens and princesses. The males were the fertilizers, rather stupid, strong in only one respect and otherwise weak.

Society was run by the masculates, who were the vast majority of Myrons born. Masculates were not quite analogous to Earth's worker bees or ants: the last are basically unsexed females, whereas Myron masculates were basically unsexed males. There was nothing effeminate about a masculate: they were hard, systematic, logical, imaginative, courageous; they felt and behaved with each other like solidly masculine men. Although they were unable to feel a man's interest in a female, nevertheless—or, perhaps, therefore—their loyalty to the females they served was intense unto death.

Across millenniums, the mutational factors which had caused these arthropoda to overwhelm their instinctive patterning with a human level of intelligence were analogous to, although different from, the series of factors which had done the same for some mammals and then for primates and finally for humans on Earth. The series of mutational strains had grown in body size. Ultimately, as their size taxed the oxygen-feeding potential of their tracheal structure, a strain of their breed developed blood and five primitive hearts (but no lungs); their hundred spiracles, fifty down each side, were able to feed oxygen directly into the blood for their five hearts as efficiently as human lungs feed it into blood for one heart. The next evolving strain had taken to rearing up on its nether four podia for better visibility in high grass, and these podia elongated; an associated development occurred in the swiveling of the head on a five-jointed neck which allowed the anterior eyes still to look forward when the body was erect. So freed, the six anterior podia began increasingly to be used as hands, encouraging claw-eye coordination: the two side eyes and the center anterior eye continued guardedly to watch for distant developments such as enemy approach, while the two lateral anterior eyes achieved binocular coordination focused on the object being handled.

The rudimentary sign exchanges common to all metazoa above the level of jellyfish gradually attained symbolic level; this development, together with the claw-eye interplay and associated factors, necessarily and reciprocally entailed the appearance and rapid enlargement of a telencephalon. Correlatively the voice discs were complicated until they could enunciate all the vowels and consonants that Earth humans can produce, and a good many more. All brain centers interplayed in their elaboration: manual, visual, eye-claw coordinative (with related enlargement of midbrain kinaesthetic feedback), hearing, speech, abstract thought, and so on. Their armor-plated exoskeletons were no more an obstacle to brain growth across generations than man's bony cranium had been: across the brain pan they developed sawtoothed interstices which yielded to infantile growth and then grew solid.

The flashing variance of their panoply colors was voluntary, dyed, corresponding to human-male clothing fashions in florid eras. When they wanted to change color, they dipped.

After enough drinks to relax them and before intoxication could begin, the black-armored admiral called the gentletens informally to attention to brief them on the final phases of their intergalactic invasion. To facilitate 'is lecture, 'e utilized the axis variability of the ship's repulsors in order to position the ship so that 'is vast enthralling background, through the transparent hull, was the diagonal spiral of Sol Galaxy.

"You'll notice," 'e chirred with the speech discs beneath 'is third shoulders, conferring icily minimal intonation signals on 'is remarks with 'is antennae, "that the galaxy behind me, like our own Mandomen, is an Sb star spiral—that is to say, it has wound itself in fairly tightly during the past ten billion years, but it is only in its early middle age and still has a long way to go before it coalesces into an amorphous fiery globule. This similarity to our home galaxy will facilitate navigation in one way, but in another way it has pitfalls: we may be lulled into false tranquillity by this quasi-familiarity. Remember, it is *not* our galaxy—*not yet!*"

There followed a casual analysis of galactic structure. The central bulge of stars and star clusters, with its inflow of gaseous energy at the north and south poles. The equatorial disc extending fifty thousand light-years in all directions: the spiraling arms of stars that were the endoskeleton of that disc, the intervening outflowing gaseous currents that were the starlight-reflecting bloodflow of that disc; the critical points—whose latitudes and longitudes were plotted on all their navigational charts, but which now were seeable and pointable although at a vast remoteness—where currents met and fought and created cosmic hurricanes light-years in diameter. "The currents themselves we can disregard," observed the admiral, "because their thrust is negligible compared to the thrust of our velocity, although we do have to avoid blisters of relative vacuum which would affect us as calms affect wind sailors by reducing our fuel intake. The hurricanes, however, can deter, damage, or even destroy us—"

Luckily, 'e added, these problems would not arise until the last two days when, after running along the plane of Sol Galaxy until they would be far out near its periphery, they would be diving in on the Solar System and Earth. And 'e gave some time to broad discussion of *those* problems—although, 'e stipulated, discussion of those problems in detail would be deferred for two more days, to be attacked just before the commencement of the entry run.

Just now it was more crucial to pay attention to factors of *time*—and of *timing*.

Their perfect attention became pluperfect. All of them were as aware as Krell that their margin had been shortened—and all the females knew as well as Maelbrug what this could mean for them.

"I would like now, gentletens," the admiral interjected, "to move just for a few minutes to the bridge where we can examine the instrumentation related to tempigation—"

The crimson commander interrupted: "Sira, there appears to be a disturbance developing in the Queens' Lounge."

The admiral swung left to look astern; the others all swung right. Through the transparent bulkhead, female hurly-burly was evident: so intent had the gentletens been on the admiral's lecture that even their side eyes hadn't noticed—but Commander Crimson had a roving side eye.

At the admiral's nod, a yeoten switched on audio, and their Officer's Clubroom was flooded with the skirring of excited women.

They all listened keenly. Presently Krell's young ears began to make sense of it, and 'e reported (loudly, to be heard above it): "Sira, a rumor has spread that we are far behind schedule, that we will not touch down before extrojection time. I get it that they are on the verge of panic."

"Captain Zl," instantly snapped the admiral, indicating the silvery flag captain, "you do not need this time-briefing. Will you be good enough to attend to the girls?"

Zl nodded, had the yeoten snap off audio, and left the room. In the blessed silence, Krell followed the admiral and 'is fellow officers to the bridge—relieved, for the first time, to know that 'is Maelbrug was out there alone aboard the *Champu*, away from this horde of survival-crazy women.

**All Actualities D minus l**

Part Four

THE TIME-DIVER

Dr. Fellanel evaded the meticulous research, testing, and inspection procedures of the Earthworld Biotherapeutic Association and of the Galactic Medicine Board by taking skillful advantage of a therapeutic computer protocol—namely, that each therapeutic instrument, including injection guns, consummate its radiological sterilization with a small shot of Antiseptane prior to each operation. He divided Anagonon into two components: the major manufactured component which exhibited the prime effects (and this was what was carefully tested and repeatedly inspected by the Medicine Board), and a secret additive which provided the invidious side effects when combined with the major component. Dr. Fellanel manufactured all the additive himself, in his Boston laboratory—an easy task, since a single drop impregnated a liter of Antiseptane; his aides and traveling programmers kept the TAC doctors and computers supplied with the treated Antiseptane. On routine sampling by Medicine Board agents, this Antiseptane appeared normal since the only effect of the additive was to slightly increase the spin of the single electron in each hydrogen atom. However, this faintly altered Antiseptane trace on an injection gun was enough to create the side effects.

—REPORT OF THE INTERPLANETARY PRESIDENT'S
BIOTHERAPEUTIC TASK FORCE (2503)

# 17

Hot on the trail of his theory, Croyd nevertheless uptimed cautiously: if his theory was right, caution was not needed; if it was wrong, he was in the past from the instant he quit the admiral's flagship, working against the stream of time, and he might at any instant collide with a frozen mass that would annihilate him.

It gave him time to collect his thoughts about the events immediately preceding the last things in 2502 that he remembered. How, at Galactic Headquarters on Nereid, he had been approached by the Secretary for Internal Affairs with a request that he undertake personal attention to the weird new Earth-drug Anagonon and its frighteningly large and growing cult. How his examination into the drug and the TAC movement had led him to arresting conclusions: the genetic-attitudinal side effects, and the nearly absolute certainty of a resulting future that threatened not only Earth people but all humans everywhere in his galaxy.

Humans? What is a human?

The Galactic Code recognized that all known self-reproducing metazoan lines had evolved as devices for increasingly complex experience. Because of the crucial importance of survival and self-reproduction, it was survival and reproductive experience that proved wholly absorbing to the individual animal up to a threshold level of neural complication—of brain.

The Code therefore defined and distinguished *human* as "having sufficient neural complexity to use symbolic language in order to sublimate survival and reproductive interests into more complex levels of aesthetic development, individual or social (but without necessarily denying the more fundamental levels of living)." This definition, in the voting, proved ultimately to have more substance than several proposals based on a criterion of symbolic communication.

Although theoretically the required sublimation could be totally asocial and without communication, it could not be known to exist without communication. Consequently, law specified a minimum communicating language consisting of one thousand clearly different and interrelatable symbols. This was the compromise—allowing legal control of the question in practical cases, while giving criterion priority to philosophical considerations.

This definition, which of course called for a great deal of judgment by the designated Interplanetary Board of Human Issues, had turned out to embrace a surprising spread of species on a significant number of planets. Even dolphins had profited.

Croyd now remembered subjectively his arrival at a theory about Anagonon, his filing of the theory with the Earthworld Bureau of the Galactic Medicine Board, and his decision to move in personally on Fellanel under the incognito Thoth. He had brought in Commander Greta Groen because he needed a witness, because of her experience and skills, and—most of all— because they knew each other perfectly, worked in perfect harmony, respected each other enough so that each could accept the other's risks.

He was now about to review *in present experience* the events of 2502—and thereafter. Without a sharp objective review to supplement his subjective memory, proof of his theory about Monon was impossible. Without a clear theory, he could not act—and the theory he was forming would be might hard for even himself to believe!

The rescue of Earth from Anagonon depended on this. The saving of the galaxy from Anagonon—and maybe from extragalactic invaders who were using Orpheus and his Anagonon—depended on this.

The saving of Greta—and maybe of Croyd himself—depended on this. It was perfectly clear to Croyd that both he and Greta were already Anagononic—permanently slaves to the heirs of Dr. Orpheus.

Working in carefully to a foliage-secluded place very close to the grounds of the dark-mighty brownstone house, Croyd lurked until he saw Croyd and Greta approach and enter the front door.

Utilizing an electric lead exterior to the house, Croyd then left his body and entered the computer which, as he had surmised on this prior visit that he was now monitoring, was as intricate as a mammalian brain and completely threaded the mansion.

He watched himself and Greta beard Orpheus under the menacing topless guards, uptime here in 2502. He watched the ultimatum with the Unholy Ten, watched himself trying to leave the house with Greta, mocked himself for his own stupidity when he and Greta fell in the doorway beneath an injective shot of mixed sleep gas and Anagonon.

But the sensitivities which his mind added to Fellanel's mindless computer told him something else. When his body had hit the floor, his mind had instantly downtimed out of it.

However, Greta's had not.

It was now perfectly clear to Croyd whither-whinner his mind had downtimed: there was no sense wasting precious moments checking this out, since he could remember the instant of his awakening on New Year's Eve, 4-5 EA, and every subsequent event. Obviously Fellanel had kept him in stasis during the five-year period, so nothing during that time could be of much interest—except just what had happened on this evening and the following day in 2502.

Remaining in Fellanel's computer, he watched his own body, saturated with Anagonon and soporific drugs, carried to Fellanel's laboratory for a carefully timed blood extraction before the side effects could show up. His body was then conveyed to a reasonably comfortable escape-proof suite below ground level, where presumably it was going to remain for most of the next five years. That disposed of *that*.

He then downtimed eight hours to watch his own mindless, embarrassingly assinine semiawakening. They readily secured his signature on documents which were bound to be crucial at the Medicine Board inquiry—or rather, already had been crucial.

He moved then to the room where Greta was being awakened. With grim relief, he noted that her own awakening behavior was at least as embarrassing as his own had been.

When they departed by private helijet to Earthworld Headquarters in New York, Croyd reclaimed his body and spaced intertime to Tannenport ahead of them. There he stashed his body in the control tower locker, entered the control tower computer, and monitored the conversation in the helijet en route.

Subsequently he entered the computer who was the fifth member of the Medicine Board of Review; and he followed all the testimony and laboratory work with fascination. When the time came to vote, and his computer voted *for* Anagonon and the TAC Board, Croyd had to admit that his computer was dead right on the evidence it had; being an uptime, there was no way Croyd could give it additional knowledge—and this couldn't have affected the vote anyhow.

In the computer, he watched Greta leave the courtroom on an arm of Orpheus. Well, Greta had already told him what had followed. He thought he had her movements thereafter pretty well in mind. Attacked by Dr. Fellanel, her mind had left her body and uptimed to 4-5 EA. Attacked again by Fellanel, again her mind had left her body; and when in his nontime house Croyd had created a body for her, Greta's mind had entered it. (The one-day time lag meant nothing: nontime was in or out of direct contact with any era anywhen.)

Subsequently, on Leclerc's flagship, Greta had entered the pullman, presumably to return through space to her frigate. Since the frigate wasn't there, Greta's body for sure would be headed eternally in all possible directions. As for her spatializing body, his developing theory astonishingly told him that it didn't matter. As for her mind, either it was alive or it was not, and he knew how to check this out—but it could wait.

Just now it was more in point to follow another dangerously relevant uptime trail. . . .

He watched Greta watch Dr. Fellanel and the green decapod, Sira Ssen, in 2495, deep in Fellanel's manufactured Hades and thereafter in his office. When Sira Ssen quit Fellanel's presence, having given him the formula, Croyd quit his own body and entered the decapod's brain.

It took his mind a prolonged while to adapt to this alien brain which was laid out in a manner considerably different from the brains of *Homo sapiens* or of Croyd's own similar species *croyd*

*Thoth.* Once he had mastered this brain, however, he found it entirely logical in quasi-human terms.

Croyd then began to use a time-sampling technique to get through six years in as many minutes.

Ssen, who had some kind of ability to render himself invisible (it wasn't strobotemping), continuously haunted Dr. Fellanel as time ran downtime. But as the year 2501 arrived, Sira Ssen grew restless; and presently, always with the Croyd-mind in 'is brain, the decapod went for a spaceship that 'e had secreted near an oasis in the Sahara Desert.

Taking off without incident, the spaceship rocketed outward a-mong stars at an obtuse angle to the galactic plane. Rather soon, Croyd was experiencing for the first time the turbulence incident to penetrating the metagalactic barrier—outward.

In metaspace, halfway across the intergalactic fissure, Sira Ssen established hypertelemetric contact with friends in his home galaxy Andromeda. At least, Croyd surmised from topological considerations that it must be Andromeda, although Ssen thought of it as Mandomen. And this was Croyd's first astonishing contact with Andromeda, one of the more remote among the immediate galactic neighbors of Sol Galaxy.

Ssen reported laconically as follows:

"Planted hormone formula with Earth zealot who thinks he is a demigod. Implantation has germinated and use is spreading rapidly. Estimate two Flr-years for complete Earth captivation, ten to twenty years for complete Sol Galaxy captivation. If you invade in two years pinpointing Earth, it will be safe. If you invade in one year, it will be possible but extremely risky. Have confirmed that Earth actuality is in the same temporal sector as Mandomen actuality. No time to repeat, engines heating up. Good luck to all Myrons. God bless—"

The ship disintegrated.

Hurled out of the dying decapod's world by the shattering ship explosion, adrift in metaspace void, in the infinity beyond the universe, the Croyd-mind grasped that his return to his body in Fellanel's Boston house in 2495 was going to be a bit complex.

He had to think fast. Metaspace—or any space—had a way of swiftly eroding and disintegrating disembodied minds.

What to do—fast?
Metaspace.
*Non*space. . . .
*Non*time.
*His house!*

And he was there—on his breezeway bridge, in his own brain, with Greta there talking to him.

Luckily it was uptime in nontime, and so his mind was not there to fight with his mind. Uptime, downtime, anywhere, anywhen, a mind is a mind, and it exists at only one spacetime locus—the one where it is because it has come there. It may extend itself; it may even divide itself—but then it is two different minds progressively differentiating themselves through different experiences even when they inhabit the same brain.

No time to relive this past conversation with Greta—and no point.

Leaving the uptime trace brain, Croyd returned to Boston, picked up his body in Fellanel's house, and returned embodied to his nontime house—time seriatim, Greta gone.

He had places and times to go. But first, he had some thinking to do, a practically warranted theory to consolidate.

# 18

His breezeway in nontime seemed the only appropriate locus for hard meditation—and, probably, the only locus where he could hope to be temporarily free from what was beginning to feel like a cockeyed *karma.*

It now occurred to him to wonder how it could be light here. The light had no particular source; it was ubiquitous and clear like an artist's north light. Perhaps it was mental: perhaps only out of time could one clearly think without emotion and see without perceptual distortion. *(Without emotion?* Could he and Greta ever be together again in a way that would be live and right?)

At any rate, his theory had come clear. The nature of what was happening and of what *had* happened was ruthlessly simple. It was only difficult to put into conventional language.

Monon in the year 5 EA *simply did not exist.*

The year of present actuality was probably the year 2502 AD—five years "ago"—a few days following the hearing before the Medicine Board.

The ships "from Earth" that hovered above Monon—Admiral Leclerc, Bisquit, and all—were phantom ships.

Himself, Croyd—here on the breezeway bridge—was an actual mind occupying and activating a mere probability body: a *pr*-body.

But this *pr*-world of Monon had a probability so high that it *might as well be actual.*

This probability world called Monon was the most chilling phenomenon in all of Croyd's cosmic experience. Its chill was inherent in Croyd's time theory, which he had verified by many personal invasions of time.

Real events, now-happenings, he called *germinality* or *actuality.*

Germinal actuality is not instantaneous: it is the fraction of a second during which events which might develop in more than one way come into clear one-way definition. This period of time was what Russell called *specious present,* and the development that occurred in the specious present was what Whitehead called *concrescence.*

As germinal actuality or specious present flowed onward, futurizing, in its wake it left *past events* or *uptime.* Uptime consisted of frozen event deposits: no longer uncertain, no longer germinal, but absolutely definite and done and changeless. In uptime there could be no talk of event probabilities, for all probabilities were 100 percent: uptime is what it is, forever.

Ahead of actual germinality there is *downtime:* the *future* of actuality. In downtime, for every event complex there are several ways it can go; that is, the probability of any predicted actuality is considerably less than 100 percent. In the immediate future, there is reciprocal interplay between downtime and actuality: whatever is happening *now* has a strong determinative effect on what will happen *next:* thus immediate downtime probabilities are very high probabilities. But as one moves farther and farther downtime from actuality, all probabilities decrease and grow vague, more and more potentialities are possible. (When one is so far downtime that there are no developmental trends at all, that is *nontime,* containing all possibilities and no definite probabilities whatsoever; and it was for this reason that Croyd had been able to build this house in nontime and put people into it as quasi-physical realities merely by psychic projection.)

On past occasions when Croyd had guardedly invaded downtime—that is to say, probability—he had found himself in the midst of *blurring.* If an actual event had two possible futures—for instance, if a tree might stand or might be struck down by lightning—then *both* possibilities, both trees, were seen in downtime blurredly superimposed. If there were a dozen possibilities, already the blur became impossible.

With purely physical and very massive events, like the orbital positions of stars and planets, their probabilities were extremely high for centuries of even millenniums ahead. But individual human behaviors, and (by derivation) social and political developments, were scarcely predictable even a year ahead: this was not mere lack of knowledge; it was inherent lack of determination.

Therefore the world of Monon and the city of Eurydice, five years downtime of 2502 actuality, should have appeared more hopelessly fuzzed than the wings of a hummingbird cloud.

Instead, Eurydice in 5 EA was sharp and definite and real! Oh, in small details there might be blurring—but not more than what a slightly astigmatic man experiences when he looks at something closely without his glasses. Anagonon had boosted the future probabilities of Earth to the staggering percentage of 99.901: the very probability borderline of specious present: practical certainty, and therefore, *reality!*

The specious present of Earth—which normally lasts a fraction of a second—had become five years deep! Boston in 2502 AD and Eurydice in 5 EA were, for practical purposes, simultaneous!

How?

Well, what can heighten the predictability of individual human behavior? Two opposite conditions: either the human goes mindless and becomes a purely physical victim of physical events; or, the human can form a purpose and persevere in it.

And what can heighten the prediction probabilities of *social* action? Two not quite opposite conditions: there can be fulcrum events and forces which for a while dictate automatically and inescapably which way a society will go, or, there can be concerted long-range planned programs by a society or its power structure.

With The Anagonon Circle and Dr. Orpheus, all four determinants had been brought together. Anagonon was the dictatorial fulcrum event. Dr. Orpheus had formed his program and was persevering in it. The TAC Board power structure was exercising its long-range planned program for the society. The side effects of Anagonon reduced all individual minds to one group mind; and the irresistible main effects of Anagonon made sure that all people would be ineluctably drawn to accept it. The results were as predictable as the 1-2-3 action of a computer whose programming and data are known.

Thus, at the instant in 2502 when the Medicine Board had voted for Anagonon and the TAC Board, the Monon world of Orpheus had become so perfectly predictable that it might as well be real. And so, for all practical purposes, it *was* real.

Eurydice was Boston. Monon was Earth.

But the sweep by Dr. Orpheus was trying to be so total-clean that he had changed the name of his planet; and he even taught that Earth, *another* planet, was *the enemy* of his Monon people. The hovering *pr*-fleet of Admiral Leclerc—which, now Croyd thought about it, had flickered in and out of visibility exactly as a *pr*-fleet might be expected to do—was damned by Dr. Orpheus as the invading ships *from Earth.* (In fact, they came from Nereid, the galactic capital of Neptune; but Earth was the dominant planet in the galaxy—or had been so, until this Orphic secession.)

Ancient Pythagoras had taught that beyond a mystical Central Fire (not the sun) there was a dark supermystical *Counter-Earth*—always eclipsed by the Central Fire so that it was not visible from Earth but always obscurely affected Earth. Adapting this old idea to his new purposes, Orpheus clearly identified himself and his Monon as Counter-Earth; whence, of course, Earth was Counter-Monon—the inherent Adversary. There were psychiatrically diagnosable meanings in this approach—a fact which did not make the approach any less potent.

Now, in 2502, all this *had not happened yet*—but it was so surely *going* to happen that in Croyd's and Greta's and Leclerc's *experience* it already *had* happened!

For Croyd, this situation contained four crisis urgencies. He ranked their value in this order:

First, Anagonon of itself was subverting Earthworld and was bound to subvert the galaxy.

Second, he now had *reason* to believe that intelligent decapoda from the galaxy Andromeda were planning to invade, or *even now were invading,* his drug-weakened world.

Third, his Greta was in danger

Fourth, *he* was in danger. Ranking his personal peril last, he nevertheless had no desire to discount it entirely.

At least three corners of this complex crisis were worse than mere futurities. Many millions of people on Earth were poisoned *now,* in 2502. Greta and Croyd were contaminated *now.* It was rampant epidemic, multiplying itself in a geometrically proportioned chain reaction. There was no known medical way to check the spread, much less cleanse the millions already contaminated. Croyd, with his intricate psychophysical powers, doubtless could work out a way to cure himself and Greta and some other individuals by gene alteration; but finding the way would take weeks; and after that, working on one person after another individually would be like trying to suck away a torrent with a pipet—for only Croyd himself would be able to do it. Meanwhile, each of those growing millions—including Greta, including Croyd—was already slave to every higher-ranking member of TAC on up to Dr. Orpheus.

As for the fourth corner—galactic invasion by alien arthropoda— that too could be happening *now*. Croyd's probability theory explained why Leclerc had been getting all those extragalactic idar warnings: in a situation where mere probabilities were practically realities, merely possible attacks were being picked up as though they were actualities. But— *some* of the warnings *might* be real. . . .

That corner must wait, however, Anagonon was *here now.*

Croyd's problem was to find a method of breaking up these probabilities without in any way hurting all the Anagononic people.

He gripped the breezeway bridge, peering out into the void. How was all this knowledge related to his problem of somehow addling the hard probabilities in Monon?

He tried to keep thinking. But somehow he found his thinking blocked by a queer obstacle: the bizarre anachronistic *knife* that had fallen out of nowhere into the hand of Orpheus to be driven into Greta's back, and later had disappeared from the museum case to land in Croyd's own hand which then had driven it into the back of Orpheus.

*Where now was the knife?*

Croyd tried to banish its image from his mind so that he could go on with his critical problem.

The flowing of probabilities into actualities is not, he reflected, just an automatic sequence. It is reciprocal. Present events are limited by what is past. Future probabilities are affected by what is going on now. As present events develop, they reach out into the future.

*The knife. . . .*

If one can change the past, one can therein affect present and future; but the past is changeless. If one can change the present, one can affect the future; but the present moves by too swiftly to catch and affect.

*The knife. . . .*

But if one can somehow change the probabilities of the future, one therein restricts the possibilities that the present has to choose among.

*The knife. . . .*

It is maybe a logical problem. Uptime, with its frozen set of facts permanently related in one particular way, makes perfect logical deduction possible. Actuality whips by too fast for logic: it is action on the run. As for downtime—*normal* downtime, with its indefinite mishmash of probabilities—inductive logic, of the sort first projected by postmedieval John Dewey, is the only gross approach to logic that has any sort of usefulness.

But Monon was *not* normal downtime. Monon's probabilities were so high, by reason of Anagonon, that its events could be handled by a *de*ductive logic which was *uptime* logic, practically Aristotelian!

THE KNIFE!

Electrified Croyd simultaneously grasped the central problem and the key to its solution. Not the solution—but the key.

What was the one element in his Monon experience that had thrown the logic of Monon into a tailspin?

THE KNIFE!

He had to GET the knife. What he would then do with it he didn't yet know; but that knife he had to GET. . . .

Where was it?

It was gone from the case.

It was gone from Greta's back.

Where-when had it originated? How had it got into Monon in the first place? Nobody had heard of this knife until it had dropped into the hand of Dr. Orpheus.

To find this knife, Croyd would have to invade uptime—go back to the place and time of the knife's origin.

*When* would it have originated?

Ivory handle out of Egypt, fourth millennium BC.

Bronze, knurled and fluted and riveted—later than the tenth century BC.

A hoax. Made later than the tenth century BC. Made by somebody who had enough historical and archaeological knowledge and objectivity to conceive of such a hoax. Not recent, either: millenniums old.

Made by a philosopher *with a sense of humor.* Deliberately planted some place, to be found millenniums later and confound human logic.

Confounding logic was precisely what Croyd had to do.

Where and when was the earliest place-time that could have produced such a philosopher?

Greece. Nowhere else—and no place earlier.

Thales, the earliest known philosopher of all? Probably not—no evidence of a sense of humor.

Pythagoras? But the whole sense of the knife was *counter*-Pythagoras. . . .

Abruptly Croyd knew who *might* have made this knife.

On the thought, he was already over his rail, suspended in the nongray of nontime.

# 19

His feet touched down. He opened his eyes. He was high on the side of a gentle mountain. Off to his left a blue sea rolled below. A small city nestled at the foot of the mountain.

Intuitively, he knew that the city was Ephesus. Anachronistically, he knew that the year was 502 BC.

It was by far the deepest uptime penetration that he had ever attempted. He felt like one of the primitive tree divers that he had seen in the Museum of Ancient Man. One of the winners, luckily.

Working his way down the mountain, he came to a clear-cut road for men and mules. This he followed downward.

It was evening: the moon and one star were visible. Ephesus was a labyrinth of hovels and huts. Why did it come into his mind that Heraclitus was "the *dark* philosopher"? He had a vague inward image of a gnome; he had an urge to see him, to talk with him.

Avoiding mutually annihilating contact with passersby (some in decorous tunics, some in rags), Croyd scouted the narrow stinking streets of Ephesus until a powerful brain drew him—a brain that once had housed a powerful mind. Then he zeroed in on a hovel and peered inside.

It *had* to be Heraclitus, and he *was* a gnome, and he was drinking.

Suddenly Croyd realized that this Heraclitus was about to die. Then, if Croyd could avoid contact with any other contemporary, he could not create any significant time paradox, for the chances of Heraclitus's recording anything about Croyd's visit were nil.

To be certain, Croyd downtimed delicately about thirty minutes and assured himself that nobody else would come during that time. Then he returned to the moment when he first saw Heraclitus, and he entered without knocking. An oil lamp behind him cast his shadow on the table.

Heraclitus looked up: his eyes were bleary, and he did not seem disturbed by Croyd's weird clothing. "Sit down," he said (and Croyd understood the thoughts although not the language). "Pour yourself some wine. Custom calls for me to flatter you, fair sir, inquiring whether you be some god, since no human could be so radiant; however, I can't see you very well anyhow. Are you anybody I know?"

"No," answered Croyd, "I am not. But I have wanted to know you."

"Do you want to tell me your name?"

"It would have no meaning."

"That's all right," said Heraclitus. "The thoughts I am receiving of your talk are different from the strange sounds of your talk; and I suspect that what you really are is beyond my philosophy."

"Not really, in your case," Croyd positively asserted.

"Thank you," responded Heraclitus. "I suppose my philosophy says that anything is possible, so of course *you* are possible. Are you really a god, come to take me away from this life?"

"Call me one of the gods that the sea is full of."

Heraclitus blinked. "That is a saying of mine, but I did not know that people were remembering the things I have been saying."

"Your teachings are known. I understand them to mean that everything is always changing, that change is the substance of reality; so

I am sure that my own queerness will fit into your philosophy."

Heraclitus thudded his wine mug on the table. "That's a mistake!" he growled. "I teach that everything *in nature* is always changing, that change is the substance of *nature.* But *nature is not everything!* How stupid can you get, stranger? It is the *essence* of my philosophy that *values are eternal!* Take another slug of that wine: maybe it will brighten you up a little."

"I thought you said that one couldn't step into the same river twice, because the second time it would be a different river."

Heraclitus quaffed deeply and then said thickly: "But I went on to teach that the riverness of the river was more permanent than the waterness of the water; and that, by the same token, the justness of justice was more permanent than the opinions of judges, and that one virtuous man was worth more than a thousand great knaves. What bothers me is that my full meaning may not survive me; that posterity will be as obtuse as you, remembering only my sensational discoveries about nature and claiming falsely that I applied the same thinking to the human soul."

" 'Understanding is common to all,' " Croyd quoted slowly. " 'It is necessary for those who speak with intelligence to hold fast to the common element of all, as a city holds fast to law, and much more strongly. For all human laws are nourished by one which is divine, and it has power so much as it will; and it suffices for all things and more than suffices.' "

With both hands flat on the table, Heraclitus was staring at him.

"So you see," added Croyd, "both sides of your philosophy have survived you."

"Tell me, stranger—are you from a time later than my own?"

Croyd nodded slowly, marveling at the mind that in the sixth century BC could arrive at such a concept. And in the back of his own mind there stirred another kind of marveling related to the paradoxical fact that he and Heraclitus were actually in conversation here in changeless uptime.

"How much later?" the philosopher demanded.

"Much later."

"Have things changed?"

"History has proved both sides of your philosophy," said Croyd obliquely.

"Eh." The old man nodded. "I see you do not want to say too much; and perhaps a man ought not to know too much. Why have you come to me?"

"On a blind bowshot, Heraclitus. I am seeking a knife that was made either in your era or several centuries earlier, I do not know where or when or by whom. I do not know of any man as wise as you who has lived in your era or earlier, unless it was Anaximander or Anaximenes or Thales, but your philosophy draws me first to you."

Heraclitus squinted at him. "You did not mention Pythagoras?"

Croyd's eyebrows went up. "Was he wise? Or *is* he wise?"

"He was or is a fink."

"He is or was pretty good at numbers, don't you agree?"

"His teaching involves number magic. If your time is remembering him for numbers, my guess is that he has some bright students. Thales a century ago had better mathematics—he computed the solar ecliptic."

"What is your opinion of Orpheus?"

"Orpheus was a bright shining musical demigod a thousand years ago. Pythagoras raped him for his own finkish purposes—"

It was a fascinating byway, but one that Croyd unhappily had no time for now. He required himself to interrupt: "Well, as you noticed, I did not name Pythagoras among men of your wisdom. Can you perhaps give me a lead that will help me find this knife?"

Heraclitus was frowning at him heavily. "What sort of knife?" he demanded.

"This knife is anachronistic." Croyd described it.

Heraclitus inquired: "Does the hilt show a naval battle on the Nile among ancient Egyptian galleys?"

"Yes. Then you know of this knife."

Getting up with difficulty, Heraclitus pottered into the other room of his little house. Returning, he laid a knife on the table.

It was the knife.

Croyd gazed at him.

"I made it," said Heraclitus.

"Why?"

"For fun. For a joke. To show off my wisdom and my craft." He brooded. "I had an idea. I thought I might bury it someplace; and when it would be dug up later, what delicious confusion it would cause! The best of it would be that the more a man might know, the more it would confuse him!" He sipped. "But I never did bury it," he added, "because it bothered my conscience." He looked up, squinting. "How could you possibly have known about it? Nobody else has ever seen it."

"If I were to tell you," said Croyd, "you would never believe me. May I borrow it?"

"What for?"

"I will return it undamaged in a few moments."

"Are you going to do mischief with it?"

That one stopped Croyd, who hadn't the faintest notion what he was going to do with this knife. How then could he persuade Heraclitus to give it to him? He could just *take* it, of course, but the idea was repulsive.

He said presently: "You have recognized that I come from a later time and that I understand both sides of your philosophy. I can't satisfy your question, but I can assure you that it is necessary for me to borrow this knife—that the borrowing has crucial relationship to the interplay between the changing of nature and the eternity of human values." He knew that this was true; later, he would decide why.

"Take it, then," said Heraclitus.

After brief hesitation, Croyd picked it up, hefting it.

The balance was beautiful.

Abruptly it came into him what he had to do with it. Not the whole program—but the first necessary two actions. They would give him the material situation that he needed for improvisation.

He began to chuckle without mirth.

"Chuckle with *mirth*, stranger," said Heraclitus gently.

# 20

He arrived strobotemping in the salon of the brownstone shrine of Dr. Orpheus on New Year's Eve, 4-5 EA, just as distraught Orpheus prowled up behind his reluctant Greta-victim, clasped her, and murmured hard: "If I had a weapon, Greta, I would kill you. But since I do not have a weapon, I *will* take you by force this time."

Her voice was chilly. "I will not resist, Orpheus, because I have to love you; I have no choice. But I will be cold; I have no choice. But I wish you would kill me instead."

Continuing to strobotemp—because theory warned him that even relative uptime in 4-5 EA might not guarantee his visibility—Croyd watched the right hand of Orpheus wave frantically, and Croyd gave his own intent a split second reconsideration. It meant Greta's death. But he needed her duplicate in the Morgue for what he was going to do, and he needed the knife subsequently in the Museum of Ancient Man—well, just because that was what had brought him here! Besides, Greta was Anagononic: there would be no pain. . . .

Neatly he let go the knife so that its hilt was positioned precisely where the hand of Orpheus would grasp it an instant later before the knife would have time to start falling.

Orpheus felt the dagger in his hand. On impulse, he stabbed her.

So, looking back upon his Eurydice in the Greta-revivification of One Who Had Thought Him Too Dreamy, he lost her, and lost his world. Her loss was immediate; world loss was to be delayed a bit, he had no sense of it yet. . . .

As Greta slumped, supported by an arm of amazed Orpheus, Croyd reflected that he had just created the truth of what Orpheus had recited as history the day before in the museum. But Croyd noted also that this time his changing (if it was changing!) of events in uptime had no theoretical significance; for the evening of 4-5 EA, if it was uptime, was uptime only of its own downtime; relative to 2502 actuality, it was downtime absolutely.

He downtimed twenty-four hours to the Museum of Ancient Man.

# 21

Croyd actualized on the floor of the Museum of Ancient Man near a wall behind a column—not *in* floor or wall or column, much to his relief. Had he coincided with a material object, it would not have noticed him, but he would have perished. (At least, in real uptime, he would have perished; but what of this uptime in downtime? He wasn't sure.)

It was night, the evening of New Year's Day, 5 EA; and the museum was deserted. In the center of the floor was the case that did *not* any longer contain the knife. This case was open. After the disappearance of the knife and the death of Orpheus and the subsequent clamor, the museum had been cleared, and attendants had opened the case for the curator and the detectives to see what they could make of it. The case had been left open.

Not far from the case, on the other side of it from Croyd, an armed guard watched. This presence might or might not create a problem: had he been truly in uptime, he could have swaggered over in plain sight of the guard without being noticed; but high-probability downtime was treacherous, especially in view of the disturbing knife. As a precaution, he therefore resorted to strobotemping. So flittering, he crossed the floor to the case, never staying long enough in any single time track for the guard to notice him.

Swiftly he entered the case, which was large enough to contain him; and there he uptimed, keeping his eyes fixed on the exact center of the case, where the knife had rested. He was aware of the force-field case cover closing over him; and, as he backed into day, of hubbub outside the case—remarkably confused hubbub, the sounds being like a tape played backward.

He poised his right hand.

At the instant when the knife appeared, he grasped its handle.

Instantaneously he downtimed to the moment when he had entered the case. There stood the oblivious guard. Croyd grasped the knife.

He examined the knife. It was beautiful in its bizarre fusion of time styles. It was also an erudite joke.

If jest was all that old Heraclitus had in mind.

Nothing is real but change, in the world of nature. But in the world of spirit, values are eternal. This was the opposition that Heraclitus had tried to teach, even though the second part of this teaching had somehow been sloughed away by later scholars of Heraclitus. Thus Plato, in seeking and finding a synthesis between the total stasis of Parmenides and the ubiquitous change of Heraclitus, had actually settled for a refinement of Heraclitus in the *total* philosophy that the old gnome of Ephesus had tried to teach—but who now recognized that Plato had made such a settlement?

This line of thought was teasing, but there was really no time to philosophize. Croyd shook himself out of it and concentrated on the knife that he held.

Circularity. . . .

Orpheus had stabbed Greta with it. Subsequently it had been put into the museum case. It had then disappeared from the case, and subsequently Croyd-Thoth had stabbed Orpheus with it. *Subsequently,* Croyd had *for the first time* secured the knife from old Heraclitus, imported it into Monon, and handed it to Orpheus so the doctor *could* stab Greta with it. And the knife had disappeared from the case because *subsequently* Croyd had gone uptime and snatched it downtime—but in the course of that uptiming, the knife was *already* gone, for Croyd had not found it in the case at any instant subsequent to his snatching of it!

The indefinite regress of the circularity was possible only because paradoxes were inevitable in this Monon world which was merely although highly probable.

This Heraclitus-knife, which intentionally symobolized *paradox,* was in itself no paradox but hard intentioned reality. Hence, in this Monon, it catalyzed multiplication of paradox. If, with the knife, Croyd could sufficiently multiply paradox—*could he end by reducing the probability?*

He gripped the knife, grinning grimly. There was a third time-paradox that remained for him to bring off. It was going to be whimsically central to the colossal program that had crystallized for him—the action program that would save Earth and the galaxy from alien bugs and from Anagonon, provided only that Croyd would not make a single mistake along the way.

Knife in hand, Croyd actualized on the museum floor (New Year's Day, 5 EA) behind the column that had been his first hiding place. The museum was full of people, a number of whom were around the central exhibit case where the knife that he carried was on exhibit. He glanced upward: there on the TV screen were the hovering ships from Earth.

He studied the crowd near the case. Then he picked out Orpheus; and beside Orpheus, chatting easily, stood

*himself!*

His nose wrinkled a little in self-disapprobation: it was what he had anticipated, what he had come for; nevertheless, he supposed, the small shock at seeing himself in striped clothing and cap-and-bells was human enough.

Strobotemping, he moved invisibly to a point behind the two men, just as the disappearance of the weapon from the case was detected and the excited people crowded around.

This was the point of departure. This was the moment when Dr. Orpheus had gone down, stabbed by the knife which then had been found in the hand of this Thoth who was Croyd.

Croyd was sure that Orpheus was worth killing. But if now Croyd were to kill Orpheus and slip the knife into Thoth's hand, Croyd would only be confirming a probability and throwing everything back into repetitive *karma*. Besides, Croyd wasn't much for murder.

Instead, Croyd settled for creativity. He thrust the knife into the back of Thoth, and dropped the knife into the right hand of Orpheus.

# 22

He did not wait for the sequel, knowing that he would be able to return to it. Instead, he moved into downtime.

An instant later he stood in the admiral's cabin on the flagship of the Galactic Fleet that hovered over Monon, timing his arrival for the same number of hours following his departure that he had actually expended.

Admiral Leclerc was writing at his desk. Croyd cleared his throat conservatively. The admiral turned instantly.

The admiral leaped to his feet. "Croyd!" he exclaimed. *"Épatant!* Sit down, *mon ami!* Wait, I will call for Hennessey; the Bisquit we liquidated yesterday—"

Croyd raised a hand. "I'd like to sit and chat, but I think that minutes may count. Admiral, it is time for you and me to exchange identifications."

Leclerc's lips went tight. "I agree, it was indiscreet of me not to think of this before."

They went together to the admiral's computer and deposited their ID cards one by one in its slot. Having compared each thalamic pattern with the owner's thalamic pulse and with its own memory, the computer, a French model, said dramatically: *"Celui-ci, il est bien Monsieur Croyd. Celui-là, il est bien l'Admiral Leclerc. Sans doute! Soît, messieurs! Fin du communiqué!"*

Having reclaimed their cards, they stared at each other.

Croyd said faintly: "Please send for that Hennessey."

"No time," snapped Leclerc. *"I* will get it." That he served it himself from his own bar, instead of sending for a yeoman, proved the urgency of the moment.

They sipped moodily. It was unusually good Hennessey, and Hennessey is usually pretty good. Croyd allowed himself to speculate for a moment about the significance of good probability cognac being appreciated realistically by a probability palate owned by an actual mind. He decided to forget this problem which seemed secondary to the major concerns of the moment.

Then suddenly he saw that this problem was totally relevant.

Setting down the glass, he told Leclerc calmly: "My friend, I do not believe that you exist. Not here, anyway."

Leclerc puzzled over his little glass, holding it with six fingers (three of each hand). Then he said softly: "If I know Croyd, he is not going to confuse our thinking at a moment of concern by committing the comical fallacy of teaching me that solipsism is the true philosophy."

"Thank you," Croyd responded. "However, I am going to teach you a time theory." Rapidly he sketched the gist of his theory about the projective relationship of downtime to actual present.

Then he was silent while Leclerc thought. Once the admiral asked a curt question; Croyd answered tersely and adequately; there was silence again. Leclerc finished his cognac. He thought. He glanced at Croyd's half-full glass, shrugged, and got more for himself. Croyd waited, although it was hard to be patient.

Halfway through the second shot, Leclerc set down his glass decisively. *"Bien,"* he declared. "I follow you well enough for now, although we must talk later. Now: I think I see what you hint at when you say that I do not exist here. You think that I am really in—*comment vous dirais-je?*—in actuality, five years ago; and that this seeming of me here is only my future probability uncertainly engraved in downtime space. Am I right?"

*"Très bien, mon ami. C'est ça.*

"Then how can I be conscious of this unreal instant? How can I feel that I am here arguing with you, when in fact I am somewhen else?"

"I'd guess, as a possibility, that your phantom brain is generating a phantom mind which experiences phantom consciousness and exercises faint volitions and choices and judgments, as in a faint dream that will be forgotten. But for practical purposes, in the unusually high approach to certainty of this probable situation, it is enough to notice that your brain can work with computer precision, and therefore we can argue; and among other ideas that your high-probability brain produces and tries to communicate to me, there is the idea that you are conscious, that the full actual force of the Leclerc-mind is here—which it isn't."

"If it is like this," Leclerc tightly challenged, "why do you bother to argue with my seeming?"

Croyd answered firmly: "Because I have to be sure to keep you operating here in a stable and fairly predictable way until I have done what I intend to do. And even a phantom mind of a Leclerc-brain is sure to be such that it must understand and consent before it can be predicted."

Suddenly Leclerc seized and drained his cognac; and then he shattered the glass against the metal floor. "Now you have lost me entirely," he asserted, "but I think I have to believe you and obey. One of three states of affairs is the case: you are real and I am not, or I am real and you are not, or both of us are unreal: the fourth possibility, that both of us are real and you are talking like this, is unthinkable. I eliminate the third possibility: if both of us are unreal, none of this matters anyhow. Of the remaining two possibilities, the first is more likely, for you are coherently teaching me ideas that I would never have thought of; and so I accept your thesis."

"Do you understand it, my friend?"

"As well as I can understand myself—which is not an exciting measure of understanding. What are you about to do, Croyd, that I must hold still for?"

"One question first. Where was Commander Groen five years ago?"

"Name the date."

Croyd named it. The date was what he believed to be germinal actuality, *now*, but in 2502.

"Commander Groen and her frigate were then in exercises off Nereid." The reply was instantaneous.

"Good. And where is she now, Admiral—now in 2507?"

Leclerc's eyes widened, and with the little finger of his left hand he touched a corner of his moustache.

Croyd's *pr*-face colored, and he grinned. "What you are thinking," he said, "is only probable." Losing his grin, he added: "I have lost track of Commander Groen—mind *and* body. But at least, you have told me where she *was*—and, if you follow me, that is where she *is*. I'll pick her up soon—probably."

"May I ask a personal question?"

"Pray do."

"Are you two married?"

"Probability question?"

"In 2502, I mean."

"Officially, you mean?"

"*Oui.*"

"That," Croyd declared, "is between Greta and me and the Galactic Register—which you may research, of course."

Pulling gently at his long proboscis, Leclerc declared: "There is a limit to my nosiness."

"Then it is my turn. Now while we are asking and answering questions that will in fact never be asked or answered in a future which I mean to annihilate—how did Greta ever get to be a commander in five years from 2497 to 2502, starting from scratch?"

Placing his hands on his knees, Leclerc looked Croyd straight in the eyes. "Personal superiority," he asserted. "Nothing else at all. *Parôle d'honneur, mon ami, le* Temporary Galactic Chairman." Then he smiled a little. "I suppose the next logical question is: If a commander in five years on personal superiority—why not now a captain five years later?"

"I was not going to ask it, and I will not. In a probability world, her continuing commandery confers a certain stability that I prefer not to question."

Leclerc frowned. "While we are talking about what is only probable, you may wish to give some attention to the numerous extragalactic alarms that this fleet has been receiving. Since you tell me that we are only probable, I deduce that these alarms are only probable. On the other hand, in plain Gallic logic, we must concede that some probabilities are more probable than others. Now, today, there is a hint of a developing concentration quarter—"

"*Where?*" Croyd instantly demanded, leaning forward.

Leclerc gave him the coordinates. "Still beyond the galaxy," he added, "and, as you read from the coordinates, tending toward Sagittarius and therefore toward galactic center—but moving in toward us, on a large diagonal."

Croyd stood. "Be good enough," he swiftly requested, "to take me to your cabin and guard my body personally while I explore this. If you spot them coming in, destroy them if you can. But I think you will not spot them coming in."

# 23

Guided by the rough coordinates of Leclerc's alarm concentration, Croyd's mind (which he had learned to keep
self-contained and integral during a limited number of disembodied
minutes) rose at an obtuse angle from the plane of the galaxy; and at
the correct latitude and elevation, allowing for probable error but
correcting intuitively by means of brain-draw, he sensed (being unable
to see anything) that he was in the presence of a large number of
brains. Drifting with them for several seconds, he recognized two
facts about these brains: first, that they were the same species of
decapod brain that he had haunted in Sira Ssen; second, that they
were not really in this spatiotemporal locus—only probably so, with a
probability around 60 percent, much lower than the 99.901 prag-
matic reality of Monon.

Experimentally he uptimed, moving always toward Sagittarius. The
probability grew higher. And when he reached 2503—a year downtime of present actuality—he found himself in an actual living brain.

Then this invading fleet from Andromeda was in fact coming in on
Earth—only, weirdly, not in 2502 actuality, but a year later!

The task of orienting himself to this enemy brain, which was
humanoid in level but alien in structure, was eased by his experience
with the Ssen-brain; but it was rendered more difficult by his desire
to avoid letting the brain's owner know that he was here. In Ssen's
case, it had been uptime, absolute past with absolutely no fear of
detection; but in this case, it was *now*, and the brain was alive and
minded.

When he had himself adequately oriented, Croyd positioned himself unobtrusively in the brain's abstraction area, extending unnotice-
able processes into its visual and auditory centers.

For practical purposes, he then *was* the brain's coowner, except
that he could not will action. The owner was named Krell, and Krell,
along with other multicolored decapods, was listening intently to the
chirring speech of a black leader whom Croyd through Krell's brain

identified as a fleet admiral. They stood on a remarkable bridge all of whose walls were transparent, and through the forward wall Croyd clearly identified a star sector centered on Sol and extending perhaps a thousand parsecs in every direction.

This fleet, then, was diving in on Sol. And while Croyd could not immediately read the instrumentation even with the aid of Krell's brain, he judged by analogy with his own fleet speeds that Sol, and presumably Earth, were not more than a day away.

This black-armored admiral was saying: "And so, gentletens, it does appear that our unforeseen difficulties with the lack of turbulence in the metagalactic barrier, together with several unexpected space hurricanes that we had to skirt, have eaten up every bit of our margin. If nothing goes wrong, we will touch down on Earth inside of twenty-four Earth hours, in approximately the heartland of the continent where Earth is richest and most powerful. It is the task of each one of us to see that nothing goes wrong. Am I understood?"

Krell joined the others in saying, "Aye."

Croyd scanned 'is brain. With horror, Croyd abruptly grasped the female nature of their urgency and what it would do to Earth people.

"Now, gentletens," said the admiral, "I turn to the critical factor of our time attitude. And I am afraid that this time attitude is possibly linked with the lack of turbulence in the metagalactic skin; and what worries me most is that I do not know exactly what this linkage would be.

"Let me draw your attention to these key instruments which are replicated in each of your ships, including even Sira Krell's. I am referring to the time dials, with their associated adjustment controls."

'E pointed with a prime claw to a row of ten vertical long-rectangular gauges. Each gauge resembled an ordinary thermometer or barometric pressure gauge—only upside down, since each thin crimson-glowing indicator column started at the top of its gauge and extended downward.

"Tell me, gentletens," the admiral demanded, "do you see anything unusual about these time bands?"

As they drew close, studying the gauges, Krell's brain told Croyd why it was a life or death question.

Each gauge indicated the temporal status of the ship's target: the gross gauge to the left was calibrated in millenniums, the precision gauge to the extreme right in seconds, and the eight intermediate gauges in progressively correlated intermediate units ranging from centuries down to minutes. The zero point at the middle of each gauge was *ship's now.* If the meniscus end of a band hovered above the zero, it meant that actuality at the target was uptime of the ship, so that the ship was going into the target's *downtime;* conversely, if the meniscus descended below zero, the ship was entering the target's *uptime.*

The gauges worked on probability conventions that approximated Croyd's own. The meniscus of each band extended to the target's specious present, defined as the temporal range where the average probability of events at target fell between 99.901 and 99.998+; averages 99.900 percent or lower counted as downtime, averages from 99.999 upward were taken to be frozen actualities in uptime.

Usually—and now—a commander wished to enter his target in its present actuality; but time slippage in transit, or slight wavular variations in simultaneity between stars and galaxies, might throw a ship slightly into the target's past or future. The time bands revealed the error, which rarely exceeded a few hours one way or another, being unrelated to the velocity of light. To correct it, the commander would adjust the ship's ATN (Automatic Temporal Navigation system) by moving a red arrow beside each band until it pointed to the meniscus. If, however, the ship was to enter uptime (first calculating carefully the possibility of lethal collisions), the arrows would be moved upward of the menisci; if downtime, downward. (Never very deep into downtime, though!—for there was no theoretical return from a probability situation below 51 percent.)

The admiral's question was a mortal question for two reasons. Generally, if they were to err too deeply into Earth's downtime, they would perish beyond the point of no return. But specifically, the females were so close to extrojection that there was no time for any error: they must strike instantly and accurately into Earth's actuality!

Croyd shared Krell's tension as the officers examined the gauges. On the millennium and century gauges at left, the crimson bands came down to the central zero; on the decade gauge, the band descended below the zero nearly halfway to the +1; on the year gauge, the meniscus hovered farther down at the +4; and the bands entirely filled, from top to bottom, the six precision gauges to the left. (Myron time units corresponded closely to Earth units, their planet having a similar orbit and velocity around its star, and naturally, decapoda would use a decimal system.)

For nearly half a minute, now, the captains had been scrutinizing these gauges, looking for something unusual. One antenna after another negated. Only two sets of antennae held quietly hesitant: the blue antennae of the blue commander (who awhile ago had detected Russell's Paradox about noticing no turbulence) and the golden antennae of Croyd's host, Krell.

A green captain asserted: "I am looking particularly at the year gauge which is the one most frequently useful for gross tempigation. This band entirely filled the gauge all across the galaxy, as did the decade band to its left; and now, as we approach the star Sol, both bands are withdrawing into adjustment. Since the instrument works by detecting gross probabilities, this would be expected."

Even without Krell's brain, Croyd would have seen his point. In the behavior of astral and planetary bodies, in their positions and orbital motions, the regularities are so high that the probabilities of any reliably based prediction are well into the specious-present probability range far into the future. Hence, as far as this instrument was concerned, galactic downtime might as well be actuality or even uptime: the bands of definite events had filled the year dial entirely and the decade dial entirely; most of the time they had even filled the century dial, while the millennium meniscus had fluctuated near the bottom. So these bands had told the Myrons very little while crossing the galaxy; they had until now paid scarcely any attention to them.

Krell had beckoned to a yeoten and whispered something to 'im. The yeoten had departed. Croyd's opinion of young masculate Krell went splendidly upward.

"Very good, Captain," responded the admiral. "But now I wish to introduce another variable into the discussion. Until a few hours ago, we have been out of instrumental range of Earth; we have been detecting only gross galactic and galactic-sector probabilities. But during the past two hours, this instrument, and the corresponding instruments on your own ships, have all been focusing on Earth with increasing precision; and by now they are excluding practically all other galactic influences. Any comments *now*, gentletens?"

Nervously clearing 'is discs, Krell spoke without any prompting from Croyd, whose presence 'e did not suspect. "My esteemed green colleague is impressed by the fact that the year and decade dials have been filled all across the galaxy, and he assumes that they are now withdrawing into normal adjustment. But I seem to be thinking that this adjustment is abnormally slow, that by now both menisci should be approaching zero."

Croyd's attention to the debate that followed was absolute. These aliens, by his definition, were *human.* He was witnessing the most thrilling phenomenon that he knew: human minds driving their brains at peak intensity, seeking a coda of meaning in a cacaphony of conflicting indications.

The green captain countered: "It is only a little time since the instrument has been targeted on our Earth objective. High galactic probabilities would slow the meniscus withdrawal."

Krell retorted: "But the admiral has just asserted that the instrument is by now excluding practically all other galactic influences. Admiral, how long have the menisci remained at this four-years-down-time level?"

The admiral turned to the silver flag captain, who replied tersely: "They had withdrawn to this level thirty-seven minutes ago. Here they have stayed."

The blue commander interjected: "Wait, gentletens. I see what Krell is getting at. Don't *any* of you see? The gauges seem to say that actualities on Earth are four years in the future of our actuality here! And yet, by intergalactic temporal theory confirmed by our martyred pioneer Sira Ssen, all actualities within the metagalaxy are absolutely contemporaneous with probable errors not exceeding one week!"

During the silence that followed, the others did mental double takes eventuating in something like physical shock. Only Croyd knew the truth—and Croyd wasn't talking (but he wondered whether the science of the Myrons had actually refuted Einstein-type relativity or had merely ignored it). The black admiral waited.

Krell came into the silence. "So, then, these abnormally long time bands are presenting us, as the admiral has already seen, with a mortally dangerous problem. Consider two alternatives—"

'E paused as the yeoten approached 'im and murmured something. Krell nodded and resumed: "Either something is making the instrument misbehave, in which case we cannot use it. Or else our objective, the planet Earth, has a specious present which is an incredible four years in length—in which case we *still* do not know how to tempigate or when the actual present of Earth would be located in this monstrously long specious present. Am I still correct?"

After a moment, a low-pitched buzzing began, but the admiral silenced it with a peremptory antenna-flip. Seeing how it was going, the Croyd-mind took this instant to transfer to the brain of the black admiral. Peering from the admiral's eyes, feeling 'is tension, Croyd appreciated the worker-warriors in their assortment of challenging colors. For him, the golden armor of young Krell stood out gloriously from the mass.

"Now," said Krell, pursuing it, thinking on 'is feet, "let us look at the possibility that the instrument is misbehaving. This seems unlikely, sira, at least in its time detection: a moment ago I sent a yeoten back to my *Champu* by flttr to check my own time dials, and 'e returned just now to report that they are behaving the same way. Since time detection on our several ships is *not* locked into detection on the flagship, then if all our instruments are behaving the same, the disturbance has to be external, affecting *all* our dials. However, one notices that all *other* instruments on this bridge are performing as expected, and it is difficult to imagine an electromagnetic disturbance that would affect only the time dials. So one has to conclude that what is affecting the time dials is a *temporal* disturbance. And that puts us squarely into the other alternative—namely, that this damned Earth has a multiyear specious present, as opposed to the normal planetary specious present of a few clicks. Indeed, this specious present may even extend into Earth's downtime, so that the menisci would indicate not Earth's *now* but Earth's nonexistent *future!* So, gentletens, the mortally perilous problem in a pupa is: *Where* along this extrojecting time band do we set the ATN indicator, to get us into actual present instead of landing us in nonexistence?"

The admiral said gravely: "Admirably presented, Sira Krell. You have stated precisely the decision that is mine to make. It is a question of *racial* survival, not merely our own survival—and of extrojective relief or hideous and prolongedly painful death, thinking about the girls. I must make this decision within moments. I entertain your advice."

Krell answered promptly: "I think the meniscus this time represents not actual present but future. In a preliminary way, I therefore advise that we aim not at the meniscus but at some point above it. Beyond this general idea I haven't yet pinpointed my thoughts."

With faint melancholy, Croyd reflected on an unsavory fact of life: one galaxy's meat could be another galaxy's poison. The reflection did not slow him down, however: he knew which side his own galaxy's bread was buttered on.

He therefore threw a doubting thought to his host the admiral.

Turning to the silver flag captain, the admiral demanded: "Captain Zl?"

After deliberation, Zl asserted—as Croyd had thought 'e might, in the nature of conservative intelligence everywhere: "I applaud the penetrating analysis of young Lieutenant Krell. I do not find myself in accord with his action judgment. I see no reason to begin distrusting the frequently confirmed and never-denied assumption that the meniscus denotes the start of present actuality, even when the following specious present is abnormally long."

The admiral inquired: "Sira Krell?"

Krell addressed Captain Zl directly. "Let me remind you, sira, that we were disturbed by the lack of turbulence as we penetrated the metagalactic surface. This, I am now realizing, is a very improbable state of affairs. It now occurs to me that our master ATN on this flagship, into which we *were* all locked during the crossing, may have undergone some slippage. We would not have noticed this because in extrametagalactic space, where nothing special ever happens and so no significant probabilities take shape, the time dials behave in a random way. If this slippage did occur, it has thrown us either into uptime or into downtime. I believe it was downtime, and that when we hit the metagalactic skin, there was no turbulence because no events that we were penetrating were real yet.

"And this possibility bothers me most of all, for two reasons: one you all know, but let me explain the other one. As you see, the ATN *indicator* is now pointing to zero, where we have kept it set for the entire voyage. But if the basic ATN has slipped us into downtime, while erring in its pickup so that the *indicator* says we are in actuality, then we do not know how far into downtime we may be! If this is so, then the four-year apparent specious present of Earth may in fact be five years, or ten years, or a hundred!"

Croyd admired the young masculate's intuition. In fact, their ships had slipped one year into downtime. The specious present of Earth—owing to the astonishing Anagonon compulsion—was not four years long, as the dials showed, but five years long: from 2502 to 2507 AD (or to 5 EA). The Myron ships were operating in 2503.

Croyd also felt the shock in the mind of the admiral, and saw it slowly double-taken by the others, at the suggestion that the ships had slipped into downtime. He perceived that the admiral had the same suspicion but had hoped it might be rejected. There was no return from deep downtime—except by the untried Zed Maneuver for which only Krell's little *Champu* was equipped! Croyd wondered a bit why none of them, not even Krell, was thinking of doing a control check by focusing the time dials on another star system: the planet Alpha Centauri III, for instance, had a human civilization that would tell the Myrons the temporal facts. But in the heat of argument and concern, none of them thought of this.

"Captain Zl?" queried the admiral.

"Sira, if such time slippage occurred, it could as easily have been uptime, since extrametagalactic space offers no resistance either way. Improbable experiences do not necessarily mean downtime: it would be an improbable experience if we were to meet with our ancestors of a million years ago, and that would be uptime. Not only that, but if we have slipped four years into uptime, then that is precisely what the time dials are telling us. To me, the key influence in this inscrutable dilemma is the convention that the meniscus shows target actuality. Since all other reasoning is self-contradictory, I would hold to this."

Krell cried: "If we are in uptime, then the ATN indicator is still wrong in pointing to zero, and we still do not know how deep into uptime we may be! And if improbable experiences do not necessarily mean downtime, then this instrument is contravalid anyhow—so why hold to the meniscus?"

Unexpectedly the blue commander helped Croyd's cause by admonishing: "Excuse me, Sira Krell, but you are guilty of a slight semantic sideslip. The instrument is valid on a basis of epistemological probabilities: when they are low, it is downtime; when they are high, it is present or uptime. But when things are actually happening to you and me, for us it is *now*; and if they are unlikely things, then whether they are uptime or downtime or merely phantasmic relative to other events is a matter for judgment on internal context."

"Nevertheless," Krell passionately fought back, "we *have* to be downtime, not uptime. The key point is the lack of turbulence back there. If we had been uptime, not only would there have been no turbulence, but we would have been increasingly slowed and finally stalled and permanently stuck there by the impactedness of frozen lightwaves."

"In fact," Captain Zl pointed out, "we *were* slowed going through. We interpreted this as being due to the lack of pulsation thrust—but it could as well have been due to pressure of frozen events in uptime, which, by the way, need not necessarily stop us entirely when the events are nothing but photons. Admiral, I conclude my discussion by stating my judgment that we are in uptime, not downtime, and that we should follow convention and aim for the meniscus if we want to hit Earth actuality."

At this crisis of the argument, Croyd intervened. He threw a decisive thought at the admiral.

The admiral said quietly: "Then we will aim for the meniscus."

Before Krell could interject, the admiral nodded at the silver flag captain who said: "Thank you, gentletens. Formation dismissed." And he followed the admiral through the officers and off the bridge.

Croyd took just a moment to reexamine the brain of Krell. He found this brain in a state of dejection—as well it might be!—but, at least, in a perfectly normal state of compliance with command decision, as might be expected in a member of a race whose genetic hormones included the formula for Anagonon.

But Croyd could not linger. Departing Krell, he spacetimed to pick up his body on Leclerc's flagship.

His own mood was as dejected as Krell's, but for a different reason.

True, he had saved his galaxy from the alien threat by influencing the Myron admiral to follow the temporal course which would lead the Myrons to downtime destruction.

But what he had done was an act of genocide, and it left a bad taste in his heart.

Had he remained a few moments longer with Krell, his conviction that he had saved his galaxy from the invading Myrons might have been undermined a little.

# 24

In Admiral Leclerc's cabin, Croyd picked up his body which
the admiral had been personally guarding. He sat up on the
admiral's bunk, swinging his legs over.

Leclerc queried: "Sleep well?"

"Well enough," Croyd bit, "to have destroyed a race."

"You destroyed them? Who were they?"

"Andromeda," he snapped. "Not destroyed, but doomed—can't
miss. I don't want to talk about it now, Admiral, I'm a little sick. Let
me brief you on the program. Ready?"

"Ready."

"For you, it culminates in fleet suicide."

*"Comment?"*

"We were pincered between two crises for Earth and the galaxy:
invasion and rather hideous enslavement from outside, Anagonon and
lotos-eating slavery from within." (He neglected to mention the personal crises for Greta and for himself.) "I just nipped off the invasion
prong thanks to your intelligence, sir. Now between us we tackle the
other problem of liquidating The Anagonon Circle and more than a
hundred million Anagononics without killing them."

"Killing the fleet, however?"

"You stay on duty here while I perform the following sexigesimal
series of one dozen gambits. *Imprimis,* a check on Commander Groen.
*Item,* a duplication of my body. *Item,* a body switch for me. *Item,* a
body switch for Commander Groen. *Item,* a mind fission. *Item,* a two-
Croyd ploy. *Item,* a catalytic marriage between Anagonium and an

anachronistic knife. *Item,* a pullman adjustment. *Item,* an alteration of certain papyrs. *Item,* a two-Greta caper. *Ultima,* a rerun of Orpheus and the Bacchantes—"

"*Ultima* means last. You have mentioned only eleven."

"I'll give you *Penultima* in a moment."

"Why twelve, by the way? It is a magic number in the wrong system. Pythagoras was a decimal-system character."

"Exactly."

"Ah."

"Be it added, Leclerc, that the first ten gambits merely build a rather complicated spring machine. With *Penultima* and *Ultima,* we trigger the machine—and it all pops off in thirty minutes. I hope."

"And *Penultima* is?"

"Your fleet suicide."

Leclerc merely held silent. Croyd went into more detail: it involved spacetime and probability theory.

Having digested it, Leclerc touched his moustache and inquired: "The destruction of my probability body will be a reality?"

"Probably."

"*Ah, bon.* Meanwhile I merely sit here?"

"Prior orders hold: sit tight, and stall if Derien gives you a destruct— it would be premature. By the way—if my guess is right, the concentration of extragalactic alarms will continue and strengthen from the same quarter—but you don't have to worry about it."

He disappeared.


Leclerc, blinking, reminded himself that some day he must pin down this Croyd long enough to learn about up-down timing. Croyd had remarked that any sufficiently intelligent human could catch on to it, and Commander Groen appeared to have learned the rudiments.

As nearly as Leclerc could gather, time was only analogically a fourth dimension; ontologically it behaved like a stream. Old Isaac Newton had thought of it as a stream; but he had the direction wrong, supposing that time streams from the future past us into the past. Modern science, unable to grapple with the resulting paradoxes, had dropped the stream idea and substituted the dimension idea. Well: time as a fourth dimension was fine for epistemology but silly for ontology; in discarding Newton's whole concept, science had thrown out the baby with the bath water.

In fact, according to Croyd, time is a stream and *we are parts of it:* we flow *with* time. If Croyd wanted to reinspect the past, checking the debris that had dropped out of the current, he had to exert extra energy to swim *up*time; if he wanted to foresee things to come, insofar as decreasing probabilities let them be foreseeable, he again had to exert extra energy, this time to pick up his pace and swim ahead *down*time. Such action he accomplished, as a volitional mind, by acting through a specific and delicate integration of forebrain, midbrain, and hindbrain into which necessarily all nerves and soma were swept like matter into a vortex. . . .

So, at least, Leclerc understood it. Scratching the bridge of his nose, he reminded himself that it was like knowing how we think: enough comprehension to seem to understand it, not enough detail either to teach it or to do it.

He glanced at what was left of the Hennessey bottle. Blinking, he decided instead for the bridge. Even if he was only a *pr*-admiral, it remained that his probable duty was absolute duty: by staying with it, perhaps he could increase his own probability. And this was morally desirable, for a man who was about to die: there was no valor in volunteering to die as a phantom.

## Greta Actuality D minus 2: then
## All Actualities D-Day

### Part Five

### SHELL GAME

At the climax of the Anagonon incident, it appears that no more than two hundred doctors, or about one doctor in five hundred, were members of The Anagonon Circle. These doctors controlled about a thousand interns, about six thousand trained aides, and about ten thousand traveling program-checkers, all Anagononic. However, the two hundred thousand computers that these two hundred doctor-teams controlled were Anagononizing and banding approximately ten million new TAC members daily in the middle and lower orders, without reference to the average of one new doctor member and three new high-ranking official members per doctor per month. The immediately subsequent organizing procedures were accomplished by a highly trained cadre of lay "noncoms."

To the credit of our profession, it must be said that the overwhelming majority of doctors were holding aloof and even developing a mounting organized resistance. It was a losing cause, however: they had no real evidence, only inferential behavioral suspicions, and the calamitous Medicine Board decision of 2502 presented an almost insuperable obstacle. . . .

—REPORT OF THE BIOTHERAPEUTIC TASK FORCE

# 25

**D-day minus 2:**

Having stepped into the pullman of Admiral Leclerc's flagship in a routine electromagnetic jump to her frigate to put
on her uniform, Greta was disintegrated into space. Her frigate wasn't
there any more.

Her mind had to do something. Already it had downtimed as far as
the specious present of Monon would allow. This time it uptimed—into
her own actual 2502 body, the body that had mindlessly left the apartment of frustrated Orpheus after yesterday's Medicine Board hearing.

She found herself facing Admiral Leclerc, at attention, while the
admiral lectured her roundly on absentminded behavior in his presence.

She looked down at herself: she was in uniform. She looked up and
blinked. The admiral paused, seeing that something was amiss.

She managed to summon up feminine sweetness. "Admiral, please
don't think I'm nuts, but—just tell me what year this is."

Moodily the admiral considered her. Then blandly he asserted:
"2502. I curse myself for revealing this top-secret information."

"Thank you. And the month and day?"

Pursing his lips, he dated the day.

Greta began to tremble. In an automatic gesture, she dug into a
uniform pocket, produced a book of matches, lit one, and studied its
flame, trembling as the flame trembled.

The admiral touched a corner of his moustache. "Pardon, Commander, but this is not the first time I have watched this match act. Do
you wish to explain it, or do you prefer that I do so?"

Wide-eyed, she stared at him across the flame. She blew it out. She
said primly: "I know what it means. I did not know that you knew."

Wordlessly Leclerc gestured at his Asimov flashtray.

Dropping the match there, blinking at the little flash, and pocketing the booklet, Greta said: "Thank you for your answers. Please do not ask me why I have asked the idiot questions, and I apologize for any inconvenience I may have caused. I have been ill, but now I am all right. Will you be good enough to repeat my orders?"

"Croyd ordered you in from Alpha Centauri. You tell me your orders."

Anagononically unable to betray Orpheus, she improvised: "Croyd left hurriedly. He sent me to you for new orders."

Somewhat later she was on maneuvers in her frigate off Nereid, away from Dr. Orpheus for a while, tied to him nevertheless. Her downtime maneuvers she dismissed as transient psychosis.

**D-Day, H-Hour minus 12 hours:**

Returning to his nontime house, Croyd spent several hours in the catacomb that burrowed into nothingness behind his first-floor dining room. In this cavern he utilized the random energies of raw space to construct two dynamic fields. When they were done, he tested them theoretically; and then he had to trust them, despite the considerable personal risk entailed, because there was no reliable way of putting them to empirical test prior to the business use that he contemplated.

He was now ready to begin his series of twelve gambits—some of which would involve these fields in crucial ways.

He uptimed to 2502 actuality.

**H-Hour minus 8½ hours:**

The place where he appeared was two billion miles from Earth—in the captain's cabin of Greta's frigate which, as Leclerc had advised him, in 2502 was cruising off Nereid, Neptune's little satellite which was the seat of Croyd's galactic government. The actuality that he homed in on was three days after the Medicine Board inquiry and two days after Leclerc had ordered time-confused Anagononic Greta onto this duty. (Greta had paused only long enough to pick up, as auxiliary ship's doctor, an intern who wore an Anagonium bracelet.)

In the cabin, Greta's yeoman opened her eyes rather widely at the materialization. But when Croyd swiftly adjusted her mind, she lost surprise and obediently went to fetch Commander Groen.

Greta entered from the bridge, and her mouth broke wide with pleasure. "Croyd! How did you get away from Orpheus?"

He took an instant to clarify her meaning. Greta of 5 EA *knew* that he had killed Orpheus. This, however, was Greta of 2502 *in actuality:* four days after she and he had been felled in the doorway. What she meant was: He was holding you in stasis in his Boston house—how did you get away from *that?*

However, his visit had a precise purpose. "Never mind that," he said crisply. "Listen, Greta. I want you to put your ship into an immediate suicide dive. You are to crash on the surface of Neptune."

Greta swallowed, cleared her throat, and said without showing emotion: "I assume that the crew and I can bail out along with you."

"Well done, Commander: I thought you might ask *why,* and I can't tell you why. No, the crew may not bail out."

Extremely pale, Greta asserted: "Then neither can I."

"And neither can I," he told her.

She stated: "Now I must ask why."

"Understandable. However, I may not tell you why. But it is an order."

Her arms were straight at her sides, but her little fists were clenched. Presently she said: "I will accept *our* deaths. However, I am sworn to preserve the life of the Galactic Chairman at all costs, even against his own will. I will crash the ship, and the crew and I will go with it, but you must bail out."

"I am telling you flatly that I will not bail out. Nevertheless, you are to do this."

"Perhaps I forget that you are after all Croyd. Are you going to survive somehow? Do you have a way of surviving?"

"No. I will die with you."

She studied him.

She ran to him, embraced him.

She stepped back, trembling but at attention. "This is for sure?"

"This is for sure."

"Then I must refuse the order."

Silence.

Croyd: "Court-martial, you know."

Groen: "Of course."

Silence. Croyd was convinced that she meant it. He had therefore completed his control study: apart from Anagonon, Greta was willing to kill herself and her crew for a command, but she was also willing to

take a court-martial by refusing a command to kill the Temporary
Galactic Chairman. (He chuckled inwardly: the court would of course
find that she had acted properly, but he was sure she hadn't thought of
this.)

He went into the experimental study by producing the dagger: he
had left it in the hand of Orpheus, but he had retrieved it by a simple
time replication in the museum case. "Have you ever seen this?" he
challenged.

Puzzled, she studied it. Then she looked up, shaking her head no.
(That meant little: it had been behind her when it had stabbed her, and
she had been distant from it when she had watched herself being stabbed.)

He hated to do what he had to do next, but there was no substitute
for this testing. Seizing her arm, he slashed away her uniform at the
shoulder and, while she watched with anxiety, he deliberately cut a
zigzag wound down her upper arm. Blood flowed freely. The watching
yeoman was paralyzed.

In a wondering voice Greta demanded: "Why did you do that?"

"Didn't it hurt?"

"Of course not. Anagonon, remember? And death won't hurt me
either, or any member of my crew: we've *all* had Anagonon—so that
pulls the rug out from under my heroism, doesn't it? But also it won't
hurt you, since you've had it too—so that shows my refusal was a
matter of straight duty, not sentiment, since both of us would have
died in the crash anyhow. Doesn't it? Anyhow, I won't crash you—period."

Having wiped the blade on a part of her uniform that was not
blooded, he replaced the knife of Heraclitus in his pocket. "Yeoman,"
he snapped, "get the doctor to stitch this up before Commander Groen
bleeds to death. Immortality requires blood." The yeoman whipped
out.

Croyd now demanded: "Show me your rank."

Understanding that he did not mean Navy, Greta bared her left
wrist. On the Anagonium amulet of her bracelet was indelibly inscribed
a $\Lambda$—the eleventh rank in TAC.

"Lambda!" Croyd muttered. "He might have done better for you."

Greta said quietly and with conviction: "It is what he did for me,
and I am happy with it."

Croyd asserted: "I rank you in TAC. But I have a reason for not showing you my amulet. Do you accept my statement, Commander?" Now, in 2502, she would not have understood his ironic O.

Greta responded with a twisted little smile: "He is wise, and therefore you would *have* to rank me. Of course I accept this."

"Then," said Croyd, "my order takes irresistible force, Greta: it is not an order by the Temporary Chairman to a commander—it is an order by a ranking Friend in TAC to a subordinate Friend in TAC. Crash the ship, and me with it."

"Will do," said Greta. She started for the ship's audio.

"Wait," said Croyd—satisfied now not only that Greta was Anagononic but also that the compulsion of Anagonon was invincible.

Greta turned.

"Forget it, Commander—and forget this conversation. I've arranged for your wound to heal rapidly now; it will be healed by the time the yeoman and the doctor arrive here. I can't quickly fix the tear in your uniform; but just tell them to forget it, and they will—you rank them. Good-bye, Greta. I love you, I'll be back."

He disappeared downtime.

Obedient to her ranking Friend in TAC, Greta forgot. She therefore forgot to tell the yeoman and doctor to forget. However, as it turned out, it didn't matter.

# 26

**H minus 8 hours:**

Thoth wavered down, stabbed by Orpheus, his special friend. The time intervention by Croyd had reversed *pr*-history. In true uptime, or in actuality, it could not have happened.

Croyd, back still *another* time, strobotemporally witnessed it again.

Orpheus turned, registered shock, then waved back the crowd and called for help. Guards came running. (Even in Anagonized Monon there were guards: they were love objects to keep people from vandalizing and pilfering as outlets for Anagonon-repressed aggression.)

Orpheus cried out in treble excitement: "I did not do this! There is a *deviate* in this crowd! Lock the museum and call the police!"

While they were doing it, Orpheus knelt over Thoth, confusedly fingering the dagger haft.

The dagger haft shimmered and disappeared. But Thoth continued to lie dead.

Awkwardly Orpheus got to his feet and wiped a sleeve across his brow. The police were here. Orpheus ordered: "Get Thoth to the Morgue, and take all these people to the internment suite of the palace for examination. Treat them gently: there can be only one deviate among them. Anagonon is, unfortunately, not perfect: one miss in ten thousand cases—"

Croyd grinned grimly. The replicate of the dagger reposed in a belt beneath his clothing. Unfortunately neither he nor Greta had been a miss.

Proceeding immediately to the Palace of Pythagoras, he descended to the Morgue where that very morning he had visited Greta's copy-body. (That very morning? Well, yes, as of *these* coordinates.) He waited, ready to play Gambit Two.

Presently they appeared, bearing the body of Thoth. This body was impassively received by the blond receptionist and the brunet demonstrator. It was brought into a side room (not the many-tiered vault where Greta reposed) which had the air of a dental clinic, bearing only slight resemblance to mortuary clinics that Croyd had seen in a couple of twentieth-century uptimings. Here the body was suspended in a force field; and the senior mortuarian (a classic type) entered and inspected this body. He was followed by two young men in white surgical dress. The receptionist and the demonstrator vanished.

Duplicating operations on Thoth could begin immediately: the case load was light in Anagonistic Monon.

Stifling his impatience, since he had to wait, Croyd watched with technical interest while the interns undressed the Thoth-body, positioned it for camera, and floated up the equipment. There were several species of camera, utilized at several angles, all of them taking four-D samples of durations ranging from ten microseconds to ten seconds. It was of particular interest to notice how the icroscopic cameras (modifications of a model which Croyd had developed a number of years before) handled replicative details, such as the genetic structure which was replicated with minor variations in all of the trillions of body cells. There was nothing so crude as a photo of a single cell standing for all cells, nor anything so impractical as photographing each cell individu-ally. Instead, submaster photographs were taken of epithelial samples (for each cell in the sample, 440 shots of minimal ten-miscroseconds duration each—that is, at each of forty depth levels, one shot at each of ten atomic periodicity dimensions, plus an eleventh icromacrosopic shot of the gross genetic structure); corresponding photographs of the ten sperms in the random sampling were then blended; and the resulting 440 masters were translated into quinary symbols and fed into the computer as controls for replication according to the several parameters for the numerous other classes of cells.

The procedure was going to simplify Croyd's problem with respect to the Thoth-body—which, now he thought about it, was *himself* in an alternate line of probability development. And he believed that he had a corresponding ploy for the Greta-body.

When the procedure was completed, the Thoth-body was floated out for the routine autopsy slicing, whereafter it would be atomized. This part of it did not interest Croyd. Abandoning his strobotemping, he settled into *their* time, becoming visible to them; and his perfect resemblance to the Thoth-body produced the expected effect of shock in the senior mortuarian and his interns.

Croyd tapped his Anagonium bracelet with a finger: the O confused them, but intuitively they took it to be superior. Croyd said: "Don't be disturbed, Friends. This unusual rank symbol is uniquely mine by reason of my unique relationship to Dr. Orpheus. Yes, I am Thoth's doppelganger. I only want to inspect the icrographs before they are reified; and of course I have particular interest in the master icrographs of the epithelial controls."

Without resistance, they led him into the dark chamber and left him alone with the projection equipment. Before they left, he had the foresight to warn: "Dr. Orpheus wants this kept secret from everyone, even from himself—he does not want his judgment influenced by knowledge of the procedure." Assenting, they closed the door on him: they would obey.

Croyd remained there for several hours. When he emerged, he had altered the genetic patterns of the 440 master control icrographs to make the probability better than 99.9 percent that the reconstructed genes would be identical to Croyd's *before Anagonon,* with the remaining error probability blurred so that the Anagonon configuration was astronomically improbable.

He had purified the Thoth-body of Anagonon. His own body remained contaminate.

Also, when he emerged, he found himself face to face with towering Dr. Orpheus.

It was a crisis. With his present *pr*-body Anagonon-contaminated, there was nothing hostile that Croyd was able to feel or do to this Orpheus who ranked him and everybody.

Said Orpheus grimly: "I don't exactly know why there should be two of you, Thoth; but I do know that one of you is dead and you are the other. So if you were in there with the master controls, there was something you were doing that I need to know about. Tell me what it was."

Unable to lie to him, Croyd managed to temporize: "The answer is complicated. Give me a moment to formulate it."

"Of course," Orpheus pleasantly answered. Unless his Anagonon had miscarried on Croyd also—the second case in one day, which was simply out of the question—Croyd would have to answer truly. Orpheus confidently waited.

Croyd disappeared.

# 27

**H minus 6 hours:**

He downtimed two hours. When he rematerialized, Orpheus was not present: if Orpheus was going to come here now, he had not yet arrived. By now the Thoth-body, which he had just purified of Anagonon, should be completely replicated and in its vault drawer.

He organized himself for Gambit Three.

Transiently he found it interesting that he had so far been able to resist the influence of Orpheus by temporizing and fleeing instead of confessing. The reason for this resistance might be studied later; for now, he briefly hypothesized that his vital *mind* in this imperfectly concresced *pr*-body had partially weakened the Anagonon influence, although not enough to really free him.

Now he moved directly through a communicating door into the vault. Tiny in the distance, the demonstrator with the little black moustache sat at a clean desk, looking busy. Surprised at Croyd's entrance from just that private door, he arose hastily and came forward. He had not seen Croyd in the mortuarium, and he had paid little attention either to live Thoth visiting Greta this morning or to dead Thoth in a drawer; he merely reacted with respect to Croyd's apparent Anagonon authority.

The demonstrator drew out the drawers: the two bodies were not far from each other. (The *pr*-time when Thoth in his nontime house had stolen Greta's Serenitite duplicate from this morgue was a dozen hours in the future.)

'Good," said Croyd. "You are to close and lock the drawer containing Mr. Thoth; and you are not to open this Thoth-drawer for anyone except me. Do not even open it for your chief. Do not even open it for Dr. Orpheus: he does not want to know about this until afterward; and if his curiosity should temporarily overcome his will, it is his desire to be refused."

The demonstrator nodded, accepting, believing. The poor man would probably go into neurosis if his chief or Dr. Orpheus *should* demand that the door be unlocked; but whatever the outcome, there would at least be delay—and his neurosis would be only probable.

"As for Miss Groen's body," added Croyd, "please remove it from the drawer and bring it into the mortuarium."

The demonstrator complied. Presently Greta's *pr*-body was floating nude in the force-field. At Croyd's bidding, the demonstrator departed.

(Croyd could not help reflecting ironically that this same Greta-body must now be departing into space in all directions, atomized and subatomized as the square of the distance, never to stop until it would reach the metaspace barrier whereupon its component positive and negative electrons would enter upon an eternal roller-derby around and around the banking of the curvature. . . .)

Having watched the filing and recreative procedures once, Croyd
assured himself that he had them minutely memorized.

Alone in the mortuarium, he went to the drawer that contained
Greta's tape. Working more rapidly this time, having been through a
similar process once, he altered the genetic engrams of the 440 masters.
There was a slight difficulty here, since he had not memorized Greta's
pre-Anagonon patterns quite as well as he knew his own; nevertheless,
with delicate minimal work, he was able to blur off the known Anagonon characteristics without doing any significant violence to the genetic patterns of Greta herself.

Having done this, he fed the tape into a computer. He then altered
the force field in such a way that the facsimile of Greta which hung
therein was atomized. Activating this computer, he made a new facsimile from the altered tape.

He had purified the Greta-body of Anagonon.

Then Croyd called the demonstrator, who removed the body from
the force field and floated it back into the vault.

Croyd said: "The next thing is very simple, quite routine. I want
both the Thoth and the Groen bodies vitalized and conveyed to—well,
say Room -493. And send up a tray of drinks and snacks. And some
clothing, by the way."

The demonstrator permitted himself a knowing wink. Then he
asked: "May I inquire—what you did in the mortuarium?"

"I checked her out," Croyd responded, "and she is perfect."

"And did you not wish to check out Thoth also?"

"This I had previously done."

"Are you sure that—checking her out—was all you did with her, in
that floating force field?"

"You are well suited for your job, sir."

"Thank you."

"You are welcome. So will you get on with it?"

Merely by touching a button on the drawer of each facsimile, the
demonstrator latently activated both bodies. Thus he had infused them
with electrochemical charges which would continue to function in the
bodies, continually regenerated as the bodies ate and drank, until such
time as these charges would be withdrawn by pushing another button.

This procedure had been superficially explained to the demonstrator during his three-week training period. Not understanding it, not really caring, the demonstrator nevertheless basked in the status superiority of his technical knowledge. It was with real professional flair that he touched the buttons for Greta and for Thoth.

He then used light-duty tractor beams to lift out Thoth and Greta and to lay them on transporters; and he called the receptionist to convey them aloft.

"Lock their drawers again," cautioned Croyd, "and remember what I said about your chief and Dr. Orpheus."

He followed the bodies out of the vault, up the force field elevator shaft, and down the perfumed corridor with its translucent living-color walls. The blond receptionist palmed the doorknob of Room −493; and the door, psychogalvanically deactivated, simply disappeared, revealing a boudoir done in a demure blue. The receptionist led the floating body-transporters to bedside, where tractor beams lifted and laid them on the bed. She then turned to Croyd.

"When you are ready for the latent activation to become actual," she said, "touch this button; the bodies will be irradiated from the ceiling. I should caution you, though, that they are not always willing to be *de*activated later. If these two are willing, have them lie on the bed again, and touch *this* button: it will deactivate them and at the same time summon us. If they are *not* willing, you have only to scream: we will knock out all three of you with a shot of gas, and later we will awaken *you*, sir, harmlessly."

"Thank you," Croyd acknowledged. "And the clothing?"

Her eyebrows assumed curious curvatures. Then she went to a wall and opened a closet. "Several sizes here, male and female," she told him. "They aren't often used—but some like to dress them."

"Thank you again. And by the way—skip the drinks and snacks."

"You realize that their energy flags rapidly without drinks and snacks?"

"They will be all the more ready to accept deactivation."

"True—" She paused, fluttering a little.

Croyd inquired: "Was there something else?"

She said impulsively: "He must be your twin brother, sir. I know how you must feel."

Croyd dropped his head and veiled his eyes.

She left, reactivating the door behind her.

Returning to the Morgue, the receptionist found the demonstrator locked in a tearful vise between Dr. Orpheus and the Chief Mortuarian on the one hand, and the restrictive command of Croyd on the other. Leaving quickly before she could be involved in discomfort, she took a thoughtful seat at her desk with her back to the vault door. Now that there was no longer any physical pain, psychic discomfort was mortal agony.

It would be necessary for Croyd to activate both the Thoth-body and the Greta-body before the next step could be taken.

A difficulty was that the man and the woman lay nude; and in their mindless condition, their response to each other was likely to be automatic and primitive, creating a state of affairs which would interfere with the efficiency of what Croyd intended. He therefore expended some precious minutes finding clothing that would fit them, and dressing them. Fortunately they were not dead weight: their latent condition allowed them to respond sleepily as he put on their clothes.

Now Croyd readied himself for fast action.

Touching the activating button, he instantly left the *pr*-body that he had been investing—his Anagonon-contaminated body—and entered the *pr*-brain of the purified Thoth, who now became Croyd.

A period of disorganization followed. Timelessly the befogged Croyd-mind struggled to regain control, as a sleeping mind caught in a smothering nightmare seeks to free itself.

Control came abruptly. He opened his eyes. Some of the smothering, as it happened, was being contributed by the now-activated mindless body of purified Greta, whose instincts did not seem dampened by the obstacle that both of them were dressed.

He managed to pin her, although she continued to heave and struggle aimlessly. Standing near the foot of the bed, the now-mindless *pr*-body that he had just deserted—the one he now thought of as the Thoth-body—swayed, a vital automaton, creating further embarrassment. There was no way to destroy that shed body tainted with Anagonon: he would have to leave it here.

Then he comprehended what would happen if he were to scream. The shed body would be knocked out by gas, put into a drawer, and deactivated.

Filling his lungs with fresh air, Croyd used only so much air as he needed to shout "HELP!" and he instantly uptimed with Greta—but not before the shot of gas had knocked out not only the shed Thoth-body but also Greta.

# 28

**H minus 4 hours:**

The doctor and the yeoman were leaving Greta's cabin, shaking their heads a little. Greta was examining the torn sleeve-shoulder of her uniform. Only a few minutes of actuality had passed while Croyd, having left this frigate, had supervised the copying of his Thoth-body, reconstructed it, reconstructed Greta, and returned here. The apparent paradox had nothing to do with relativity or subjective time: it was an outcome of the random factors in probability, and it might have gone the other way.

Greta looked around and saw Croyd. He stood at the inward wall of her small cabin, in front of a built-in sofa, holding the inert Greta-body in his arms.

Commander Greta blinked. Then she said unsteadily: "She seems familiar, somehow. May I come near?"

"Of course."

Gambit Four had been set in motion.

Commander Greta came to them and examined the Greta-body which Croyd was holding at a level somewhat lower than the commander's eyes.

Having inspected the Greta-body minutely from stem to gudgeon, Commander Greta raised her eyes to Croyd's and said: "She's me. Who dressed her?"

Croyd cleared his throat.

"I see," murmured Greta, and she set about doing what she could to fix little things here and there. Then she stepped back to appraise, and her little frown took on a nuance of puzzlement.

"She seems a bit blurry," the commander reported, "and so do you. Maybe I'm weak from loss of blood?"

"No, we *are* a little blurry. We are only 99.901 percent definite. You are about 99.98 percent definite."

"You *sound* definite."

"My mind is as definite as a mind ever is. She has none."

"Oh." Pause. "Why don't you—sit down?"

Croyd turned and gently deposited the Greta-body on the sofa. Then he turned to Commander Greta and took her hands. "But you are sure that I am Croyd?" he inquired.

"Yes. You are Croyd." Pause. "And yet you are different, somehow. Not the blurring, I mean. You are different from—the Croyd who was here just now."

"Tell me how I am definite."

Pause. Then: "I do not get the Anagonon feeling now."

"Then I am no longer a Friend to you?"

"Not in the TAC way, no. In the *old* way, thank God! You are Croyd, the way you were before Anagonon—almost."

She came into his arms. Their embrace was long. Presently she moved away and observed: "If your *pr*-body is a problem for you, I would not have noticed it."

He said: "My Anagonon-body you *had* to obey, no matter what I might tell you to do. But now I am no longer a Friend. Will you obey me?"

Her brows flattened. "I will not kill you, Galactic Chairman."

"But in every other way, Greta?"

"I—I think so."

He told her briefly what he proposed to do.

Folding her beautiful hands, she tapped lightly at her front teeth with her thumbnails. Then she bit the thumbs lightly, looking up at him.

She queried: "What are the hazards?"

"Your death or your insanity."

"Are these hazards great?"

"Significant. I am willing to risk them."

Softly: "For you, is it much risk?"

Croyd hesitated. Then he asserted: "For me, it is a great risk, to risk you. The greatest."

*"Well!"* she responded, dropping her hands and smiling with restraint. "Never did I think that great self-sufficient Croyd would ever say *that!*"

He spread hands a little. "I've said it."

Turning her back to him, she leaned on the worktable, musing: "But if it works, I will just be Greta again, the way I was before Anagonon. Normal energy. Able to feel pain. Entirely mortal."

"And, also, entirely free of slavery to Orpheus-Fellanel."

"True." Suddenly she turned to him, concerned, leaning back against the table. "Tell me, Croyd—does he plan to *use* me?"

"You and I both know this—to a certainty of 99.901 percent. And we know something else, Greta. It is probable that in five years' time, he will kill you. With a knife in your back."

"But I'm immortal—practically!"

"There's going to be an unexpected thing about kidneys."

Standing erect, she bowed her head, folding her hands before her. "I almost wish you hadn't told me that."

"Why?"

"I would have preferred to make my judgment on a moral basis. But now you leave me no personal choice. In plain self-preservation. I have to do what you say."

Again Croyd cleared his throat. He said, half apologetically: "Then I guess I have to tell you something else. If he kills you—which is almost but not quite certain—he will kill you with a knife which I will hand to him. But I don't have to hand him that knife. So now I tell you flatly that if you do not do what I say, I will not hand him that knife. So now your choice is purely moral." He meant the promise sincerely, though he groaned inwardly at the reentry into *karma* that would be required to cancel out this future history.

Her head came up slowly, her eyes narrow, her lips tight. She enunciated: "You are a devil."

"That's as it may be, Greta. But your choice has to be free of compulsion."

"What do I have to do?"

"Does that mean yes?"

"You say I may die or go nuts?"

"It could happen."

She repeated: "What do I have to do?"

He told her.

"Croyd—"

"Greta?"

"Hold me tight while you do it."

He took her mind into his brain.

It was not the first time. She was half asleep; she stirred comfortably in his brain. Meanwhile her mindless body, responding automatically to his body, was getting a bit out of hand.

He put it to sleep. It slumped in his arms. Carrying it to a chair, he deposited it there as decorously as he could. It looked as though Commander Groen had drunk too much and had passed out.

He then went to the sleeping *pr*-Greta and roused her. She opened her eyes, stared at him, leaped to her feet, went tightly into his arms.

He put Greta's mind into the *pr*-body.

It threw *pr*-Greta out of control. She went catatonic, her arms bruised his neck. Then she slumped, breathing heavily.

He waited tensely, holding her.

Greta's eyes came wide open. They gazed into his eyes. Her delicate brows arched high. Then deliberately she softened and kissed him.

Suddenly she pushed him away, breathing hard. She looked down at herself. She said: "Turn your back, you idiot, while I rescue my Navy clothes!" Breaking from him, she ran to the somnolent mindless body in the chair and began to strip it. She paused and looked frantically about. Then she went back at it.

Turning his back, Croyd chuckled silently; but the lump in his throat was large.


Uniformed, she stood behind him. "Turn around, Croyd."

He turned.

She commanded: "Hit me."

"Pardon?"

"I did what you said. Now you do what I say. Hit me. Hit me *hard.*"

He slapped her face, spinning her half around. For a moment she held her head, evidently dizzy. Then she recovered and turned back to him, her face grim. Swinging from the floor, she smashed his cheek with her fist. Then, massaging her hurt fist, she stood back to watch.

She'd actually drawn blood, a little.

Croyd nodded, his face tranquil. "I'm happy to say it hurt me. Did I hurt you?"

"Real bad, thank you. God bless pain. What do we do now?"

"Go to the intercom and tell your exec to take over for a little while—you have some heavy thinking to do, you don't want to be interrupted, he should pretend you're not aboard, he's in command."

Not even pausing to wonder, Greta did it. Then she came to him.

"Grab hold, now," he ordered, seizing her waist with his left arm. Obediently she hooked an arm around his neck. He went to her discarded body and took it in his right arm.

He downtimed with Greta and the Greta-body to the reception room of the Morgue—Eurydice, Monon, 5 EA.

The receptionist gaped at the triple apparition.

Croyd said pleasantly: "Miss Receptionist, meet Commander Groen—this one, the live one. You girls get acquainted while I dispose of this body."

Opening the door behind the receptionist, he carried the discarded Greta-body into the Morgue. The demoralized demonstrator went haggard. He was alone, Dr. Orpheus and his followers having just gone up to Room −429.

Croyd said: "Here is the facsimile of Miss Groen. Please put her back in her drawer and deactivate her."

The demonstrator managed to formulate the following question: "Which one of them are *you?*"

"Not the one for the drawer. Him you'll find upstairs. Better go get him and put him away. First, though, please drawer Miss Groen."

Reduced to automaticity, the demonstrator opened the drawer, activated the tractor beams to place the body inside, closed the drawer, deactivated the body.

Greta hurried in. "Croyd, here comes Orpheus with another body that looks like you. Let's get out of here."

Having examined live Commander Greta carefully, the demonstrator went into the fetal position.

"Not yet," Croyd cautioned; "we mustn't waste our human resources. And, Greta—remember that you aren't Anagononic anymore."

Ranging herself beside him, she squeezed his arm, and they waited together.

The discarded Thoth-body floated in feet-first, flanked by a white-uniformed intern, followed by a concerned Dr. Orpheus. The small procession stopped fifteen feet from Croyd and Greta.

"Keep clinging to my left arm," Croyd advised Greta quietly. "There is no sense in making a big scene."

He advanced with Greta until he flanked the Thoth-body on the far side from the receptionist. Gravely he contemplated the twisted face of Dr. Orpheus.

Then Croyd stooped, hooked his arm about the waist of the Thoth-body, tightened his other arm on Greta's arm, and nontimed.

"What are we doing here, Croyd?"

"How do you like my house?"

"All I am seeing is the exterior, and this bridge that we're on. It looks nice. It's for you, all right—you could have dreamed it up yourself."

"I did."

"The scenery, though—the landscaping—it seems to lack something."

"You mean, this nondescript void effect? I'll correct it when I have time. By the way—you talk as though you had never been here."

"Have I been here?"

"Think, now. *Have* you?"

She puzzled over it. "I confess there is a sort of a sense of *déjà vu.* Otherwise—well, tell me."

'Your mind has been here, Greta, but in a later stage of your body history. In your mind there is an engram of the particularity of this place, but in your present body-brain it finds no responding symbolic storage, because your brain hasn't yet been here before. It will all come back when your new combination shakes down. But just now, you and I have problems that are much more pressing."

"Name of?"

"First off, our bodies are only *pr*-bodies. This we have to correct—and this is perhaps the only place where it could happen without creating difficulties with respect to the rest of the material world."

"Why?"

"Tell you later. Just now, I have to lift this Thoth-body. I never realized I was so heavy."

Bending, Croyd grappled the inert Thoth-body and with an adroit twist and swing slung it over a shoulder. Straightening, he clasped Greta's waist and transspaced to the dim catacomb behind his dining room. There he stripped the Thoth-body, installed it within his force-field machine, closed the machine, activated it.

"Tell me," demanded Greta.

"His atoms are *Schrödinger*," Croyd explained, "and I am Bohring them. You know, Greta, our uptiming and downtiming has really been spacious: we have never stopped being contemporary with actuality— but we are not actual, and *he* is not actual. If this works, he becomes actual. If it does work, you're next."

"Why not *you* next?" Greta challenged.

"You'll see," he promised. Deactivating the machine, he activated an icrospectroscope and examined it carefully. Finally he switched it off, grunting satisfaction. "Theoretically it did work," he told her. "Now for the next thing."

Having opened the machine so that the Thoth-body was visible (and apparently unchanged), Croyd removed his own clothing and laid himself down on the dank floor of raw clay beside the machine.

A moment later, the Thoth-body within the machine stirred, roused itself, integrated itself, and came out. "Hi, Greta," it said.

Greta's right hand uneasily clasped her left upper arm. "Who's who?" she demanded.

"I'm Croyd now," said the emergent. "That's Thoth now," he added, pointing to the inertness on the clay.

Greta's hands slipped into the jacket pockets of her uniform. She said coolly: "One of you had better explain."

"What I just did," said Croyd, "was to test the effectiveness of this Bohring experiment by transferring my mind from *that* body to *this* one. Had the experiment failed, there might have been some embarrassment for me—but all is well, as you see. So you're next."

Greta frowned, staring at the body on the floor. Presently she said: "Look, Croyd. I'm hardened to this, now—one body is just like another body, as long as it's yours and your mind is in charge of it. But I do see one difference. *That* one was free of Anagonon. But—are *you now* free of Anagonon?"

"I'm loaded with it."

"Then—but, look, what a hell of a handicap you've shouldered all over again! *Why?*"

"Tell you later. Are you game to go into the machine now and be actualized?"

"I'm game for what you're game for."

"Then take off your clothes."

"Why?"

"I'm not sure what my machine will do to the relationships among body atoms and clothes atoms. They might fuse."

"Okay then. Turn your back."

"Why is it that a pretty woman doesn't want to be watched while she's dressing or undressing, but likes to be admired after either operation is complete?"

"I'll tell you when you explain about the atoms. Turn your back." Croyd, grinning, turned away.

Presently a half-muffled voice said: "I'm in. Close my door."

The door half-opened. The half-muffled voice commanded: "Hand in my uniform."

Croyd breathed again. He complied. The door closed. He noticed his own clothing on the floor. He dressed.

The door opened. Commander Greta stepped out, smoothed her uniform, and stood at ease, clasping his hand.

"How do you feel now?" he inquired.

"No different. *You* feel a little firmer, though. How do *I* feel?"

"Stronger. We're in."

"Then presumably the first-off problem of getting us actualized has been solved. What was the other problem?"

"Had you forgotten that by now more than a hundred million people on Earth, and quite a few people on other planets, have taken Anagonon?"

'Oh," she said, brows flattening. Suddenly she flung away his hand and stood quite straight, head up, face sober.

"Let's get on with it," said Commander Groen.

156

# 29

Nestling close to Krell, Maelbrug rested four podia on three of 'is shoulders. "Why so quiet so long, my friend?"

After thought, 'e turned all 'is eyes upon her. "How do you feel, princess?"

She confessed: "Very—stuffy. And edgy."

'E patted her podium. "Don't worry. We'll make it." 'E turned 'is head away and went back into thought. She noticed that all 'is forward eyes were concentrated on the time dials.

She demanded: "What worries you about those things?"

'E tensed a little but said nothing.

A fifth podium rested on a fourth of 'is shoulder—and then the five gripped him tight. Her voice was taut: "The time *is* tight, isn't it. Is there any *doubt,* Krell?"

Incisively 'e told her: "It is a gamble, Maelbrug."

Her head went down, and her podia fell from 'is shoulders. 'E continued to study the time dials.

She instructed 'im quietly: "As soon as you are sure it is hopeless, please kill me."

After digesting that, 'e turned to her again, inquiring: "How much delay can you stand?"

Forcing herself to think straight, she said: "I have talked to nurses. They say that a female can theoretically stand up to three days of delay. There are five problems. Three are psychological: the genetic lust to extroject, the genetic drive to get the extrojecting done in order to keep the species going, and the individual fear of what may happen if one does not extroject. The fourth is partly psychological, partly physical: *pain*—first mild, then severe, then intolerable, the limit of tolerance depending on the individual's physique and will power. The fifth is purely physical: in a maximum of three days, there will be rupture and toxic death. I do not know whether I can stand up to three days, my friend—it will be up to me—but in three days it will no longer even be up to me."

She was honest about the pain. The "anagonon" hormones that were genetic in her blood prevented her brain from registering pain-receptor stimuli as more than a telltale vibration; but since she had never known anything different, her mind took it as pain.

All 'is eyes were on her. 'E was marveling at her intellectual objectivity—*her. . .intellectual objectivity!*—in this matter which was supremely the concern of females.

It emboldened 'im to demand: "Maelbrug—what if I should make a decision—and it should turn out to be wrong? Would you curse me while you were suffering?"

She brooded. Presently she asked: "What if you do not make any decision, Krell?"

"If I do not make any decision, I will be merely obeying the admiral's decision. And the admiral may be right. So if I make a decision, it will be different from 'is—and it may be wrong."

Silence. Then: "I won't ask you what kinds of decisions we are talking about, all this is beyond me. I know you all want to get us there in time. Do you doubt the admiral, Krell?"

"Yes."

"I will not ask you if you love me, Krell. I know you do."

"Yes."

"Whether the admiral is right or wrong, since you doubt 'im, it will tear you to obey 'im. Whether 'e is right or wrong, it will tear you to disobey 'im, since 'e may be right. I can tell that for you there is no such thing as making no decision: you *have* to decide one way or another. Whether you decide for the admiral or against 'im, if it comes out wrong, you will suffer at least as much as I. Krell, I have heard that human fathers suffer as much as their females when their females are bearing children; and until now I never understood this, but now I think I do."

Suffering silence.

"Here is a thought, Krell. If you decide for the admiral, and 'e is right, all of us are saved; but if 'e is wrong, all of us—all our race—are gone forever. If you decide against the admiral, and 'e is right, I suffer and die, but the others win and our race wins; but if 'e is wrong and you are right, I am saved, and maybe the race is saved through me. Shall we look at it objectively, Krell, the way you are always saying we should look at things? Does objectivity dictate that we divide the chances?"

'Is misery was ultimate.

She whispered: "I love you, Krell. Whatever you decide, however it may come out for me, I will only praise you for the courage of your decision."

'E brooded.

'E nodded once.

Leaving her, 'e mounted the control pole. Clutching it, convulsively 'e did what was necessary to position the ATN indicator two years uptime of the meniscus.

# 30

H minus 2 hours:

√ Gambit 1. Check on Commander Groen
√        2. Duplication of Croyd's body
√        3. Body switch for Croyd
√        4. Body switch for Commander Groen
          5. A mind fission
          6. A two-Croyd ploy
          7. A catalytic marriage between Anagonium and an anachronistic knife
          8. A pullman adjustment
          9. An alteration of certain papyrs
        10. A two-Greta caper
    *Penultima.* Fleet suicide
       *Ultima.* Orpheus and the Bacchantes

The first four moves in Croyd's program for the liquidation of the Anagonon circle he had now brought off successfully. As a result, there were now three Croyd-bodies: his original body, mindless, Ana-gononic, in stasis in Fellanel's basement; the purified Serenitite dupli-cate of the Thoth whom Orpheus had stabbed, mindless and in stasis in Croyd's nontime house; and *this* body, the one that Orpheus had a-wakened, Anagononic, now animated by the Croyd-mind. As another result, there were also two Greta-bodies: her original body, mindless, Anagononic, in stasis in the Eurydice Morgue; and *this* body, the puri-fied Serenitite duplicate of the Anagononic Serenitite duplicate of the Greta whom Orpheus had stabbed, now animated by the Greta-mind.

The last eight gambits would be most hazardous, would require the tightest timing. Hazardous? The last two would be deadly.

He could not take these last eight gambits in strict ordinality. He had to intersplice them a little.

He began by setting the *Ultima* in motion. It would involve Greta in mortal peril—and she had to do it alone—and her body could die as easily now as any other human body.

He briefed her on the task and the dangers. She reiterated the task and the dangers: he was satisfied that she understood both. He said: "Will you?" She said: "Kiss me." They kissed. She said: "Let's get with it."

Uptiming, he dropped her in a secluded place near Fellanel's house just at dusk, in 2502. In a few swift words they agreed on their timing: she would wait thirty minutes, and then she would approach Fellanel. They squeezed hands.

He left her, uptime.

Twenty-four hours uptime of the *Ultima* that Greta awaited, Croyd invisibly and intangibly entered Fellanel's laboratory. Fellanel was at work.

Croyd executed the mind fission that was the beginning of four-part Gambit Five.

Holding his time track, Croyd moved immediately into Gambit Six by teleporting himself through walls and a floor into the underground dungeon where Dr. Fellanel had confined the original and mindless Croyd-body after knocking him out with a shot of Anagonon and gas in his doorway. The original Croyd-body was in stasis here. Croyd re-moved it from the stasis chamber, and he devoted a number of minutes to an accelerated hypnopaedic imprint upon its brain of the entire series of cognate and connate memories that were in his own brain from the moment of his awakening by Orpheus in 4-5 EA.

Having thus assured himself that his original brain knew all that his present brain knew, Croyd-the-mind departed his present brain and entered his original brain, animating his original body. And now, again, he was *home*: wholly Croyd—mentally, neuronically, somatically, spermatically Croyd.

Turning to the inert body that he had just departed, he performed a number of physical transfers. Notably, he used the Heraclitus-knife to sever the chain of the O bracelet, removing it from the inert wrist, and on his own wrist he psychothermally fused the jointure.

Shouldering the body, he downtimed twenty-four hours and inserted the 5 EA body into the stasis chamber. He then moved downtime another fourteen minutes.

His invisible-intangible strobotemping entry into Gamit Seven in Fellanel's private laboratory was tightly timed: fourteen minutes downtime of the planned *Ultima* with Fellanel and his TAC Board. What Croyd was about to do would require about ten minutes of time coasting—that is, allowing himself to drift on a sort of diagonal uptime line which would bring him minute by minute ever closer to actuality. The four extra minutes were minimal allowance for error.

Dr. Fellanel was poring over papers at his desk. Approaching him from behind, Croyd drew the bronze dagger from his belt inside his clothing. With his other hand, Croyd slipped a jeweler's glass into his right eye socket. He examined the dagger tip, to satisfy himself once again that he had ground and polished it to the micropoint that was necessary.

A dagger so improbable that it would throw all the logic of Monon into disarray. . . .

Fellanel was a nervous man: the powerful left hand that wore the bracelet kept twitching and broadly gesticulating as he worked. Croyd, adapting his body to featherweight, caught hold of the restless wrist with two fingers of his left hand. He was thrown about a bit, but his right hand remained steady as with the dagger point he methodically filled in the crossbar of Fellanel's A. The bronze was so very soft, compared with Anagonium, that the dagger's microground tip crumbled into the Anagonium and molecularly bound itself in.

Seven minutes later, he felt that it was done. He scrutinized the A through his jeweler's glass. Perhaps it was not his best work—there were minute featherings—but to the naked eye, the symbol on the talisman had become Λ.

Croyd now performed upon Fellanel the mind introjection that was the second part of Gambit Five.

Then Croyd moved to another part of the house and made an interesting adjustment in Fellanel's private TAC Board intercom and pullman. That was Gambit Eight.

He downtimed with two minutes to spare. His diagonal uptime drifting from fourteen minutes downtime of *Ultima* had required six minutes on the *Ultima* time track. This meant that it was still going to be twenty-four minutes before Greta would be approaching Fellanel.

For Gambit Nine, he did not change his spatial location: still he was in the house of Dr. Fellanel—who by now, he knew, would have legally assumed the name Dr. Orpheus, for it was two months downtime.

Strobotemping, he established the location of certain files, and established also a two-hour period when Dr. Orpheus would not be present. He went to work at the start of this period, now operating in a time drift that would carry him radially downtime so that, on the *Ultima* time track, no time would elapse at all.

At the end of half an hour, he had brought together the crucial descriptive formulae that *were* Anagonon.

What he was attempting, really, was utilization of a wild hypothesis that had been put forward in the postmedieval twentieth century by a freethinker named Dewey: namely, that not merely the meanings of history change, but that history itself changes—past events change—in terms of future developments. Dewey had proposed this theory in the context that no such thing as "past" ever exists: only *present* ever exists. Croyd was now qualifying Dewey's theory in a way that Dewey would not have accepted. Croyd was hypothesizing that in the day when the present—actuality—would be this very day in the year 2502, the only facts that would be true about the history of Anagonon would be the only facts that would then be knowable about Anagonon.

Utilizing now the iphotographic equipment in the laboratory of Dr. Orpheus, Croyd photographed all these papyrs.

Projecting the photographs, he made certain minimal changes. He dared not go further. By tampering too profoundly, he might introduce a galactic warp that could have tragic consequences.

Having satisfied himself about these changes, Croyd reified them on papyr that precisely duplicated the original papyrs.

He inspected the new papyrs. The only change was the introduction of a terminal period for the effects of Anagonon which in the originals were permanent.

He then used other equipment, which Orpheus had thoughtfully provided for himself, to destroy the original papyrs. And he placed the new papyrs where the originals had been.

Now Croyd downtimed to Room −429 of the Morgue in 5 EA. Having no time to throw away, he bypassed the Morgue personnel, and by remote control, he telekinetically filched the latent Greta-body out of her drawer and dropped her on the bed.

Again he drew the bronze knife. Anagonium was theoretically uncuttable except by the methods of Orpheus; but bronze, a metal totally unknown for centuries, had not been considered. The effect on Anagonium of the cupric content in bronze was devastating.

He now used brain-projected electromagnetics to harden the soft tip of his dagger, a tip which had been only microscopically blunted by his operation on Fellanel's bracelet. Again wearing the jeweler's glass, he used the dagger point to carve a crossbar on Greta's $\Lambda$, converting it into an A.

Lying then beside Greta-Beta, he departed his own body and entered her brain. He disciplined himself to be patient while he programmed a portion of the left frontal lobe (it would generalize to the right lobe when she would awaken).

Withdrawing from her, he touched the wall button that completed her activation; but she did not immediately awaken, for he had arranged that she would sleep normally. Croyd now reentered her brain and passed another precious parcel of minutes stimulating the superswift generation of a minimal mind whose attention was concentrated on the programmed frontal region: the programming was flexibly furnished with if-then contingencies that the minimal mind could use.

Withdrawing again into his own body, he was about to awaken her when. . .

Clothing! When Commander Greta had stripped her uniform off Greta-Beta, she hadn't bothered to trade!

He quickly checked the closet. Nothing suitable. . . .

Irritated at this dangerously time-consuming oversight, he committed another telekinetic filch. The female demonstrator in the Morgue Vault, as he remembered her, was young and about Greta's size and dressed mod; and when she materialized pop-eyed in Room −429, so she was.

Croyd suggestioned her. The bewildered girl began to undress. He turned his attention to Greta-Beta, awakening her. Greta sat up, saw him, clutched the sheet over her bosom, then smiled and dropped the sheet.

"Do you know me?" Croyd demanded.

"Of course."

"Don't be physical, now! Be intellectual!"

She frowned, concentrating. Then she looked up. "I'll be intellectual with *you,* Croyd. After that, I know what I'm supposed to do. When I do it, I will make a point of feeling just sexy enough to be convincing, but not enough to lose my head."

"Very good," he snapped. "Put on these clothes in a hurry."

Obediently Greta-Beta leaped out of bed and began to put on the scanty clothing that the demonstrator had shed. Croyd put the demonstrator to sleep and then into bed, covering her decorously. She didn't really quite exist  and in view of what he planned, she would never have anything to explain.

Greta said: "I'm ready."

"Grab on," said Croyd, clasping her waist. She clasped his neck.

They uptimed to Fellanel's salon in 2502. They strobotemped until the right moment.

Croyd squeezed Greta-Beta's shoulder, said, "Go to it, kid!" and dropped her on a sofa.

Downtiming to 5 EA a thousand miles above Eurydice, Croyd materialized on the bridge of Admiral Leclerc's flagship in order to set the fleet-fatal *Penultima* into motion.

# 31

**H minus 1 hour—and H-Hour:**

On his flagship, Leclerc called his captains together and gave them their alert orders. Within an hour after adjournment of the Captains' Call, Croyd appeared on his bridge.

Assuming an attitude which combined *at ease* with ultimate dignity, the admiral inquired softly: "Is it time, my friend?"

Croyd nodded.

"How soon?"

"As fast as possible after my departure. And that will be in a few moments. How fast can you act?"

"Assuredly within the hour. Will that be swift enough?"

"An hour would do—no longer. But ten minutes would be better. Do what you can, sir." He paused awkwardly; then he added: "I would prefer to stay here, my friend, while it happens."

"I understand, my friend. But you have your duty."

They considered each other.

They shook hands.

Croyd vanished.

Only an instant did Leclerc meditate. He then assembled his captains by visiphone and told them: "Condition Red. Condition Red. Your lead time for preparation has been much shorter than I anticipated. How long will it take you to act? We must all act together."

He could see them all without exception perspiring: it meant their own self-immolation—in this future, at any rate, and it felt like actuality to each of them.

Then a young lieutenant commander of a corvette said: "Sir, call me an eager beaver, but I am ready now."

"So am I," said a senior captain. "My compliments, Commander."

All but one swiftly chorused that they were ready too.

"How about *you*, captain?" Leclerc challenged the delinquent.

"The fact is," he responded, "that I am ready too. But I am too old to die."

There was nervous laughter, and then it quieted.

The admiral queried: "Do your crews know?"

Each of them nodded.

Brief silence.

"Well done, gentlemen," said Leclerc. "Stand by for the countdown. This is H-Hour minus five minutes. Flag officer, take over the countdown. Out."

He left the visiphone and moved to the broad, bulging bay window of his bridge. All of a hemisphere of Earth was visible below.

Monon—this Earth—to him was home. This was his own hemisphere. He could see his France, he could almost see his Paris. There was a particular woman. . . .Eh, but she was only probable. . . .

He listened to the minutes of the countdown.

He listened to the seconds. At H-Hour minus thirty seconds, he spoke into his bridge visiphone: "This is the admiral. Confirming the order. Confirming the order. Execute at H-Hour unless countermanded. Out."

Ten seconds later, idar control communicated excitedly: "Admiral, we have the strongest and most decisive alarm of all. Galactic latitude 187°, longitude 289°—in short, almost dead overhead, ten o'clock semi-high!"

Leclerc moved to his I-scope. Adjusting it to the coordinates, he saw—at a distance of a parsec, but diving in at a rate which would bring them to Earth in less than a minute—a fleet of six ships, the largest by quick estimate a kilometer in length, each ship slenderly resembling a mighty stick-insect: definitely alien, *a priori* hostile.

On the verge of changing the orders, he arrested himself. With a grim smile, he considered the implications for the invaders of what his own fleet was about to do.

He listened to the dying of the seconds, watching his homeland.

"—four—three—two—one—zero."

Just before he lost consciousness, he saw Earth curling up.

# 32

**H minus 20 seconds—and H-Hour:**

All officers, all masculate spacemen, all females on all ships watched Earth coming toward them.

The females were in a condition of delirious anticipation. A third of them were already at extrojection, although they could wait several hours before it would start to be seriously uncomfortable: just now it was only—*only!*—consuming lust. The rest of them were on the verge.

Perfect parallel: a human woman at the edge of a labor known to be not long and arduous but brief and delicious; but also, a labor that could not come except under certain given conditions—and whose deferral would mean agony and could mean death.

Earth drew closer. They could see it now as a varicolored ball, as large as an adult head, blue with water, green with foliage, clouded with wonderful rainclouds, fertile, teeming with life, teeming with mammals, teeming with *humans.* . . . Ovipositors were twitching, sending thrills through bodies. . . .

*Earth blurred.*

Numb shock. Staring. The women understood; they had been briefed: Earth's surface probabilities had abruptly randomized: inexplicable, they were in downtime.

Suddenly, almost simultaneously on each of the six ships, one gravid woman screamed.

Tumult succeeded.

It went into panic. . . .

On the flagship bridge, the admiral and Captain Zl stood rigid, having watched the blurring.

The admiral reacted first: "Check the time dials!"

Zl reported, voice hard: "They are rising. Our ATN indicators are now well below the menisci."

Sounds of female panic began to penetrate to them.

"Krell was right, it appears," the admiral commented. "What do we do about it, Zl?"

Silver Captain Zl was working. "Sira, I am resetting the ATN for three years uptime."

"Theoretically it is useless. We are too deep into downtime; there is no theoretical return."

"It is all I know to do."

"Is the ship responding?"

Zl watched the time dials. Presently 'e murmured: "No response."

After a prolonged pause, the black admiral observed: "It is most unfortunate that only Lieutenant Krell's little ship is equipped for the experimental Zed Maneuver."

"That would be a forlorn hope, sira. Maneuver Zed has been laughed out of court by every board that has reviewed it. It is self-contradictory within time theory."

"Nevertheless, Captain, there is no other hope. Perhaps Lieutenant Krell and 'is woman constitute the only remaining hope for our race. Contact 'im and order 'im to use the maneuver."

"Sira, the little *Champu* disappeared from our formation some time back."

The admiral's antennae barely twitched: as shocks went, it was minor now. The decision 'e had to make was grave indeed. It was race-fatal.

'E met all of Zl's eyes. "Captain, you know what you have to do. Do it." Moving to the open intercom, 'e told the fleet: "Gentletens, each of you do it 'is own way. God bless us all."

The commotion in the Queen's lounge crescendoed, grew orgiastic.

Standing on a table with the silver flag captain, the brown executive officer called to the queens: "At ease, ladies!" 'E paused: no response: tumult. Raising 'is disc pitch to ear-piercing timbre, 'e trebled: "AT EASE, LADIES!"

Tumult quieted, just a little. They all turned to 'im tautly.

Captain Zl's contralto chirr filled the room, completing the quieting. Somberly 'e informed them: "Ladies, it is time for courage. There is no hope left. Consequently I am going to put all of you into stasis."

The silence was deathly. Stasis would arrest their egg development, would suspend their own animation, would harmlessly end their consciousness and their misery until such time as stasis might be terminated in revivification or in fatal disaster. But also, stasis would kill all their eggs.

Suddenly an overdue female brayed, low: "Listen, girls—we have to lay these eggs—and *it doesn't have to be mammals!*"

All of them shrieked at her indecency.

Screeching back, she ran forward, leaped upon the startled brown commander, and thrust her ovipositor into 'is body—just below the third integument, at exactly the spot where her ancestresses had instinctively inserted millions of years before. Paralyzed, already in suspended animation, the commander went down beneath her while her eggs spewed into 'im.

Maddened by desire to do likewise, yet arrested by the horror, the females rigidly watched until it was done.

Eased, the renegade with difficulty erected herself off the body of the commander and looked about her defiantly.

Captain Zl impassively waited.

Another female came forward, her antennae angrily horizontal. She stared at Zl. She stared at the renegade. Then deliberately she grappled with the offender and bit off her head. Turning to the captain, she announced with dignity: "That is how we feel about this. We are all in the ship together, sira. Pray put us in stasis now; and then it will be easier for us than for you."

Captain Xl bowed 'is head a little, giving her a soft salute. Then 'e turned to the women. "Go to your beds," 'e said. 'E left the lounge.

They went heavily to their beds. Two of them carried the body of the brown commander and laid it on the bed of the dead renegade.

Having sealed off their quarters, Zl activated the stasis.

Returning to the bridge, the silver captain saluted the black admiral, saying: "Mission accomplished."

The admiral nodded stiffly and turned to peer into space.

One by one, similar reports came from the other five ships.

The six sailed on like *Flying Dutchmen*. If they could stay on this time band four years, germinality would overtake and rescue them.

They had atmosphere for another week of life.

**All Actualities D-Day**

Part Six

BACCHANALE

. . .Then he forsook the company of men. He wandered through the wild solitudes of Thrace, comfortless except for his lyre, playing, always playing, and the rocks and the rivers and the trees heard him gladly, his only companions. But at last a band of Maenads came upon him. They were as frenzied as those who killed Pentheus so horribly. They slew the gentle musician, tearing him limb from limb, and flung the severed head into the swift river Hebrus. . . .

—Edith Hamilton, MYTHOLOGY (1942)

# 33

Croyd having departed uptime, Commander Greta waited the prescribed thirty minutes while darkness deepened in her secluded place. When her luminous cutichron told her it was time, she took one deep breath and approached the House of Orpheus.

This would be *Ultima.*

She was ushered by the topless female servant into his inner salon. Presently Orpheus entered.

He paused, enjoying her uniformed figure. Thrusting hands deep into trouser pockets, he said: "I didn't think you'd be back so soon from Nereid."

Greta smiled wanly. "I couldn't wait to see you, Orpheus. I cut it short."

He came over and sat facing her: their knees almost touched. Apologetically he told her: "I am weary. But I am glad you are here."

Greta deliberately allowed herself to think of what he was thinking, knowing that the thought would make her flush and this would banish her pallor and make her more desirable. She said softly: "I love you for having given me Anagonon. But sometimes I think that—even without it—"

Fellanel shyly laid a hand on one of her knees—just at the knee, holding the hand steady and shy. He said: "I will tell you something candidly, Greta. I respect you more than you can possibly know. Anagonon has given me an unfair advantage over you. For this reason, almost I wish that I had not given it."

Greta felt a small twinge of remorse: he was being sincere; and now that she was free of Anagonon, she could recognize this clearly. On the other hand, now that she was free of Anagonon, *he* might recognize *that*; she must beat him to the draw.

She laid a soft hand on his hand that held her knee. "Orpheus," she said gently, "I am going to square with you. I think you are a decent guy—wild, but decent. I want you to know that I was kidding you. I am no longer Anagononic, and I have no intention of going to bed with you."

The immediate result was that his fingers squeezed her knee so hard that it hurt. Then he let go and leaned back stiffly, and his vague eyes were mystically terrible. He said: "I perceive now that you are telling the truth. Later I will ask how you could possibly have thrown it off. Just now I chiefly want to know: Why have you come?"

Greta leaned back too. "There are facts of life that have nothing to do with sex. I want to mention a few of them."

"I am willing to listen for a short time. But I wonder if you realize that you *are here?*"

"Meaning, I suppose, that I'm at your mercy."

"Of course—and I have none, and I want you. Even if you resist me, my servants will guarantee that it won't matter."

"They will guarantee only my rape. They won't get you my love."

"Anagonon will get it. I can give you Anagonon again."

"I thought you said you respected me."

"I do."

"If you give me Anagonon again, then all the time that I am loving you, you will be knowing that I am really just loving Anagonon."

"That's hair-splitting."

"Is it?"

There was silence. "Well," said Orpheus, smiling a little, "I won't take you tonight; I'm too tired anyway. But you are going to have to stay until I decide about the Anagonon."

Greta smiled at him a little. "You took it too, I suppose?"

"Of course."

"Why?"

"Why not? Painlessness. Energy. Immortality. Besides, if I hadn't taken it, my subordinates would not sense it in me, and they wouldn't obey me."

"Are they obeying *you*, then?"

"Pardon?"

"Or are they instead obeying Anagonon?"

Orpheus leaned forward. "You are confusing the issue."

"Let's see if I am," said Commander Greta, leaning forward also—their faces were close. "Your inner circle of Beta-rank doctors knows you, but who else knows you? *They* will obey you on sight—but *who else* will obey you on sight, if they do not know you? Here, look—you wear the Alpha on your wrist. Now suppose there was a Lambda, for instance, who did not know you. And suppose somebody switched bracelets, so that you wore a Lambda and he or she wore the Alpha. Who would have to obey whom?"

Softly said Orpheus: "That is ridiculous."

Gently said Greta: "Are you willing to test it?"

He replied confidently: "Theoretically, yes—only it isn't possible, unless I myself switch the bracelets; and if I were to do that, it would disturb the psychology of the test so that it would not be a test. So if we must talk, Greta, let it not be nonsense that we talk."

"But if there is a way of getting around this problem—are you willing? Or are you afraid?"

Pause.

He demanded: "Tell me what the test would be."

"If I were the potential dictator of Earthworld and the galaxy," said Greta thoughtfully, "I am not sure that I would be spiritually big enough to test my power in this way. Are you really that big?"

Sharply said Orpheus: "I am a doctor. What is the test? I must know first that it is not unfair."

Greta told him: "A certain Lambda is waiting, ready to enter at my signal. I have means of interchanging that person's Lambda with your Alpha. Then we will see who obeys whom."

Tense Orpheus said slowly: "It seems to me inwardly that I need this test. Go ahead and try it."

"In the presence of your TAC Board."

"Pardon?"

"Bring in the ten members of your Board as witnesses, and we will try it."

Orpheus thought prolongedly.

He said tentatively: "If there is any trickery, my Board will spot it and defend me."

"I am sure of it."

He leaned forward, bristling. "If there is trickery, I will shame you in front of them and then kill you."

"What about the test?"

Orpheus broke for privacy.

One by one the ten board Members, arriving by pullman from various quarters of Earth, entered the salon. Each of them wore a Beta bracelet.

Dr. Orpheus presented them to Commander Groen. Greta, knowing some of the medical names by reputation, was cowed into practical submissiveness.

Orpheus explained the proposed test.

The gynecological iron woman—whom Greta remembered well—inquired harshly: "Do you *want* this test, Doctor?"

Orpheus replied: "Yes, Doctor, I do."

"Ready?" Greta challenged.

Orpheus nodded.

That was when strobotemping Croyd dropped Greta-Beta and departed downtime to give Admiral Leclerc his fatal *go*.

Commander Groen informed the stricken Dr. Orpheus and his ten high priests, most of whom looked equally stricken: "Doctors, this is Greta-Beta. She is not a Beta in the sense that you doctors are Betas, but only in the sense that she is a second Greta. In the sense that you doctors are Betas, Greta-Beta is an Alpha."

Greta-Beta dimpled, making the most of her clothing shortage. "Hi, Doctors!" she called to everybody. "I see that I am in the presence of fellow Anagononics—or anyhow, I feel it."

Two of the men blurted: *"Yes!"*

Orpheus bit: "Let us not be calling this Greta-Beta an Alpha until our bracelets have been exchanged. How will you bring *that* off, Commander?"

"The exchange has already been made," Commander Greta replied. "Doctors, you are invited to examine both bracelets."

Orpheus gaped, then thrust back his shirt cuff and stared at his bracelet. Inscribed upon it was Λ, the Lambda.

Leaping across to Greta-Beta, he seized her bare arm and gazed incredulously at the Alpha-A talisman on her bracelet.

Presently the young German said respectfully: "May we look too, Doctor?"

Dropping back into his chair, Orpheus waved his braceleted hand and suffered his doctors one by one to examine first his own talisman, then the one on the seductive wrist of Greta-Beta.

Afterward the ten doctors rather clustered, watching the principals, looking worried. Orpheus appeared haggard. Commander Greta was composed.

Beside her, Greta-Beta looked brightly about at the doctors. She said: "I seem to have taken command here, but it needn't be sticky. Let's just begin with a little funsy hand-kissing." She held out both hands. "Who wants to be first?"

They stared at her. They stared at Orpheus.

Breathing somewhat rapidly, Orpheus commanded his doctors: "Two of you hold her while I remove my A bracelet from her wrist."

However, the ten doctors merely huddled a bit closer together, their faces professionally calm but evidently masking deep thought; while Greta-Beta began to preen her hands, occasionally holding out a hand and gently stroking its arm.

Abruptly the foremost psychiatrist in Earthworld—the grave gray-bearded portly man with pince-nez—sat on the floor and assumed the fetal position.

Greta-Beta stopped playing with her hands, rested them on her bare knees, and gravely considered this catatonic victim of soul-tearing conflict. Commander Greta lit a match and gazed at the flame.

The iron-woman gynecologist found it possible to speak. "Dr. Orpheus and Doctors," she said, her hard voice strained, "we are learning something here. There *is* conflict. I am feeling it too, but less than the rest of you because I don't respond to the sex lure of this Greta-Beta that is accentuating the conflict for you men. May I advise you, Dr. Orpheus? *This test should end now!* The girl is Anagononic; we all sense it or this conflict would not be paralyzing us. *She* knows that you really rank her and all of us. Why don't *you* give *her* a direct order? Command her to give you back the Alpha—to submit while you remove it!"

Orpheus stared at Greta-Beta—but she avoided his eyes, continuing to ogle the staring male doctors: hands on her bare knees, knees together, the toes of one bare foot leisurely caressing the arched top of her other foot. Commander Greta coolly blew out the match flame.

"Dr. Orpheus!" sharply cried the woman doctor. "Please *act!*"

Orpheus, continuing to stare at the bracelet on Greta-Beta, forced himself to say weakly: "Woman, sit quiet while I take back my brace-let."

Losing composure, Greta-Beta cringed, gazing at Orpheus. Com-mander Greta waited.

Greta-Beta whimpered: "This is awful. I know that I am only an Eleven. I know that Dr. Orpheus is The One. He is telling me to do something, and I feel compelled to obey him. But you ten doctors are all Twos, and I feel that you do not really want me to do this." Tearing her eyes away from Orpheus, she looked at each of the male doctors directly as she asked: "Tell me, Doctors– *all* of you rank me– *what do you really want of me?*"

After a moment of group paralysis, the most eminent neurosurgeon in Earthworld–the handsome white-haired man in his middle sixties– emitted a strangulated noise, darted forward, knelt, seized Greta-Beta around the waist, and buried his face in her bosom. Greta-Beta wound her arms around his head and pressed her lips into his hair.

The other male doctors, losing dignity, assumed various tight crouches. The female doctor stiffened into ultimate dignity. The psychiatrist wound himself more tensely into his fetal position. Or-pheus, face and hands contorted, was rising slowly to his feet like an automaton activated by a languidly uncoiling spring. Commander Greta, clasping a knee, contemplated this knee.

Greta-Beta vanished.

The neurosurgeon collapsed on the sofa beside Commander Greta, did a pushup, stared wildly about, and collapsed again, sobbing.

Seven other male doctors and a female doctor sagged, vacantly sought seats, found them, sat in them, bowed their heads, massaged their foreheads.

Orpheus, though, gained strength. Trembling, he moved forward and stood over Commander Greta. He said terribly: "That was sabotage, Commander. I will not even trouble to give you Anagonon again. You die for this–in slow pain."

Turning, he snapped fingers at his male and female servants. They came swiftly forward: each of them seized Greta by an arm and lifted her to her feet. They turned to Orpheus for orders.

"Take her down," Orpheus ordered, "and put her with that insane Croyd in the basement–and take him out of stasis. He will probably tear her apart. If he does not, atomize both of them tomorrow."

They hauled her away. She did not resist.

Having departed the ships from Earth after commanding Admiral Leclerc to do what he must do, Croyd uptimed to the House of Orpheus in 2502. Strobotemping, he inspected the late developments. A few seconds after the neurosurgeon threw himself sobbing into the arms of Greta-Beta, Croyd judged that all was developing nicely; and he plucked Greta-Beta away.

Since her frontal programming had run out, leaving her confused, it was with minimal difficulty that he quieted her minimal mind. By now, Admiral Leclerc would have destroyed Earth (or Monon) in the year 5 EA, so Croyd could not return Greta-Beta to the Morgue. Temporarily he took her to his house in nontime and deactivated her by his own methods.

He then returned to the House of Orpheus, but he did not intervene—not even to rescue Greta from his mindless other-body in the basement. That would be Commander Groen's problem: she would not welcome his intervention.

Strobotemping, he monitored the salon. Tensions among the Unholy Eleven were coming to some kind of climax: he didn't know just what it would be, but he anticipated something pretty grisly. It had to play itself out among just these eleven. Croyd had arranged for the world's physical purification, but Dr. Orpheus and his TAC Board had also to purge their spirits of power lust if they were to survive as potentially creative human-humans.

Croyd had little hope for the redemption of love-starved Fellanel, but he did not intend to expunge the possibility of that redemption by letting Fellanel be killed, or to warp permanently the souls of the TAC Board by letting them kill him. Nevertheless they all had to *live* the full catharsis—carry it *all the way through*—and at the same time *survive*, to remember and comprehend and compensate. . . .

Having sent Commander Greta to her death—either at the maniacal hands of the mindless Croyd-body imprisoned below, or tomorrow by atomization—Dr. Orpheus relaxed a little.

"Now, Doctors," he observed, "we return to where we were before this little insanity." He raised a small finger to glance at his cutichron. "Late!" He remarked; "2302 hours—and we with a Board breakfast meeting tomorrow at U800! I suggest you all go home to rest, Doctors; you know where my pullman is—"

"Dr. Orpheus," insistently spoke the metal voice of the gynecologist. Orpheus looked at her. Her hand moved: she pointed at the collapsed sobbing neurosurgeon and the fetal psychiatrist. The other seven men were watching intently, unnaturally still.

Snapped Orpheus: "All *he* needs is a sedative; but *he* needs another psychiatrist. I'll hospitalize both of them here tonight; *he'll* probably join us in the morning, but *he'll* need prolonged deep psychotherapy. Please go now, Doctors. Go now."

None of them moved.

Orpheus was wide-eyed, pupil-dilated.

One spoke: the thin, young, dark German internist, a precise man who had reached the top quickly on sheer intellect. "Doctor, I think perhaps I speak for all of us. Tonight's test appears to have shown us that Anagonon theory needs reviewing with respect to questions of authority and wider political implications. Three difficulties have appeared. The first is that although *we all knew* that you were the true Alpha while the girl was an impostor, the presence of an A on her wrist and of a Λ on yours subconsciously undermined the automaticity of our loving obedience to you—to the extent that one of us went into psychosis, a second developed a low-grade psychoneurosis, and all of us became absurdly indecisive. The second difficulty is that *your own* decisiveness was undermined by your sign inferiority to her sign superiority, to the point where you could not lead us until our gynecological colleague drove you to lead. And the third is that in the mind of the girl. who knew herself to be only a Lambda, the combined weight of us Betas neutralized your total authority as the Alpha in *her* mind, and she too was rendered indecisive.

"It would therefore appear, Dr. Orpheus—on this showing—that Commander Groen's hypothesis has been confirmed. Anagonon is compelling us to obey, *not true* superior rank, but *the appearance* of superior rank even when we know it is false! And this is *fatal,* Doctor—and it *must be talked out* NOW!"

The speaker ended and looked about him. Several of the others nodded gravely; all were watching intently.

Orpheus gripped the arms of his chair. Tightly he said: "The situation was atypical, and it is done. My authority remains—" Conscious that the internist was gazing fixedly upon him, Orpheus traced the gaze, looked down at his left wrist, and saw the Λ. Angrily he rotated the bracelet on his wrist so that the amulet was hidden beneath. He affirmed with total conviction: "I am *The One.* Each of you is a Two. Go to your homes now. Be back at 0800."

The gynecologist gravely came to him and laid a hand on his shoulder. Her voice was gentler than it had been. "Under the circumstances, my friend, it is best that we meet at a different place." She turned to the others: "I invite you all to *my* home for breakfast at 0800 hours. Do you agree?"

All who were able nodded.

She turned back to Orpheus, the whites of whose eyes were showing all around the pupils. She stroked his high forehead, and smoothed back his hair, and said: "You are our beloved master. You are invited too. If you come, you will chair our discussion and record our voting. Perhaps it will all end up as it was. I hope so, but we are too tired to know. Even the energy of Anagonon has its limits."

Orpheus gazed up into her eyes. He replied firmly: "Of course I will not go there. The meeting is here."

Troubled, she looked down at him. Then, seating herself wearily on an arm of his chair, she turned for help to the others.

They were all indecisive again. They were haggard.

There was a bit of a commotion below, rather like the sound of a bank vault door being blown in by explosive. But nobody really noticed.

For Dr. Orpheus was on his feet, seizing the situation. "Go to your homes and rest," he commanded with kindly authority. *"I am the Alpha. The meeting at 0800 hours will be here."*

The gynecologist inclined her head, defeated. Coming heavily to her feet, she started for the room where the pullman dispatchers were. Several others turned to follow. The young German stood his ground, but he was acutely unhappy.

Orpheus went to him and took him by an arm. "Go, my friend," he urged.

The German patted his arm and turned to go.

Commander Greta appeared in the doorway, uniform torn and disheveled but *on,* face bleeding but composed. She said: "Wait, Doctors."

Nine people whirled on her. (Two others did not know they were here.)

Greta challenged: "You seem to have forgotten the order by Dr. Orpheus that I be killed. I was to be killed by this mindless body of Croyd who was imprisoned below. But I happen to have some influence on this Croyd, and his brain responded to me, and he blew himself apart in the process of getting me out. However, the command by Dr. Orpheus that I be killed is still valid, and I think that somebody should do something about it now—the suspense is pretty rough."

At Greta they stared: they had done a lot of staring this evening. And then it was the young internist who turned on Orpheus. "Tell us, Doctor—how will it *serve the long-range interests* of TAC to kill this woman, instead of giving her Anagonon again?"

Perhaps it was one challenge too many for cool judgment. Orpheus angrily shot back: "I am your master, and I judge that she must be killed, and no reasons need be given you. I *order* you to kill her! *All* of you!" He lost his head and screamed: *"Tear her apart! Tear her limb from limb like Bacchantes!* DO IT—"

It paralyzed all of them. And then, as Greta restrained herself from cowering, the gynecologist went into a semibestial crouch; only she was facing Orpheus, not Greta.

She bellowed: "YOU ARE COMMANDING US TO BE MAENADS?"

Frenzied, Fellanel—Dr. Orpheus—stood on his chair, flailing fists. "MAENADS! BE BACCHANTES! KILL! KILL! TEAR—"

The young German too was in a grotesque crouch, clinging to the remnants of his reason. *"But we are* MEN!" he screamed. *"Bacchantes are* WOMEN! *How* CAN *we be Bacchantes?"*

Astonished, Greta saw that the fetal psychiatrist was coming out of his trance. He had got to hands and knees, he was gazing stupidly at the scene.

Quivering taut, fists high, Fellanel yelled: "THEN YOU ARE WOMEN! ALL OF YOU! WOMEN! MAENADS! KILL! KILL—"

Slowly like activated robots they were beginning to turn on Greta when crazy laughter arrested them. They swung back. The psychiatrist, tottering on his feet, was pointing unsteadily at Fellanel. He sang out loud and clear: "BUT HE IS THE ONE WHO IS ORPHEUS!"

And they knew the myth!

Shamefully subhuman, the gynecologist with both big hands ripped open the top of her dress, tore off her brassiere, lacerated her bare breasts with long fingernails, and released the howl of a hungry hyena. And all the doctors, totally under the Fellanel-spell as modified by the singing of the psychiatrist, tore open their shirts and drew blood on their chests and howled and talked after her.

Shocked, Orpheus fell from his chair to the floor.

The gynecologist leaped upon him and sank her teeth into his arm. The men piled on.

Clammy cold, Greta drew a small pistol from a shoulder holster and advanced on the ghastly madness, hoping to find an opening and perforate the skull of Orpheus with a mercy shot. Halfway there she paused. Orpheus was Anagononic—he could feel no pain.

Replacing the weapon, she retreated to a wall and steeled herself to watch. A military woman must be able to watch anything.

It was half an hour before the last subhuman twitch of the mania died.

Nine passion-drained people, among the most highly cultivated people that Earthworld had been able to produce, lay in semicoma.

A tenth, the neurosurgeon, was unconscious on the couch where he had clasped Greta-Beta.

There was no Dr. Orpheus. There were only scattered remnants of Dr. Orpheus.

Greta fumbled in what was left of a pocket. She drew out a tiny vacuum pack. From it she withdrew a long cigarette, new-fresh although it had been there for months: it was a kind of emergency kit. Snapping shut and replacing in her pocket the vacuum pack, she placed the cigarette tip in her mouth, struck a match (there was still in her age no aesthetic substitute for matches) and pulled hard. Ritually expelling that first drag, she burned down half an inch of the lighted end with her second drag, filled her lungs, held her breath for thirty seconds, expelled it slowly.

When, after fifteen seconds, all the smoke was out of her lungs, she dropped the cigarette on the carpet and ground it dead with her heel.

Then she went to the visiphone and called the Galactic Police Deputy for Earthworld directly. Several minutes were wasted in multiple identifications and clearances and top-secret classifications. At length she got him at his home. He would not show her a visiphone image, which meant probably that he was in bed; but he satisfied her with a thalamic pattern that well enough matched the one in her crude portable screening kit.

He said: "I recognize you as Commander Groen of the Galactic Fleet. What is it, Commander?"

Having inhaled room air, Greta said: "Deputy, you aren't going to believe this—"

The room *blurred*.

# 34

At the instant when the last doctor piled on Orpheus, Croyd performed the third part of Gambit Five and departed.

He downtimed to the probability world of Monon, midway through the year 2 EA—the temporal midpoint of Monon's existence.

As his observation point, he selected a position two thousand feet in the sky above the just-completed first unit of the Palace of Pythagoras.

Since it was night, he expanded his visual sensitivity into the infrared; and panorama of the city of Eurydice spread beneath him like a bloodshot nightmare.

Suddenly the city began to blur like a TV picture in the throes of a random set of rippling distortions.

Croyd descended now to the surface of Earth: that surface, at least, stayed firm, undergoing no perceptible distortion (although, under high magnification, molecular patterns would now surely be queasy). But everything around him that was human or manmade was a hopeless blur of coexisting alternatives.

The projected world of Monon was no longer a 99.901 percent certainty—or a 50 percent probability—or even a 10 percent possibility.

What remained to be determined was whether the other two final parts of the operation—the destruction by Admiral Leclerc and his fleet of Monon in 5 EA, and Croyd's alteration of the papyr formula for

Anagonon—would work together dynamically in the way that he hoped.

But this he could not find out by walking aimlessly about in this probability blur two and a half years in the future. Besides, there was work to be done in actuality.

## D-Day; then D plus 1

Part Seven

### TREAT HUMANS LIKE HUMANS

It was a canon of *domnei,* it was the very essence of *domnei,* that the woman one loves is providentially set between her lover's apprehension and God, as the mobile and vital image and corporeal reminder of Heaven, as a quick symbol of beauty and holiness, of purity and perfection. In her the lover views all qualities of God which can be comprehended by merely human faculties. . . .

—James Branch Cabell, BEYOND LIFE (1919)

Fortunate it was that no planetary rebellion—and no intergalactic invasion—occurred during the Anagonon crisis. . . .

—REPORT OF THE BIOTHERAPEUTIC TASK FORCE

# 35

Maelbrug, already turgidly gravid, pressed her iridescent purple forehead against the transparent forward shell of the bridge. Behind her, a tense Krell clung to the control pole, peering forward over her shoulders.

They were close above a major continent of Earth—blue with water, green with foliage, clouded with wonderful rainclouds, fertile, teeming with life, teeming with mammals, teeming with *humans*. . . . Maelbrug's ovipositor was twitching, sending thrills through her body. . . .

*Earth blurred.*

Numb shock. Staring. The misery of realization. They were still in downtime.

Krell said tonelessly: "I was wrong."

Maelbrug said tightly: "If you were wrong, the admiral was worse wrong. 'E is leading the fleet into Earth farther into downtime than you. It was a good try, Krell. Now, please kill me. I love you."

Krell came off the control pole. "No!" 'e bit. "I'm not through yet! We'll try two years earlier!"

"How can you do that? I thought it was impossible to return from deep downtime."

"Maneuver Zed, Maelbrug. Maneuver Zed." Setting the ATN indicators, 'e started for the stern.

She clutched 'im. "Will it work?"

Turning, 'e gripped her claw hard. "It is dubious. But we are going to try."

"How—how long will it take?"

'Is grip on her claw tightened. "Hours. It is slow."

Breath whistled in and out of her spiracles. She said presently: "I will take it. But Krell—"

"Maelbrug?"

"If it doesn't work—will you be sure to kill me?"

'E nodded and left her. Privately, 'e had another thing that 'e wanted done, in case it didn't work.

The alternative of stasis was not for her. Stasis equipment had been jettisoned in favor of the experimental Zed equipment.

# 36

Uptiming, Croyd entered the Fellanel salon. Greta sat there, quietly smoking. The cigarette told him that she was distraught, which was rare for her. He didn't happen to know that it was her second in five minutes.

He spoke to her, and came and sat near her. She threw him a quick strained smile and went back into her brood.

He waited patiently, his eyes roving the floored and variously overlapping doctor-bodies. She had to find her own way to composure on this one.

Presently, without looking up, she inquired: "Are the other things done?"

"Yes."

"Greta-Beta?"

"Inert in my house—beside the Thoth-body."

Short laugh.

Silence.

"Croyd—"

"Greta?"

"Would you—feel funny about holding a commander's hands? In uniform, yet?"

He sat quickly beside her and took her hands (the cigarette was in her mouth). She squeezed and puffed; she was almost trembling, not quite.

She said: "Thank God for you."

He said: "Thank God for you."

Freeing a hand, she took the cigarette out of her mouth and surveyed the room shambles. "Okay, so let's get with it. I've been checking this room. Some things are blurred, some aren't. So what gives?"

"So what's blurred?"

"That chair is, over there, a little. That one over there is terribly blurred, the blur is three times the chair width. But that chair and that one aren't blurred at all. Walls and ceiling and floor—all clear, sharp. That picture over there—blurred. That one—clear. Those curtains—an absolute fuzz."

"What do you deduce?"

"Glaucoma."

"Alternate hypothesis?"

"Downtime. Walls aren't likely to shift—chairs and pictures are—curtains blow like hell. Downtime, Croyd. Only—"

"Look at the bodies on the floor."

"The doctors? Not blurred. Clear."

"And the pieces of Orpheus?"

"Well, they're

> *gone,* Croyd! *Gone!"*

She mashed out the cigarette and turned slowly Croydward, seizing and squeezing his hands. "Tell me!"

His mouth corners were twitching a little. "You think about it. Remember that I'm seeing exactly what you're seeing. Meanwhile, I want to awaken the doctors."

"Wait!" Her eyes widened. She squeezed his forearm hard. She murmured: "You damned fool! This doesn't hurt at all, does it?"

"No."

"That's the trouble! You're Anagononic! You'll be at their mercy if you awaken them! There are nine of them—and only one of you! Remember what that group pressure did to Greta-Beta—"

"I'm not Greta-Beta," he reminded her. "And besides—by now. Commander Groen, *surely* you must have figured out the implications of the blurring—"

Then, as her eyes began to dilate, he muttered: "Cool it for now. Just let me operate. Murder me later."

He left her to perform the medical reveille.

# 37

"You know me," he said. "I'm Croyd, the Temporary Galactic Chairman."

They waited, but he was waiting too.

The psychiatrist, who had wholly collected himself, was the subtlest and most deeply cultured of the group; and now he addressed himself to the task of speaking for them. Sane reflection regarding his own part in the death of Dr. Orpheus had thrown new coils into his guilt complex, and this made him all the more effective in the cause of righteousness.

"We know you," said the impressive gray-bearded psychiatrist—making a futile motion to adjust the pince-nez which had been lost in the mass wrestle—"as the chief representative of the radical left which has wormed its way into control of the galaxy. Whatever you may have to say to us, please say it and leave; we do not wish to argue."

Croyd responded: "If by 'radical left' you mean representative heuristodemocracy, then I plead guilty. But I am surprised that you do not know something else about me, Doctor. Are you too wound up in your own defenses to *feel* what else I am?"

The psychiatrist stared.

*"Anagononic!"* breathed the gynecologist. Croyd being male, she caught it first.

Nettled at having missed it, feeling it now, the psychiatrist nevertheless could immediately assert a triumph for his group. "That the great Croyd is Anagononic," he commented, "this can only please us, for now we can and do love him, and we know that he loves us. But there is another dimension, my colleagues; for, loving us, Croyd cannot avoid helping our cause."

"Why is that?" Croyd inquired.

Deftly and significantly the psychiatrist showed his Beta wristlet. (He did not have to pull up his sleeve—it had been torn off.) "All of us here are Twos, you know. As a layman, Mr. Croyd, what are you?"

"Before I reply, explain to me why I should obey you. As my superiors, what plan do you have *for the long-range good of TAC* that gives you the right to impose your will on me?"

The seated German barked: "The question is not in point; he should not have asked it! Perhaps he is a deviate!"

But the gynecologist interposed: "Wait. He may not be a deviate—he may have strong ground for asking the question. Anyway, we ought ourselves to know. It is a good challenge, Doctors—what plan *do* we have?"

"We have," said the psychiatrist, "the plan of Dr. Orpheus."

Said the gynecologist: "We have liquidated Dr. Orpheus—in our great love for him."

The psychiatrist developed a tremor.

Croyd fixed him with strength-giving eyes. "Don't go fetal yet," he urged; "we will need you in a moment. Well, Doctors: your plan?"

The German stated incisively: "It is simply that TAC will take command of the galaxy because every human in the galaxy will be an Anagononic Friend in TAC. And then this galaxy will be filled with peace and health and growth and love, total obedience to law, total humanity—and painlessness, and energy, and immortality. What higher plan for TAC or for mankind can there be, Mr. Croyd?"

"Well," he remarked, "there is no time to argue the point; and besides, you have no disposition to argue. But I am questioning first of all whether you will really serve this long-range plan by commanding my obedience. In the nature of Anagonon, a single leader is required. Who is your single leader?"

The German responded swiftly: "Our single leader is—"

*"No!"* croaked the trembling psychiatrist.

Croyd went to him and pressed his shoulder, quieting him. "Well?" he asked the group again.

"In fact," said the gynecologist flatly, "we have murdered our single leader. And the only possible new single leader would have to come from among the ten of us. And we surely could not make a decision until the tenth of us, who is ill, could join us. And when he *can* vote, Doctors, how will we decide? Is there a doctor present who is sufficiently deviate to regard himself as better than any other Beta?" She looked about, waiting.

Silence.

"Is there any doctor present," she pressed, "who feels able to favor any other single doctor above the rest of us and vote for him?"

Silence.

"I think, Mr. Croyd," she asserted, "that you are answered. We do not have a leader—and we *cannot* have a leader. I am realizing that this is an ironical outcome of Anagonon. We are not even able to constitute ourselves jointly as a leadership council, because we cannot generate enough hostility to argue effectively or to vote for a proposal by one of us in preference to a proposal by another of us. This Anagonon, which was to be the road to perfection, has paralyzed the ten greatest doctors in Earthworld; and while it tears me to say it, the reflection causes me to doubt Anagonon." She turned to her colleagues: "Am I speaking against any of you when I say this? If so, I will withdraw it."

They stared at her. Presently the German shook his head a little.

She turned again to Croyd. *"Now,* Mr. Croyd—now that we cannot properly give you any orders at all—perhaps you will condescend to show us your rank?"

But he temporized yet a little more. "Doctor," he requested of the psychiatrist, "will you briefly recite for us the potent numbers of Pythagoras?"

"All is number," recited the doctor, "and each of the ten perfect numbers is a synthesis of a cosmic opposition. *One* or Alpha, which was the number of Dr. Orpheus, synthesizes the limited and the unlimited; and the synthesis is totality. *Two* or Beta, which is *our* number, synthesizes odd and even; and the synthesis generates plurality, or all other numbers. *Three* synthesizes one and many to produce the finite; *Four,* left and right, to produce rectitude; *Five,* male and female, to generate humanity; *Six,* rest and motion, whose synthesis is energy; *Seven,* straight and crooked, generating form; *Eight,* light and darkness, generating diurnal periodicity; *Nine,* good and evil, producing fate; *Ten,* square and rectangle, generating the Pythagorean principle of the hypotenuse which we now use to measure the cosmos. Is this what you meant, Mr. Croyd?"

"Perfectly. But now tell me about *Zero.*"

"About Zero?"

The German sat up straight. The gynecologist was frowning, puzzled. The other seven merely continued their attitudes of intense involvement.

"Yes," Croyd insisted. "What about Zero in the Pythagorean arithmetic?"

Beginning to tremble again, the guilt-ridden psychiatrist ventured: "Zero did not appear in the Pythagorean arithmetic."

"Why not?"

"Because Zero was not known until it was introduced into the algebra by Arabic philosophers nearly fifteen hundred years later—"

"And if Pythagoras *had* comprehended the number Zero—what rank would he have assigned it?"

The silence was intellectually and emotionally loaded.

The German internist fired a reply like a machine gun volley. "The question should be put a bit differently. If Pythagoras had lived today, and if in the light of all our knowledge he had projected his mystical system, which he might well have done: *then* how would he have ranked the number Zero? I say he would have recognized Zero as the number of *psi*-space, the number of the ancient Egyptian *Nun*, the formless male-female progenitor of all the gods: the root of our word *non*. Pythagoras would have accorded Zero a rank higher than One, higher than Alpha—the *ultimate* rank, with no higher rank possible!"

That was when Croyd exhibited his bracelet.

# 38

The pullman was blurred and unusable. Croyd therefore had to use about thirty minutes personally conducting the shocked doctors one by one back to their own homes and actualities.

He returned then to Greta. "I'm sorry," he told her.

Greta's little grin was twisted. "It will take me awhile to erase the memory of that butchery. I wish I'd known at the time that wasn't real."

"It was real enough, Commander—only it happened in downtime, not in actuality. If I'd told you the facts in advance, you might not have been so resourceful or so convincing. I timed the whole deal for twenty-four hours downtime of actuality—"

"And that's why things blurred, when it was done. This utterly improbable shambles tore up the high probabilities of Monon, when it was done."

"Check."

"But the doctors—*they* didn't blur—"

"The doctors were one hundred percent actual. I fixed Fellanel's pullman so that it brought them into downtime from their own time, and they just traveled back home again. In a week or so, I'll tell them the facts so they won't go mad—again."

"How about Orpheus, though?"

"Fellanel is, I imagine, safe in this house, one day uptime of when we are—in actuality, that is. The one they tore apart was downtime Fellanel. However, he was minded—because I fissioned his mind in actuality, and brought half of it here, and installed it in his downtime brain before the action—"

"Then he did experience all that?"

"He did experience all that."

"But only with half a mind?"

"With a whole mind. Mind fission is crudely analogous to cell mitosis: each half mind is a whole mind, it totally invests its brain. That's why each of the multiple personalities in a hysterical split is so convincingly coherent."

"But if—"

"I rescued the mind. It's in my brain now."

Greta recoiled a little.

"Dormant."

"Oh. Well. . . .Now what?"

"Let's go interview Fellanel. It might have been better for him to die."

Uptiming to actuality, they found themselves alone in the vaulted obscurity of the Fellanel salon. No guards or servants were in evidence.

"Think he's asleep?" Croyd suggested.

"Doubt it," Greta meditated. "He'd be a night owl. Try his laboratory."

They passed through the door, closing it behind them. The laboratory was empty, but there was a light at his desk. The room was puzzlingly haunted by remote harp music.

Or was it a lyre?

They glanced at each other. They nodded. They went to the cellar door and opened it. The music crescendoed.

Softly, Croyd in front, they descended the rotting wooden stair into the mists of Hades. Walking cautiously through curling fog, chilled by the hollow-tragic chords of the distant lyre, they forded the dry thigh-deep Stygian waters and crept hand in hand toward the shrine of Eurydice.

Orpheus-Fellanel was praying.

Croyd hit him from behind with a psychoneural block. Fellanel fell forward. Shouldering his body, Croyd carried him forward to the shrine, mounted the dais, and propped him upright on the throne of Eurydice.

For half an hour, then, Croyd used a direct hypnopaedic method of imprinting on Fellanel's brain a complete set of conceptualized facts about the duplicity of Sira Ssen and the invading Myrons. Following this, Croyd gave him the coherent conceptualization of the hard to grasp circumstance that the downtime confrontation with Greta-Beta and hard death beneath the teeth of the TAC Board Maenads would have been actual for Orpheus and *had been* actual for the other doctors. In the context of that conceptualization, and keeping in telepathic touch with Greta to supplement Croyd-witness with Greta-witness, Croyd imprinted on Fellanel's brain an unbroken, unsoftened sequential and subjective image memory of the fiendish affair, ending by making an explicit allusion to the fate of the original Orpheus. Then, just to play it safe (since the Croyd-body was Anagononic), Croyd implanted in Fellanel an unbreakable inhibition against issuing any orders to Croyd.

Then Croyd restored to Fellanel's brain the mind that had hideously experienced the bacchanale. And Croyd awakened Orpheus.

The vast eyes of Orpheus, the misty-blue inward-looking orbs of Orpheus, came open, gazing at his visitors and through them. The long arms of Orpheus came convulsively forward; the long hands of Orpheus gripped the arms of the throne, working convulsively, fraying the fringe. Croyd and Greta, shamelessly telepathing the minds of Orpheus, felt them interfusing, becoming one; felt the fused mind, with its direct subjective experience-engrams of the bacchanale, engaging the corresponding symbolic imprints in the brain of Orpheus and struggling into full-blown memory and stark comprehension of the total significance.

The grotto-filling music became a dirge. The visitors decently withdrew from telepathic contact. The brows of Orpheus were drawn together a little, and the eyes and dry lips of Orpheus were as though he were contemplating the body of an Eurydice whom he had slain by stupidity.

He wet the lips and gazed upon Croyd; and he said very softly, pleading not commanding: "Kill me."

"If I had wanted for you to be killed," Croyd responded, "I would have replayed Orpheus and the Bacchantes in actuality, instead of moving it one day downtime so you could experience it and still live to remember it."

Again tonguing his lips, Orpheus whispered: "If you do not kill me, I will suicide. I cannot live with this. My suicide will be on your head. It would be better for you to kill me quickly."

"You are not depressive. You are obsessive-compulsive. You will not kill yourself. You will live, and suffer, and seek to create a new Eurydice."

Closing his eyes, Orpheus shriveled.

Greta telepathed earnestly: "Adjust him, Croyd! Remove his obsessiveness! Be humane!"

His answer came clear in her mind: "Too easy, Greta. If he needs help, he is a doctor; let him seek a psychiatrist; but one way or another, he has got to work this out in his own mind."

"How will he know whether he is working it out, though?"

"When he finds that his reflections are less painful, he will be warm. Believe me, this is more humane than anything else."

He felt her reluctant assent.

They left Orpheus on the throne of Eurydice, racked on the psychic agony that is the price of physical analgesia.

# 39

Again fertile Earth was the size of Maelbrug's head, and growing. Now it spread broadly across the center of the forward shell. Now it filled the shell. Now they could see only the sector of the hemisphere on which they were coming in. . . .

"I think we're in," said Krell. "Are you all right?"

Her mouth parts were working convulsively, her armor was moist from the abnormal transpiration of her spiracles. She said: "Just don't fool around, Krell. As long as it isn't an ocean or a desert. As long as there are humans. After all this, I will wait until the last possible moment for a human—"

*Earth blurred.*

After a long moment of numb silence, all her voice discs vibrated in a prolonged high-pitched scream. Bringing them at length under control, she began a long vicious chant: "Kill me—*kill me*—KILL ME—" '

Krell seized her with 'is six forward podia. "Listen, Maelbrug! You must listen! Do what I say, now! *Extroject in me!*"

It silenced her. She stared at 'im wildly. Then she began to shudder and shake her antennae. "No, Krell, no! I love you! I won't do it!"

"Maelbrug, think! It isn't just you and me, it is the species! Maybe the eggs will still develop in me; we didn't use mammals always, maybe they still have the genes to develop in arthropoda."

"What do you mean, the species? It is just us, now, Krell—*just us!* If I knock you out with an extrojection, I kill the species too: do I know how to fly this ship through space or time or anything?"

"All right," said Krell hopelessly. "All right. We're doomed anyway. I will not see you die horribly. If you extroject in me, I will go unconscious immediately, and you will be out of pain. *Do* it! *Do* it—"

She stared into 'is eyes. Then her eyes glazed a little; and trembling she began clumsily to mount 'im while 'e helped her. . . .

Violently she threw herself away from 'im, pressing herself back against a corner of the bridge; and between pain gasps she said angrily: "Both of us ought to be ashamed of ourselves. Krell, try it again! I have strength for at least one more try! We ought to die *trying,* we *ought* to!"

'E contemplated her with devotion.

'E nodded and turned to the time dials and the ATN controls. "This time," 'e told her, "I'll play the final risk: 99.9989 probability—the very borderline between specious present and uptime. If I miscalculate and drive us into uptime, even if we encounter a mammal your extrojection will be useless; but at least, you *may* be able to extroject into *something—"*

But the time bands had been unaccountably disturbed, either by the cosmic dissolution of probabilities in Earth's neighborhood, or by the Zed maneuvering: all of them extended almost all the way across their dials. A millimeter back on any band could mean a moment, a year, a century, a millennium: there was no way to tell what a millimeter might mean.

Resolutely selecting the year gauge for 'is control, 'e set the ATN back one millimeter and went astern to activate the Zed Maneuver.

# 40

"I do not entirely understand," murmured Leclerc, "this thing about the water."

"Admiral," Greta returned, "You may sack me for this, but I think that's a pretty stupid question. Croyd wants to find out for sure whether and when the effects of Anagonon will die out in people as a result of his alteration of the formula in future probability. So he and the TAC Board doctors went on worldwide TV and ordered all Anagononics on Earthworld to turn on all their water outlets for five minutes every day at 1100 hours Greenwich. All governments on Earth are now going to report the daily water drain at 1100 hours Greenwich. For the first three days it is going to be frightful in the cities of America and Western Europe where most Anagononics live; and it will also probably be bad at 1000 hours and 1200 hours because of people who won't quite understand 1100 hours Greenwich. Then on the fourth day the drain should begin to taper off, and by the tenth day it should be normal. If so, we can conclude that by the tenth day the effects of Anagonon will have completely died in everybody on Earthworld who has ever received it. What's so tough about *that* line of reasoning?"

"Nothing," the admiral answered; "and if I sack you, Greta, it will be for a reply that was *assez stupide.* I understood the test. What I do not understand is—what is being tested? In other words—how can the effects of Anagonon in more than a hundred million people die in ten days?"

*"Pardon?"*

"Let me press the *right* question precisely. How did Croyd kill Anagonon? *That* is what I want to know."

Greta defended: "Ill-formulated questions evoke irrelevant answers."

"This," Leclerc told her, "is a noble generalization, worthy of a fleet commander. But *not* worthy of a fleet *captain."*

"All right," Greta plainted; "so I've been scrubbed; so I keep my darned old frigate. Croyd, explain to the man."

Croyd said: "Here is what I did, Leclerc—and what I hope the results will be, although it is only a half-well-grounded hope. When your fleet destroyed Monon in the year 5 EA, you did not damage any of Monon or Earth prior to that destructive instant; but you did set up thereby a kind of temporal zero screen, and this is what I am counting on. Then, at a time point just a little in actuality's future, I altered the master formula of Anagonon just to the extent of eliminating its permanency; but this in itself, just on an isolated set of papyrs, could hardly affect any Anagononics. What triggered the change was Greta's operation in actuality—the one that ended with the slaughter of Fellanel-Orpheus and the demoralization of the TAC Board. This action sent a wave of probability disintegration rippling up through the future, carrying with it a disintegration and a random distribution of the altered formula papyrs. When the wave hit your time barrier at 5 EA, it rebounded and started back; and one effect of this backlash was that the new probabilities entailed in my change of the formula worked backward to affect prior probabilities. Now, if you couple this with the realization that immediate future probabilities affect the progress of actuality, perhaps you can see how—"

"Cease fire!" commanded Leclerc. "My mind tells me that my brain has registered all this and must work it over before my mind can understand. Meanwhile, I accept, since it seems to be happening. So Earthworld is about to be freed of Anagonon—although there are still seedlings to be extirpated on a few other planets, but no Anagonon for them to use for propagation.

"I have another question, though—and a hard question, I think. Five years from now, am I going to destroy Earthworld?"

Croyd responded thoughtfully: "I'd say that while Anagonon was alive, you did; but now that it is dead, you probably won't."

"Then if I probably won't, how can my improbable action five years from now be helping to destroy Anagonon?"

Archly suggested Greta: "Maybe the probability that you will is inversely related to the remaining prevalence of Anagonon."

Leclerc frowned at her. Then he turned the same frown upon Croyd. Croyd spread hands. "I could not have said it more economically."

Leclerc drained his cognac. Then he growled: "Perhaps you two have business elsewhere. I know *I* have."

"Just one more thing, Admiral," Croyd said, "before we go. As a little postmortem, or premortem—what is your opinion of the Anagonon idea? Just think, Admiral: all hostilities destroyed, endless loving progress: one peerless leader, counseled by a loving council each member of whom is counseled by *his* loving council, and so on down to the lowliest human—all working for human benignity, all immune to pain, all endlessly energetic, practically all living practically forever. Now that we've destroyed this dream—what do you *think* of it?"

Leclerc pondered. He replied eliptically: "I *learned* through pain. I *grew* through the fencings of limited hostility—though I admit that hostility is frequently carried too far. As for the energy and the immortality, though—I have to confess that I do not find these repulsive, provided there is no senescence, and provided there is no pressure of younger people for whom I ought to be making room. What do *you* think?"

Croyd pondered. "You've criticized mainly the advertized effects," he noted. "Consider the side effects, Admiral, in their relationship to what is human-human. If you *have* to obey your leader, what happens to mental integrity and independent operations? If you *have* to be gregarious, what value is left in people-contacts? If you *have* to be a friend of everybody, does caring have any meaning? Does sharing have any conscious significance? What does the pleasant but obligatory ten-day sex claim do to the pair instinct? And if you have no territory that you can call your own, doesn't it leave a hollow place where your territorial satisfaction ought to be? And with all these values canceled out, who wants to create anything? Indeed, why live at all?"

Leclerc pondered. Then he turned to Greta. "What do *you* think?"

Commander Greta raised a beatific face. "I agree wholly, oh, so wholly, with my wise admiral!"

Leclerc said gruffly: "Your battleship, Captain Groen, is waiting in moondock. Get out of here!"

# 41

Of course they went to Croyd's nontime house.

For a while, hand in hand, they walked corridors, explored rooms, waltzed in the ballroom to private music.

Ultimately they were leaning side by side on the slender rail of the nontime breezeway bridge.

She commented: "You are positively going to have to do something about that nonexistent landscape."

"Can it wait until tomorrow?"

"Of course."

They brooded over the void.

She suddenly stiffened.

"What is it?" he demanded.

She turned to him. "Croyd—you're Anagononic!"

"How's that again?"

"That body you're in—it's your Anagonon body—you left the purified body here in stasis! And now that you're out here in nontime, you aren't in the world to get purified with the rest of the change—"

"I don't see where you're leading me."

"Croyd—doesn't it *bother* you to be a slave?"

"So to whom should I be enslaved?"

Gazing at him, she thought it through. Her lips compressed. She said harshly: "Pray, rip off my stripes."

"Only so the admiral will replace these three with four."

Her voice came small. "Suppose I were to decide that I didn't want *any* stripes?"

He took her upper arm, looking down at her solicitously. "Was it for kids that you wanted me to landscape?"

She looked away. "I don't know."

He said flatly: "I think you'd rather be a captain. Am I wrong?"

She looked at him earnestly. "I think you ought to have a son. Would you be willing for him to be raised by a yeoman on my ship?"

"What would he use for playmates?"

"Mm—"

"Besides, Greta—before he was eight, it would interfere with you; and after he was eight, it would interfere with him."

"Don't you care?"

"I would if there were. I won't if there isn't. You know that all of this is true."

Down went her head again, and she kissed the back of his hand on the rail. Without looking up, she whispered: "We never needed Anagonon, you and I."

Silence like that.

He said presently: "I think you ought to realize that there are two other bodies here."

Up came her head. "How's that again?"

"My non-Anagononic body. Also Greta-Beta. They're in stasis."

"Does that mean we can—"

"Any time we choose."

Greta's fist beat the rail. "You're always making these damn problems for me! In this body you're immortal, you'll never grow old, and I don't suppose with you the other body makes much difference. But me, I'll grow old in this body—but not in Greta-Beta. But if I enter Greta-Beta, then I'll have to do any damn thing you ever tell me to!"

Swinging to him, she seized both his forearms: "Croyd! What shall I *do?* I don't want to *have* to do what you tell me to do! *Tell me what to do!"*

He smiled, and his hands gripped her upper arms. "Greta-Beta is your original body, and I happen to be in *my* original body. How does this affect the discussion?"

Her head went down. She said low: "Go ahead. I'll take the gaff."

He led her below. They effected the mind transfer. *"That's* Greta-Beta *now,"* he specified, pointing to the inert body that her mind had just departed; and he eased it back into the stasis chamber beside the Croyd-Two body.

Clasping her waist, he said: "Welcome home, chum. Let's visit a friend of mine called Heraclitus."

Croyd and Greta touched down with accuracy inside the hut of Heraclitus of Ephesus, at a moment that Croyd judged to be less than an hour after his departure with the knife. Greta stood slightly to his left and rear. The old man looked up at them blearily.

Said Croyd: "You are a strong-minded man. Will it bother you if I tell you that you are about to die?"

"Not at all," said Heraclitus, "since it is what I thought myself. But who are you? Are you some god?"

Croyd's left eyebrow went down hard: then didn't the old man remember his visit an hour before? He produced the knife. "Have you ever seen this?"

Heraclitus took it, studied it. "Fascinating!" he exclaimed. "It is a hoax: it looks like a blend of eras, but it is actually quite new. But the wonderful thing is this: it is perfectly a knife that I had planned out in my own mind. I was going to bury it as a jest for the future. Only, I never got around to making it. Who did make it?"

Pondering his reply, Croyd studied the old man.

The old man dropped dead.

The knife shimmered and vanished.

Presently Greta said softly: "Sometimes men should be alone together. I'll wait outside." She left the hut.

Croyd brooded. There was something definitely wrong with the concept that nothing could change in uptime. The paradoxes of the EA years could be discounted—they were all probability multiplications:

even when in 2 EA he had seemed to be uptime of 5 EA, he had been downtime of actuality in 2502. But Heraclitus was a different story. Either he was uptime absolutely *—or actuality was downtime!*

The latter hypothesis Croyd dismissed for working purposes: it was not impossible—Heaven knew that Monon had so demonstrated!—but until paradoxes should multiply to the point of denying common sense absolutely, the most fruitful working hypothesis would be that the spacetime situation in which one was continuously conscious was. . . .

Eh? How does one say it—one who can go uptime or downtime while remaining continuously conscious?

Face the central problem. Uptime—absolute past—should be change-less. Yet it almost seemed that his two visits to Heraclitus had been visits to two different old men, that the knife both had and had not existed.

Perhaps the things that actually have happened constitute changeless uptime whose mass is continually increasing to approach absoluteness of mass. But also, perhaps—since every lifestream and every subatomic particle is continually making choices or having choices forced upon it—perhaps in some phantom way abandoned potentials build them-selves in uptime on the *if-nodes* that are left by settled choices. . . .

Croyd shook himself back into reality, if that was what it was. This quality of meditation was the finest possible kind of funeral service over the body of the great natural philosopher who had tried to make synthetic sense of the dichotomy between stability and flux—but who had been remembered only as the prophet of flux. However, Greta awaited outside. Later he would get into this—with her, probably.

Perhaps he should arrange the body decently on its bed.

No; it would be more decent to leave it this way for its own time to compose and decompose.

He told the body awkwardly: "I have been honored far more than you could ever have known."

Head down, he strolled out of the hut.

Greta screamed.

His head snapped up. In the uncertain moonlight, the long, stick-shaped, possibly transparent object in the background appeared to be an alien spaceship. In the foreground, a man-sized decapod—pale in moonlight, possibly golden—held Greta's arms locked behind; while a dark moon-gleaming decapod, possibly purple, advanced swiftly upon

Greta with unsheathed ovipositor.

Seeing Croyd, Greta yipped: "Okay, Croyd—let's see you get me out of *this* one!"

Croyd yelled: " KRELL!"

Krell turned 'is head. Maelbrug came on, laying podia on Greta.

Comprehending, Croyd threw a mental motor block at Maelbrug, paralyzing her: impossible for him to do accurately, had he not sojourned in three Myron brains. Then he threw a swift persuasive telepathic message at Krell: *I understand your trouble. For your female there is no time to lose. Get her into the ship, and we will follow.*

Confused, concerned, disturbed, responsive, Krell lifted Maelbrug clumsily and half dragged her into the ship. Greta, not quite in shock, followed at Croyd's insistence. Croyd entered and had Krell close the hatch.

Croyd nontimed the ship. It hung in nonspace just off his bridge.

*Open the hatch,* Croyd commanded Krell. The Myron maneuvered Maelbrug through the hatch and over the rail.

Leaving the ship, Croyd helped Krell carry Maelbrug down into his house, with Greta hovering behind them. In its depths, they laid the body near the stasis chamber: this Croyd opened and began to remove his alternate body.

Ineffectually Greta protested: "Croyd! You're not—"

Ignoring her, Croyd laid out his alternate body beside the stasis chamber and turned to Krell, whose antennae were pinned taut down against 'is body. Croyd said telepathically: *Stasis, Krell.*

The Myron studied Croyd with all five eyes. *It means the end of our race.*

Telephathic sympathy is totally convincing, because either it is real or it is not there. Krell felt it as Croyd told 'im: *I know. I am the one who engineered the admiral's downtime decision on your flagship. And if I could do so, I would use all my powers to find another way out of this. But there is nothing that I can do. The life of your species is the death of mine: our species have evolved past points of no return: not for ideological reasons, but for inherent biological reasons, we cannot coexist in this galaxy. Can you think of an alternative, Krell?*

Antennae motionless, 'e responded: *Only to kill you. But then I would not know how to bring Maelbrug out of your motor block.*

Croyd told 'im: *You could not kill me.*

*Then,* Krell stolidly asserted, *I will be the one to put her in stasis.*

Tenderly 'e lifted her body in six podia, eased her into the chamber, and closed the door. By the door 'e stayed crouched.

*How long will it take,* Croyd asked, *for the eggs to die?*

*Only a little while,* responded Krell's toneless thought. *And then I will strip her of the eggs. It is a thing that we masculates are trained to do, when the eggs die—*

Croyd snapped: *Let's get her out! I've thought of an alternative!*

Maelbrug lay sleeping on the floor beside the inert alternate body of Croyd. Stern Krell stood guard.

Greta whispered: "Put your body back in, Croyd."

He replaced Croyd Two in stasis.

Greta frowned down. Having cleared her throat, she mumbled: "You could have wiped out their species; but what you did instead—well, it was as though they were human."

"It can fail, of course," he mused, "but Krell stripped her eggs into a thermal jar; and if I can just reproduce that Monon icrophotographic apparatus and mutate their genes so that they become ovoviviparous with no more than one or two eggs at a time—"

"I get it. Then they *will* be able to coexist with humans."

Unguardedly, Croyd had left his telepathic output open: Krell was apprehending also the meanings of Greta that Croyd was hearing. And Krell heard Croyd reply: "By our galactic definition, Myrons are humans too. There is no anatomical specification, but only a psychological specification, for humanity."

Silence. Maelbrug appeared to be comfortably asleep.

Krell told Croyd heavily: *I would like to live with her somewhere. But I suppose it cannot be anywhere in your galaxy.*

Greta, tugging at Croyd's shirt, whispered something.

*You do need some temporary solitude,* Croyd admitted; *your eventual presence among our people will take some getting used to. So just for a while—Krell, how would you and Maelbrug like to stake out a bit of territory near here in nonspace—mutually private but accessible, with a communication channel between us?*

Slowly the amazed Krell turned all 'is eyes on Croyd.

Greta, dimpling, murmured: "Won't it be nice to have neighbors? Now you'll *have* to landscape."

*Krell?* inquired Croyd.

Studying Croyd's chest, Krell diffidently responded: *Is your non-space big enough also to accommodate nearly two hundred sterile masculates and dead-egg females who are lost now in downtime?*

Croyd studied Krell's third integument. Croyd nodded.

Krell's expression never changed, of course; but 'is antennae assumed an impossible angle. *You would do this—for us?*

It somehow echoed a rich line from a postmedieval Hecht-MacArthur-Coward play. Croyd wondered whether *The Scoundrel* might be found in his library below. . . .

A third tug came at Croyd's shirt. Greta whispered.

"She wants to know," Croyd explained, "What you are going to do about your females and their frustrated mother instinct. Of course, if my project works, there'll be some males for them eventually—"

On the floor, Maelbrug mumbled drowsily: "What's a mother instinct?"

Croyd's lips were fay as he led Greta away, leaving Sira Krell to guard his goddess. If Croyd's project worked, Maelbrug would learn.

High on the breezeway bridge:

Croyd: "We have to face it, Greta. There are two loose ends."

Greta: "I know. But they are aces in the hole for us."

"Wouldn't you rather go back to playing it human-risky?"

"Maybe. And besides, maybe I don't cotton to owning a zombie."

They brooded.

The idea hit them conjointly. They looked up, four eyebrows elevated.

Croyd: "Admit that it would be a form of reproduction."

Greta, after a moment: "I have two questions."

"Mind fission and fusion answers the first. What is the other?"

"Who gets the house?"

"Just as pointedly—who gets the Myrons?"

"Another solution would be to destroy our doubles, Croyd."

"Would you buy that?"

"No. They are alive."

They brooded. It was an ultrabaffling version of an old whodunit problem: how to dispose of two embarrassing bodies.

Croyd: "You and I inhabit the original bodies. That leaves our doubles for the Myrons. He can build for them and for himself and Greta-Beta, and lead them, and help them to come to new terms with themselves. To avoid any argument on this, I can imprint both of them for this purpose before minding them."

Greta: "Have we the right to tamper with their brains?"

"She's you. He's me. Who has a better right?"

*"They* have."

They brooded.

Then both of them simultaneously saw the light, and the simultaneity communicated itself telepathically between them. They squeezed four hands; and, arms around waists, they descended to the bowels of the house to awaken their doubles for minded colloquy.

They comprehended that individual human fulfillment depends, among ten or more prime requirements, on mental integrity. If Croyd and Greta had it, then Croyd Two and Greta-Beta had it; and two pairs of mirror heads are better than one, if all four have it. The discussion would be an honest four-way argument, with differences of opinion to be mutually resolved; for duplicates cannot possibly be identical (Leibnitz to the contrary notwithstanding) because of, at least, indexical differences and mental spontaneity.

But if mental integrity should lapse. . . .


CODA

7/69

WALLACE                    28461

# RULES
## OF THE
## MARPLE PUBLIC LIBRARY
### TELEPHONE: ELgin 6-1510

1. Books may be kept 3 weeks, unless otherwise specified, and may be renwed only at discretion of Librarian.

2. A fine of two cents a day and cost of recovery must be paid for books kept overtime.

3. The owner of a card is responsible for all books charged against him.

4. All books lost or injured must be paid for.

5. Notice of change of residence must at once be sent to the Librarian.

DEMCO